Laurence

Laurence

A Novel by France Théoret

Translated by Gail Scott

THE MERCURY PRESS

Copyright © 1998 by France Théoret and Gail Scott

ALL RIGHTS RESERVED. No part of this book may be reproduced by any means without the prior written permission of the publisher, with the exception of brief passages in reviews. Any request for photocopying or other reprographic copying of any part of this book must be directed in writing to the Canadian Reprography Collective.

The publisher gratefully acknowledges the financial assistance of the Canada Council for the Arts and the Ontario Arts Council, and further acknowledges the financial support of the Government of Canada through the Book Publishing Industry Development Program for our publishing activities.

Translation of this novel from French to English was made possible by a grant from the Canada Council for the Arts.

Quote page 124 from *Les Misérables*, by Victor Hugo. Translated by E. Charles Wilbur. Toronto: Knopf (Everyman's Library) 1997, p. 987.

Edited by Beverley Daurio
Composition and page design by TASK
Printed and bound in Canada
Printed on acid-free paper

1 2 3 4 5   02 01 00 99 98

Canadian Cataloguing in Publication Data
Théoret, France
[Laurence. English]
Laurence : a novel
Translation of: Laurence
ISBN 1-55128-060-4
I. Scott, Gail. II. Title. III. Title: Laurence. English.
PS8589.h42l3813 1998   C843'.54   C98-932200-9
PQ3919.2.T494L3813 1998

The Mercury Press
Toronto, Canada   M6P 2A7

Constant comparing is really the quintessence of vulgarity.
— Hannah Arendt

I
A YEAR OF HAPPINESS

1

Rachel, the maid who wouldn't look at you, opened the kitchen door. Laurence entered, her arms laden with farm produce that she deposited on the table. Madame Fournier appeared from the dining room, greeting her.

Laurence straightened. In the warm September light, she was a tall woman who appeared taller by virtue of her carriage. Her dark hair was pulled back in a chignon that showed off her neck. Her uniform's stiff white collar flagged her profession. The stretch of calves between hem and white square-heeled shoes alone clashed with her bearing and manner. They were clad in thick beige stockings, betraying rural origins.

She communicated the essential. The birth was long, but without complications. To the mother's relief, the baby presented itself in the proper head-first position. The patient cooperated, pushing long and hard, so the doctor barely used the forceps. The baby girl was born at about three o'clock. We swaddled it and placed it in its mother's arms, then left, Laurence added. Her love of recounting, a habit born of solitude, belied a self-confidence she would have had a hard time explaining.

Now the three women are stationary in the large kitchen. Madame Fournier and Rachel have contributed their opinions regarding the main event of the waning day. Nothing more was required. Madame Fournier informed Laurence that Rachel had earlier taken a telegram to her little suite.

Laurence walked toward the corridor off the dining room, skirting the doctor's office to reach the tiny bed-sitter: a peaceful haven. The envelope was propped up in its usual place. Filled with foreboding, she broke the seal with her fingers and read: "Mother sick. Need your help. L. Naud." The words printed in capitals trembled before her eyes, dancing with a gravity that made them seem false. Standing by the window, she looked out at the dirt road and the still-green field running along the river's edge, at evening advancing in the distance. Maman is ill, maman is confined to bed, she repeated. Life here and now superimposed onto life down there. She imagined her mother, having reached menopause, white hair loose, white cotton nightgown, lying between white sheets. To think of her mother staying all day in her room, instead of attending to her chores, required a vocabulary she did not possess. Head raised towards the radiant evening, she clenched her fists, crinkling the slip of paper abruptly into a ball between her fingers. Several minutes passed. She put down the ball of paper, opened the casement window, and breathed deeply. She would go immediately. By the next train. There was no alternative. The call for help was unambiguous. Father would be waiting at the station.

Laurence told them at supper, served in the kitchen. She didn't know how long she would be gone. The doctor thought there was a train Sunday afternoon. He would check— it was already Saturday. The young nurse looked at him gratefully. It was hard for her to say she was leaving. He predicted a month's absence, adding that the days were still long enough for him to set out on the bad country roads unaccompanied. He lowered his voice. He would limit his travelling until her return. Laurence knew she would not lose her job.

The doctor was her role model. He expressed himself clearly, reasonably. She knew by intuition that one did not seek to justify oneself. She imitated him. A man of reason is a man who does his moral duty. The two went together. The thumping of her heart at the thought of her mother's illness drowned out the sound of her own voice.

On Saturdays, the doctor made routine visits in the village. Madame Fournier suggested shortening the itinerary, to give Laurence time to prepare her journey.

The two formed a successful team. The doctor valued attentive and meticulous service. The accident at the sawmill made him appreciate his collaborator's moral fibre. Four men had entered his office carrying a blood-soaked worker. A leg would have to be amputated. Though still conscious, the patient was extremely weak. No time to transport him to Québec City— the amputation had to be done immediately. During the operation, Laurence applied chloroformed towels, gripping his jaw tightly to keep him from biting his tongue. Three of the men held down his arms and good leg, which was jerking nervously in the patient's semi-conscious state. He tossed and turned violently until his leg was severed. At the end of the operation, the man sighed and stopped thrashing. His violent spasms of pain reverberated through each of them. They each experienced deliverance when he relaxed.

The youngest of the men returned several times with documents that needed signing. He cracked jokes about bureaucratic red tape. Laurence's frank dark-eyed gaze sparkled, meeting his. Years later, she would evoke their encounter with the romantic outdated cliché: we looked into each other's eyes.

Dr. Fournier questioned her about her mother's illness. She wasn't sure.

Fatigue from overwork, age, numerous pregnancies. Her mother had never been ill. From his bag he selected remedies for the liver, the stomach, the intestines, an iron tonic and sleeping pills, to supplement her nurse's kit.

The young woman hoped she would not have to explain why she needed a salary advance. She had no money for a train ticket. Without her asking, the doctor put the equivalent of a month's salary on her desk, for unexpected expenses. Laurence was touched that he was making it easier for her. The evening before, he had received produce from a farmer who was unable to pay for his wife's delivery. Today, while she cleaned instruments and locked away the medicine, he was noting paid and unpaid visits in a bound ledger. Even-tempered, silent, he fastidiously recorded debits and credits. It never occurred to her that debts were forgiven in his year-end accounting. After the noonday meal, they would all accompany her as far as Québec City.

Laurence put her suitcase on her bed. The metal clasps no longer held. Inside was the leather strap for tying it shut. With brusque, nervous gestures, she packed outer garments, underwear, stockings. Every item was second-hand, except a skirt and some underwear. She was trembling. She tried to slow down her movements by washing with care. She didn't feel like sleeping. A night in bed, plus the time it took to get down there, seemed an eternity. The mother, in the five years since Laurence had left home, was relegated to the shadows in her father's letters and occasional visits. An excessively discreet woman, her memories surfaced in sparse phrases, reifying her mother's image. The older woman's soft voice, her belaboured gestures devoted to the serving of others, had become disincarnated. She was a statue in the distance. When Laurence pronounced the word maman, the sound was one of *veneration*.

Filled with lofty sentiment, she refused to dig deeper. She choked back the spectre of chronic illness, the shadow of death lurking in the background.

Despite her fears, one can imagine a young woman content with her lot who boarded the train that day. The rituals of departure and good wishes soothed her. She chose a seat by the window, eyes wide, taking in the A-l-l-l A-b-o-a-r-d, the clicking of the wheels over the rails. She pulled down her too-short suit skirt, folded her hands on her lap, and let herself relax.

Laurence remembered something that amused her greatly, that seemed, with hindsight, a naïvely comic moment. It was the day last January when Dr. Fournier had come and proposed that she leave the city of Québec to go and work in Beaupré. What was naïve about it was that she had no idea he had even noticed her.

Few men ever entered the women's pavilion of Saint-Michel-Archange Hospital. She and the doctor had hardly spoken. New faces supplied a means of escaping routine, particularly when it was possible to strike up a good conversation. She responded to him with sunny common sense, even joviality. The smile faded when he offered her a job. Her face tightened into a suspicious mask.

The doctor said that he frankly didn't understand what she was doing working as an admissions' clerk. She took the compliment as a rebuke, not foreseeing or anticipating what was coming next. The fortuitous offer, the unsolicited opportunity, appeared to offend her. Her artlessness shamed her. The man's reserved manner was accompanied by a remarkable presence of mind. She could see, in the quality of his bearing, that his type was not easily fooled, and she was certain she'd lost enough face to discourage even the best-intentioned individual. Her discomfort was written all over her face. She stammered and stalled, an apparent refusal. The doctor left as he had come, his back headed, in her gaze, towards the glass door, withdrawing.

The memory stuck, the certainty she'd appeared awfully rigid. She remembered the doctor's disappointed expression. Now she could laugh.

From the earliest days at Beaupré, it was clear she was going to be blessed with a material comfort never before imagined. A woman used to taking care of herself, she did not know whom to thank for this abundance: the doctor, God, or life. She got used to it.

A bourgeois house is designed to preserve everyone's privacy. Her two-room suite included a kitchen with a door opening onto the left wing of the house, and a comfortable bed-sitting room. Her quiet evenings, one or two hours of free time before sleeping, seemed empty, and she wrote two long letters to her father, justifying her departure from Québec. The idea of writing to her brother Edouard crossed her mind, but she didn't. The clock's hands ticked dead time, like in the convent-hospital residence.

The room's sturdy furniture, bed, bedside table and dresser, were covered with impeccable bedspread and runners. The cupboard blocked part of the thickly curtained window. The whole arrangement breathed calm and safety, stolidly guarding over peaceful sleep. Laurence entered on tiptoe. Her possessions, chiefly uniforms and yellow cotton underwear, took up little space. She quickly unpacked, trying not to feel like an intruder. She who had nothing would live, from now on, in the house of a village notable.

She accompanied the Fournier couple and Rachel to high mass at ten a.m. Without excusing or trying to justify herself, she said she preferred walking to going by buggy. She also preferred the eight a.m. service. Wearing mittens and a rough wool hat had never bothered her before. Now it was better not to draw attention to herself. She stood apart from the group of villagers.

In the dining room, Madame Fournier handed her a pale grey suit, almost new, that no longer fit. Laurence, troubled by such unexpected kindness, ran her hand longingly over the fine smooth cloth. Madame Fournier led her to her bedroom to try it on in front of the mirror. Laurence's dark eyes lit with happiness. The jacket was elegant, the short skirt would be fine with the hem let down. She was stunned by the transformation. The mirror reflected a sexy, feminine woman with a striking face and a straight well-proportioned body. She cried out in astonishment, followed by a choked laugh. Madame put a pink shirt on the dresser, and took a felt hat, a purse and gloves from the cupboard. The masculine brim emphasized her coquettish air. Laurence giggled and raised her head. She was metamorphosed by the city outfit. Her frank gaze made her seem taller. Her reflection mirrored her delight.

She contemplated her luck, her destiny, as she called it, the opportunity of choosing between the hospital where she was a live-in employee, and the job of a nurse with a real salary, plus lodging. The nuns had tried to make her stay. Her high spirits, kept in check by five years of submission to the rhythm of convent-hospital life, made her choose otherwise.

She soon relaxed her rigid manners, turned into the nurse the doctor wanted. She was young enough to cope with irregular hours and rough country roads in winter. She wasn't bothered by his hackneyed notion that young convent girls were polite, unassertive. His conventional attitude implied respect. She felt no need to be critical of his attitude, given her own indifference to moralizing, and to public opinion in general. It was normal for him to have certain expectations. With age, the doctor was becoming, increasingly, a man of common sense. Educated in the humanist tradition, he observed human nature from a distance, speaking seldom. He was a little boring, but she could see he was wise. He accepted each person at face value, and treated illness without moral or social bias.

Might anyone have detected her fear of madness back when she left her village of Broughton? She had hidden it, had suppressed her morbid self-doubt. The nuns who took her in made no allusion whatsoever to mental illness. They found in her a conscientious obedient employee to whom they could entrust sensitive tasks. Such severe mental confusion must leave immediate as well as long-term traces. Someone had surely noticed, and they might lock her up with the madwomen. The chance to work at Saint-Michel-Archange Hospital turned into a plot against her. Out of fear, she bowed to rules and regulations. Only thus could she escape notice. If, being new, she committed some mishap, her self-effacing manner and her obedience were proof of good intentions. She was a young impressionable woman when she entered the employ of the psychiatric hospital, trying to make herself small, to pass through the eye of the needle. She found her feet, stood proud again. But she was never able to laugh at her panic.

The train was taking her home. She thrilled at the thought of telling them all about her new life. She pictured her mother, an unflagging worker, worn out. Aline, who was fragile and secretive, didn't help enough, to the distress of Laurence, who felt torn in two directions by the immensity of their neediness. She could not be cut in half. Either she could stay home and second the mother, sparing her exhaustion, or, as was now the case, send the family the economic support it needed, in the form of her monthly salary. Thinking about the conundrum bewildered her, felt like an examination of conscience: was it good or bad to have left? There was no perfect solution. She had chosen to the best of her ability, and judged her current choice reasonable, if not ideal.

Laurence detested being caught in the middle. She reconsidered her abrupt departure, rationalizing it until, with hindsight, the economic imperative eclipsed the original motive. She had left them, but all they had to do was ask and she would again be part of the fold. She owed them life, an unacquittable debt. If good judgement required serenity, she still remained excessively vulnerable when it came to family woes. A tender sense of duty was guiding the independent single woman towards her mother. To do otherwise than respond immediately to the call would seem blasphemous.

Through the open window, she breathed the forest air. Men smoked, a grey cloud floating above their heads, travellers sitting erect, girded in their Sunday best. She observed them, men among men or with their families, trying to hold still in their seats. She automatically imitated them, settling in by the window.

Sooner or later, young women had to decide between the two options: marriage or religious vows. Some Gordian knot, some insoluble quandary had caused her flight, but the fleeing Laurence knew she was not destined for convent life. She must keep her distance. She had the reputation of being able to work like a man. She toiled from dawn to dusk, without noticing she was tiring, forgetting herself in her drive to get the job done.

By family standards, she wasn't pretty. The elder sister, a blue-eyed blonde, had clear skin and dainty manners like the mother. Amanda was blossoming. Her angelic face was enhanced by feminine ways, which delighted the father. Laurence, the second daughter, was no snob, didn't mind getting her hands dirty. Even on Sundays, she maintained her austere appearance. Her charm was of the sober variety.

It saddened Laurence that the father preferred Amanda. Laurence was the one, after all, who listened to his tales of a travelling salesman, who worked with the boys in stable and field. How to rival the elder sister with a face like hers? What could she do with her mass of dark hair, mobile features, the oddly shaped beauty marks, including one on the end of her nose? The father was said to have an Indian grandmother from whom she inherited her olive skin, her dark eyes. A savage, a squaw, mocked Amanda.

Beauty, though not deemed essential for young women, permitted the plotting of secret loves, spontaneous attractions and rejections. Religious law did not forbid affairs of the heart with their unpredictable ups-and-downs, provided they were not acted upon, expressed only in moodiness. Someone once described Laurence's gaze as impudent. Though shy, she never lowered her eyes.

Gaston flirted with her on a whim. She, taken unawares, responded uncertainly. The saw-mill worker was attracted by her uniform with its starched cap. Hearts beat, but the music did not resemble a sentimental waltz. The cool efficiency of Dr. Fournier's dispensary both ignited and tempered the spark between them. Both had remained strong and calm during the amputation of the injured worker's leg. Out of a sense of decency, neither spoke. Surprised by the mutual sexual attraction, they over-corrected with briskness.

Before drifting off to sleep, Laurence's mind was full of the handsome six-footer with the solid gait. She felt she had never met anyone quite like him, and was on her guard. Night veiled his image.

To flirt, to have fun during a get-together, preferably with family members, was fine. Keeping company without paternal sanction was not done. It was up to the father to grant visiting rights to the young man, and if marriage was in the offing, he authorized it by giving consent. The girl idealized the tradition. It seemed to her respectable, right. Love was not flaunted, it was ritualized to mask ardent feelings, fiery passions that might exist. The advantage of such rites was that they accommodated marriages of convenience, too, something to avoid if still in your twenties.

Laurence had never read romantic novels. Convent life had reinforced her idealized view of tradition, excluding rendezvous or dating. Increasingly, she imagined for herself a marginal existence, knowing full well she would never be a nun. The dowry demanded by clerical orders of girls entering the novitiate was repulsive. It should be enough that Amanda, as a teaching sister, would enrich the community while earning her keep. To say so would be considered scandalous. Amanda was called by God. Léon Naud would find the money he didn't have. He had promised to make a priest of one of his sons, but there was no sign it would happen. His daughter's choice was a consolation for his long wait. He would provide a trousseau. Amanda would not suffer the shame of being poor. Dowry and trousseau arrived at the novitiate before her, and she received the welcome due those who would be future teachers. Aline, in her turn, felt the call. Amanda asked the father to grant her sister the same privileges, for the sake of family honour within the religious community. Laurence thought to herself that the second sister would not be dishonoured as long as the first one was not defrocked.

When she envisaged marriage, obstacles multiplied before her eyes, not only those thrown up by custom, but also those of a material order. She herself would help pay the costs. The requirements had increased during her cloistered life. The gap between her natural spontaneity and conventional reality as she imagined it seemed to be widening. But once out in the world, Laurence's clear mind no longer entertained overblown fantasies. In time, she would learn how to make tradition work for her.

Too good to be true. The gloomy popular expression haunted her. She thought of writing her family about having met Gaston and the outing to the arena in Québec. She decided against it, repressing her sadness at not sharing this new happiness. Could it all really be happening to her? Laurence was no sentimental dreamer. He was so handsome. She felt swarthier than ever, her finger lifting to touch the strange beauty mark on the tip of her nose. The thought of writing them about him made her giggle. She had no one to talk to, had never experienced the sweetness of exchanging confidences. The money sent home in the envelope was accompanied by a brief note.

The nurse had been seen with Gaston Ramsay. The fast-driving *sportsman,*★ as he was known, left a trail of dust behind him. Sitting erect, he flew over the rough patches in his convertible. Laurence didn't need to ask to know he supported his mother and sisters. People gossiped. They said he had two sisters and a mother who, since the death of the father, never stepped outside. A bad drinker, the father was presumed to have left debts.

Whether in the doctor's office, or on home-visits, all Laurence disclosed about herself was her training: she had studied at Saint-Michel-Archangel Hospital in Québec. No, she had no relatives in the region. If the busybodies persisted, she named her place of birth. Her taciturn manner made her seem unfriendly. Her uniform protected her. Rachel, the Fournier's servant, laundered it. A second white garment hung ready in the cupboard. The doctor's slow methodic manner, his dryness, also helped fend off gossip.

The summer air swept away the remaining traces of stuffy convent-hospital life. Laurence reorganized her room. The sun didn't shine in and the window was partly blocked. The dresser and the cupboard changed places. She asked that the drapes be removed so that she could breathe the air of the river. The gardener planted some flower borders. She gathered pots and earth to plant geraniums and filled her room with the potted flowers. They looked good.

She was dogged by the desire to run free along the river at dusk. The damp odours and the river wind beckoned. She breathed it in deeply before going to bed. She learned how its moods, its cadence punctuated the household's daily rhythms, and held herself back, a model doctor's helper. Learning seemed an endless struggle.

At the beginning of summer, she turned twenty-three, feeling neither old nor concerned about the future. She had no plans, only the certainty that her new status set her a cut above others. Social standing gave you a role to play, regardless of age. The villagers presumed she was educated, questioned her

---

★ In English in the original.

about their aches and pains while waiting to see the doctor. Appalled by the general lack of hygiene, she dispensed elementary advice. She saw illnesses due to insanitary conditions that she had never dreamed of, notwithstanding her own back-country childhood. She examined the cases, spoke in strictly medical terms, refraining from moralizing references to laziness or to physical or psychological defects.

Gaston invited her to a fair. The animal show and the craft exhibit were ending on Sunday. They entered the throng. Two men were arguing over a steer being auctioned, each pulling the animal in his direction, until the fat man fell, his hat flying up into the air and landing in Laurence's hands. The steer took off. Some men ran after it. People were killing themselves laughing, surrounding the angry man, still on the ground. Someone helped him to his feet. Laurence stepped forward with the hat, her hand on her mouth to keep from laughing in the face of the man who was crying: it's mine.

Gaston teased her about being a good catcher. The last animals were being led towards the carts. The crowd was regrouping into families. Shouting and hailing rose from the chaos that followed the auction. Mothers pulled their youngsters out of the way of horses' hooves. Ladies smoothed their hair. The wind and the action raised a fine dust. The commercial part of the fair was over. It was time to have fun.

Half the village was there. She recognized people without feeling any particular emotion. Gaston took her arm and led her towards a field where some young men were playing ball. Their muscled bodies reminded her of her brothers. Sweat soaked the backs of their shirts. The boys showed off their brawn, exerting themselves. The game resembled a battle. Gaston was looking for recruits for the Québec hockey team. He sized them up at a distance.

He said in a low voice that he was here with her and took her for a soda. If he waited until the end of the game, it would be impossible to avoid the obligatory post-mortem. He literally sneaked away. They crossed the area exhibiting women's handicrafts, from quilts to linen sheets. The exquisite uselessness of fine embroidery made Laurence think of Amanda, who had a knack for it. The warm woollens, knitted clothing conjured up the cold seasons, the fullness of time. Laurence did knit, using patterns cut out from women's magazines.

They ate jam doughnuts and drank tea. Several women came up to inquire after Mrs. Ramsay. They could hear fiddlers warming up. There would be music. Laurence clapped her hands. They walked towards a tented area, its entrance guarded by a guy with a mouth organ. He stared with vacant eyes at the young woman, and stepped aside to let them pass. Some seated men were gambling with dice. The game's organizer held a purse of silver. Around them, people smoked and drank, awaiting their turn. Gaston offered her a mug of beer. He whispered in her ear that you should try everything once. A shiver ran up her spine. Gaston nodded at acquaintances. The players bet higher, not wanting to lose face before the audience. Gaiety alternated with silence. It took a sharp eye to see the coins changing hands.

Laurence took a slug, the pungent taste making her grimace, followed by a surge of well-being. Gaston finished his beer. They left the way they had come. The village idiot, as he was known, blew on his mouth organ. They recognized the tune, an old English tune called "Greensleeves."

They swelled the ranks around the fiddle players. People were clapping. A dancer jumped up on the platform, launched into a stepdance, followed by someone else, with whom he danced a complicated jig. The Irish tunes came thick and fast, with men jumping up to dance solo, the platform being too narrow for groups. Several women tapped out the beat with their feet. She listened, impassive, daydreaming. A fleeting memory of music and dancing in the huge family kitchen distracted her from the present. Music softens people's rough edges, brings them closer, Laurence reflected. She shared this thought with Gaston. Her enthusiasm overcame her wave of nostalgia. We should teach children this, she said. Merrymaking made her melancholic. Invariably, she projected herself towards the future, dreaming of those who would come after. This left the impression that things were over for her, that she had lived, that the future belonged to others. Gaston spoke of his brother who lived in Holland, of all the instruments he played.

She was in a bubble, standing still, distanced from the music and foot-tapping villagers. She wished such moments could last, could be perpetuated, transmuted, so each one among them could carry them within. The couple waited for the end of the reel to move on, Laurence's thoughts still floating between past and future.

She moved closer to her companion, the sleeve of his shirt touching her jacket. They stood motionless for a minute. He burst out laughing, a deep laugh. Her hand went up to her face, hiding the disgraceful spots, the beauty marks that caricaturized her features. The corners of her lips relaxed into a smile, conquering her shyness. He told her she looked mischievous.

They had brought in fair rides from Québec, the smaller ones that could be set up in the morning and taken down at night. The eagerness of the children contrasted with the stiffness of the adults, including themselves. They felt irrevocably cut off from childhood. At the candy stand he bought popcorn and several suckers that he thrust into her hands.

Gaston attracted her with concrete gestures, wooed her, elected to be alone with her in the midst of a crowd. She told him her story about leaving her hometown of Broughton, explained, spoke of life's necessities, a euphemism that he appeared to interpret in a similar fashion.

Their complicity in face of the crowd suddenly became apparent to her. They had greeted people who had not stopped to talk. You have to experience everything once, he had said, under cover of the racket of people indulging in risky pleasure. A big idea, so new, so contrary to what she had been taught, it startled her. She refused to compare the moment to any other. Gaston judged her by her eyes. It takes living through real despair to know that happiness means being in touch with yourself. She was not one to run away from life, on the contrary, she figured that learning requires trying out different ways of being.

She would not be able to meet him tomorrow. She stepped out of the garden half-running, and was embarrassed to be wearing her mended skirt, her thick stockings, when she ran into him. His convertible had broken down. He greeted her casually, happy to see her, though taken by surprise. She told him she was leaving, without saying why. At dusk, they strolled side by side along the main street that crossed the village, the windows of houses lit up. He was walking her home. Yesterday, today, tomorrow, time stopped— her family required her presence. They shared a similar sense of priority. Their conversation was limited to platitudes. He asked how she was travelling. At the doorstep of the white house, he took her in his arms, and said: *goodbye, take care, I'll wait for you.*★ His footsteps faded into the night, and she climbed the stairs.

In the train on the way to Broughton, Laurence knew she was in love. Love changed her, made her less self-conscious. The newness of the situation stirred doubt within. She refused to indulge in sentimental conjecture, pon-

---

★ In English in the original.

dered what course to follow. Those who say uncertainty is the child of unhappiness are wrong.

She felt comfortable with Gaston, was getting used to his probing gaze. Maybe she wasn't so ugly. A woman's beauty is a gift. Her charm attracted those who knew how to look. It wasn't surprising that the *sportsman* had noticed her, he who had a reputation of being more confident than most in tight situations. His attitude seemed protective, fraternal. She appreciated his attentiveness, a new experience that made her feel like a woman beside him. Her present attitude outweighed her initial mistrust and hesitation. Being in love made the future look rosy. She was speaking too soon. Love made one light-headed.

2

All villages looked alike. So thought Laurence. Being slightly better off than the next place didn't change things much. Every village had its share of old houses, bereft of galleries and front steps. The bare wooden square or rectangular structures were weathered by the harsh climate. Blackened by sun and storm, they looked abandoned, except for the curtains hanging in the windows. She meditated on the huge amount of work it would take to fix them up. Poverty was largely responsible for their crude state. The visible dilapidation was a smudge on the lovely landscape, the grassy and wooded hills speeding by under the clear sky.

Humans fared worse than trees and animals. No effort sufficed for extracting a reasonable living from the earth. Destitution contrasted harshly with the landscape. It's hard to put a place into words when you're born there. You live according to the cycles of nature, you have to. Laurence, a thousand times more interested in people than in forests and valleys, contemplated the latter, punctuated by stark dwellings, from her train window.

She didn't know if she'd like to live on one of these sparsely settled concession roads again. The way things were going, she might not have a choice. She hadn't got to know the city. Being in residence had meant only quick return trips. The city attracted her, without knowing why. She had no idea what it was like. Her family had always lived on the last concession road. Town or city, it was the people around you who counted, who made life livable, or not. Wherever you were, the main thing was to rise above misery and servitude. Laurence felt certain that as long as people had to work their fingers to the bone for a piece of meat or a pair of winter boots, happiness was impossible. The weathered houses, lacking, like her father's house, galleries and even front steps, looked sinister. She wouldn't want her sisters and brothers to live in places like that, and in her mind, the family home was excluded from the comparison. She imagined all these houses of rough wood fixed up with coloured siding and painted galleries. In her opinion, the religious notion that the poor are always with us was a self-fulfilling prophecy that sanctioned indolence. The poverty of these tumble-down shacks wasn't at all comparable to her family's situation. The father's high ideals kept the children unaware of their own misery.

Good food and a roof over your head gave you the right start in life. The worse off they were, the more intractable he became. He wouldn't tolerate the parish priest or the school teacher knowing they were in narrow straits. His stubborn efforts to maintain the family image made him complain bitterly to his elder children, demanding their salaries and their understanding. The father was changing. He talked less about the need for basic comforts, asking for money without explanation, supposedly in the name of a better future, of family unity. Ideals and obligations became one and the same, and he took, not caring any more whether it was from a son or a daughter. He salved his conscience by demanding reassurance that the money was clean, from respectable sources, legitimately earned by hard labour.

It used to be that he would hold forth self-righteously about the future. Time would be on his side. The religious vocation of his eldest daughter was a sign. But heavenly grace was doing nothing to improve daily life. He made fewer speeches. The combination of moral victories and material frustrations were making him bitter. In a letter to Laurence, he stressed the pitfalls of her too-independent life at Beaupré, warned her against her spontaneously curious nature, her tendency to avoid anything resembling domestic work. Casual encounters, this was how he put it, led to sin. She was bartering a sheltered life against an uncertain future.

She wouldn't mention Gaston. She quietly made up her mind, confident and at peace with her decision. The young man had neither suggested nor requested any such thing, and she would behave according to her intuition.

The inordinately strong emotions surging through her at the mention of his name gave her pause. Never in her wildest dreams could she have imagined anything like the bond, so tangible, between them. She didn't know why Gaston's presence made her feel like singing, a song of the heart and the senses. Her happiness made it right to say nothing.

Laurence would not have linked her rebellious tendencies to feelings of dissatisfaction. It's hard to say why, at twenty-three, she had not felt love or its lack. She was not obsessed by the fact that she was getting older. Unmarried women of twenty-five were considered old maids.

For a long time, her sister's religious vocation kept the family going. It was understood Amanda would enter the convent from the age of fourteen. The father's enthusiastic endorsement made turning back inconceivable, and the adolescent followed the straight and narrow towards a goal that justified his words and deeds, conforming to the letter of religious law. Amanda's vocation took on such proportions, any other plans for the future paled by comparison. Her bombastic attitude was rivalled only by the father's pride. Or vice versa. It was the family's first religious calling, and as such, it morally sanctioned the quality, the integrity of the parenting. Laurence observed the complicity between father and daughter and had to keep from laughing out loud when Amanda entered a state of exaltation, her eyes floating up, her blonde head lifting towards the kitchen ceiling. Impulsive girl that she was, Laurence was always at risk of bursting out laughing. She had to contain herself.

Now it was her turn to be all aquiver. Why did Gaston like her? She thought him so charming. He spoke French and English, switching indifferently. His deep voice struck a powerful chord in her. Gaston would teach her to skate, he would take her dancing. He would teach her how to have fun. She thought Gaston the nicest name for a man.

There was no commitment, except one that grew within her. Their relationship was lived in the intensity of the moment. She went along with that, knowing a bond was forging between them. She would see him in a month. Her hands fluttered at the very thought.

Love's new delights reveal the heart's desires. She had questions it was impossible to answer. Why is he interested in me? Why is this happening to me? Here she was, she who did not seek to be grand or exceptional, she who was sceptical about notions like fate or destiny, seeing herself in a completely new light, the light of love.

Was she naïve to never have thought of love before meeting Gaston? The large family of fifteen demanded unflinching sacrifice from each. The general good required an amiable harmony. She believed in this, in word and in deed.

Early marriage was not highly valued in the Naud family. A union with a young man of the parish was excluded, as long as the clan needed her assistance. Neither the mother nor the father approved of acquaintances. Although concerned about what people thought of them, they were independent enough to set their own standards. Their economic situation had deprived them of a son in the priesthood. The priest was replaced by the nun, who cost less. Amanda was the only example the father could hold up.

During her adolescence, Laurence's disinterest in feminine pursuits grew. Contrary to the blonde Amanda, she wore sober clothes and black cotton stockings to Sunday mass, combed her hair like a little girl's or like an old lady's without regard for her age or the opinions of other young people. Some appreciated her wit. No one took particular notice of her. She overcame the lump in her throat with parody and humour. The guys were alike, so like her brothers that she never felt the spark of desire. Although inexperienced, she had an increasingly clear perception of reality, and kept an ironic distance. The need to help her brothers was different than being the helpmate of a local. She couldn't help seeing in any potential suitor some poor bugger who would boss her around.

About Gaston, she would say nothing. But she planned to have a discussion with her brother Edouard about whether she should finish her nurse's training.

She turned over in her mind what she would or would not say to each, was already talking to them and feeling sorry she couldn't say all. She wouldn't speak of her happiness; she wanted to protect it from becoming the object of gibes. Suffering was relegated to the past. Why return to it? They had had their share of grief, the chronic lack of money and concerns about the younger children. The mother's sickness would overshadow the usual bevy of complaints, real or imagined. How to know which was which when they had so little in common?

Keeping mum about Gaston distressed her, but they would react suspiciously. At best, the father would want to know if the young man's intentions were honourable. There would be misunderstandings. Both on the subject of her precipitous departure from Saint-Michel-Archange Hospital, and the equally unexpected encounter with he who moved her so— she would remain true to herself.

Love is violent. It excites the senses and one could behave indecently. It was true, she had flirted with Gaston. She felt like laughing again. She didn't, overwhelmed by a flood of sensuality that made her want to give of herself, body and soul. She felt dizzy, and knew that giving over the body to hard physical work was of an entirely different order than giving it over to love.

It occurred to her she was having naughty thoughts, but she didn't think so. If there was confusion, it was due to her fertile imagination. She had been told often enough that curiosity killed the cat.

An image of her mother, bed-ridden, exhausted, replaced her sentimental drifting. A calm, precise woman, her mother was the first up in the morning and the last to bed at night, if the father was not there. Rosalie, the heart of the household, she on whom each depended. Her presence was taken for granted, she belonged to them.

Goodness personified, Laurence thought. Her mother emanated a sweetness expressed in caring gestures, bordering on self-denial. The daughter mythologized her. In this, she followed the example of the father, in word and deed. The picture of a woman given over entirely to her family reinforced behavioural taboos, sanctified everyday relations. Notwithstanding her little romantic secret, her mother came first in her mind. Rosalie's image was unbesmirched. She lived entirely up to their expectations, to the point of being speechless. The mother, in all her functions, welded the family together. Nobody would deny this.

The train trundled through village after village. Laurence sat erect in the large comfortable seat, hands palm-up on her long lap, face toward the window. After a five-year absence, it was a poised young woman who was returning home.

On the morning of July 2, 1923, a defiant adolescent had boarded the train, her only baggage the name and address of a nun who would let her sleep the night. The idea to leave was born in a moment of anger, of panic. Thomas, home on vacation from the seminary, had told her he had an aunt in Québec who happened to be in charge of the woman's pavilion of a hospital. It immediately occurred to Laurence that hospital work would suit her, she was sure of it. She could think of nothing but leaving. As her boldness grew, so did her faith in the neighbour's son. She asked indirect questions because she had to be discreet. Did the sisters hire young girls? The seminarian saw through her, and yes, he was familiar with the psychiatric ward, the difficulties of recruiting staff, the heavy turn-over. He took care to use the exact words of his aunt. Laurence kept her thoughts to herself: there was work available, she had to get her nerve up. If she could meet the nun, she could persuade her she was not afraid of hard work.

The very next day, she intercepted Thomas during his walk, spoke of her secret plan and her wish to be interviewed by the pavilion director. He had already guessed and he would write his aunt. He reassured her he would keep quiet about it. He was like a brother, better than a brother!

She crept out of the house. He took her to the station. A convent employee would meet her. There was nothing to fear. She stuttered her thanks in a choking voice. Their eyes met, aware of the risks.

Time raced by, the train wheels clacking out the rhythm of her flight. She sat bunched up in her seat, motionless, tiny, dazed by her quiet gesture of rebellion. Her servitude was over, her dependence on them, as well. She chanted the two syllables of the verb go-ing, staring at the window's copper handle. The chant became pure sound. The syllables separated, making the word meaningless. The green sunlit Appalachian forest emitted a somnolent clarity. She awoke at the next station, arms numb around her canvas bag. They were halfway. Hunger and the smell of food reminded her it was lunchtime. She devoured her pork sandwich and quenched her thirst at the travellers' fountain.

For sure, someone would have noticed by now she was gone. She reread the letter from Québec, received the week before. An employee in a blue uniform would be waiting on the platform. If the employee was not there, if the nun had forgotten, what then? Anxiety welled up in her. She was behaving insolently, provocatively, taunting chance. It crossed her mind she would be punished. Her trust in Thomas, the seminarian, preserved her cool-headedness. He had helped her. The mechanical sound of the moving train filled her ears. If-the-employee's-waiting-I-did-right, if-not-I-am-wrong, she kept repeating, obsessed by the childish ritual. She arrived, palms sweating, tense. As the director had promised, she was given a night's shelter.

The next day, she got off the train back in Broughton and walked the seven miles to the farm. A broken sole cut into her foot, and she limped from twisting her left ankle. Supper was over and Rosalie was mending in the kitchen when she opened the door. Laurence said she had been at Edouard's. The father's absence made it easier to lie. Nobody had ever dared lie to him. The father claimed that falsehood was a sure sign of a child who would go wrong. But you just had to look the child in the eye to get the truth. The rough trek through field and forest was minor compared to that. Her excuse, plausible enough at the time, was that Edouard needed her. Summers, she sometimes stayed at the brother's place. She was helping him set up a household. The mother did not notice her Sunday clothing.

Laurence let on nothing in the week that followed. Her fugue had gone unnoticed. The director wrote a letter to the father, confirming her job at Saint-Michel-Archange Hospital. "Mademoiselle Naud will live in our residence, and will be fed and clothed. Her salary will be fifteen dollars a month." Laurence gave him the letter the day she turned eighteen.

He looked her right in the eye, she looked back. He was speechless, seconds passed without a response. The daughter addressed her father, according to family custom, as "vous," and formally asked him to authorize her departure. The silence affirmed the authority of the father, who placed the handwritten letter on the table. The printed letterhead of the hospital, and the signature followed by the nun's title made a strong impression. He granted his permission on two conditions: she would send her entire salary each month; and she would not go before early August, after the haying.

A bitter mix of sadness and joy welled up in Laurence. She felt her father's terrible coldness, his anger. Only the rapidly approaching date of departure gave her courage and loosened her tongue. Amanda, who had been getting ready to enter the convent forever, handling every item in her trousseau with the greatest of care, couldn't believe it. She, who took impeccable care of each piece of her trousseau, had a dim view of the job offer. Her jealousy kept her from commenting; she sought out the father to ask if it was true. Laurence also had but little success with Edouard, who grumbled about losing a helper. However, he promised to buy her a new pair of shoes. Rosalie waited until the others had gone to bed. She was sorry about their poverty and endless deprivations. She couldn't let her daughter go to the nuns empty-handed. She took a long white linen table cloth with white embroidery at the corners out of the cedar chest for them. For Laurence, she chose a woven bed cover.

Something happened that troubled her. She had never openly considered talking back to Amanda. The elder sister was known for her pride. Everyone acknowledged she was the father's favourite child and treated her with a sometimes ironic deference. The elder sister put on a white apron and took on the tasks most compatible with keeping clean. On wash day, Laurence washed, scrubbed, rinsed the laundry in the kitchen, while Amanda took the basket and stepped out to hang things in soldierly order on the line. The brothers joked: oh, it's Amanda's washing day! Laurence savoured the mocking note, implying she was taking on the easy part of the job.

The sticky heat of late morning made her go faster. Laurence, leaning over the tub, sweated in her damp clothes. Amanda appeared in the doorway, announcing she was going to change her apron. She got a mocking snigger, ringing with sarcasm, in response. When you go to Québec, maybe the sisters will shut you up with the madwomen, intonated Amanda, head high, moving in the direction of the linen closet, the disconcerting laugh still echoing behind. She took up her station behind a basket. Laurence eyed the white apron. In her hand was a well-filled diaper. She threw it. Amanda cried out for the mother to come. Nobody heard. Humiliation reduced her to silence.

Laurence left home the following week. She experienced, for the first time, loneliness and fear. The separation was a trial. Her rebelliousness was spent. The father's consent freed her, leaving a gap soon filled by an inexplicable sense of anguish.

It troubled her to have reaped success from disobedience. That she loved her mother, brothers and sisters was unquestionable. She even loved Amanda, despite her arrogance. In the simpleness of her heart, Laurence believed that the religious vocation had changed Amanda, who was to enter the convent in the fall. Laurence, unable to wait, stole the initiative. She was the polar opposite of her sister who foresaw, planned, justified. Laurence acted on impulse, got carried away by curiosity. She felt certain her way of going about things was that of a stupid woman who didn't know where she was headed. Her own ignorance sickened her.

Some families are more painful to leave than others. Laurence had listened day after day to her mother's fears, fanned by the father's pretensions. He protected them all from disaster, from devastating catastrophe, which always just around the corner. His pessimism foretold an apocalyptic future. As proof, he held up the war, which mobilized and decimated life. The country's economic situation was improving, but the Naud family saw little benefit. The family head was no longer young, which, coupled with living in the back country, meant they could only expect crumbs.

The father's words had left their mark. She fantasized negatively, obsessively. She expected the worst. Amanda's words came back to her, muddling her thinking. Perhaps they will lock you up with the madwomen. Her irrational fear grew to immense proportions. She panicked. She was headed towards disaster. By fleeing family ties she was tempting fate. Her decision was motivated by her rebellious, scheming nature. Amanda had put a curse on her by predicting she would be shut up. She was haunted with guilt. She was walking into a trap. The asylum doors would close on her. Amanda's words poisoned her journey.

Laurence arrived at the hospital, exhausted and in a meek state of mind. She eagerly gave herself over to the most demanding tasks. Later, she forgot the perpetual nightmare lurking in her psyche. She was assigned to the common ward. She had nothing to compare with her new reality. She washed patients, changed beds, cleaned chamber pots, helped with the laundry, served midday and evening meals and scoured pots and pans. She was given routine tasks, as it had been decided with Sister Agnès. She worked six days, more than fifty hours a week.

Laurence observed the patients: some were extremely apathetic, others highly agitated. She noted which was which, and tried to spare them frustration as much as possible. Washing and caring for the women gave her confidence. With smooth gestures and reassuring words, she could approach all of them, even those with a phobia for water.

Sister Agnès was favourably impressed. She ran the pavilion with authority. New recruits, to their distress, were never asked to explain their errors. The even-tempered nun was observant, uncompromising about blunders. If an employee, caught in the act of doing something amiss, tried to make excuses, the nun considered the explanation coolly, neutrally.

The pavilion contained minuscule rooms in which, on doctor's orders, aggressive or suicidal patients were isolated. They were tied to their beds during psychotic episodes. If this didn't suffice, strait-jackets were used. Among those in isolation were women considered to have disgusting sexual habits. Cries and moans came from behind closed doors.

Sister Agnès held forth solemnly on the causes, effects, and signs of madness. She forewarned Laurence of abnormal behaviours offensive to a young girl. Her new duties would expose her to bad habits she didn't know existed. Providence would provide her with the grace to accomplish her work. No less than absolute discretion was required. If the work had an adverse moral affect on Laurence, she would be removed instantly from the ward. To a Christian, the deviant behaviours of madness were odious. Sister Agnès named each patient, noting that they were not aggressive, but could be subject to compulsive, morbid perversions not to be tolerated in the common ward. Onanism, in particular, was a sign of insanity.

The nun assigned her certain patients confined to cells. The employees said there was an asylum within the asylum. The madwomen heard howling, but never seen, conjured up terrifying images.

Behind a door, Laurence saw an emaciated woman penetrating herself with her fingers while her other hand jiggled her pubis, eyes bulging, mouth opened to cry out. Laurence had outrageous dreams that awakened her. Crossing the threshold from dream to reality, the cries were confused in the night, some, distant, creeping under her door. People were moaning. Insanity didn't stop at bedtime. The patients did not sleep. Their illness was forever with them. She shivered. The gloomy shadows of night underscored their dementia. Destructive insomnia, apathy beyond words, madness was a punishing scourge, emptying the body of its vitality.

On the first of each month, Laurence wrote her family about such happy events as a quick outing to the city, a visit from Thomas, the seminarian, and apologized for her spelling. She enclosed banknotes in the envelope. A nun gave her a letter from the father, and the girl smiled, naïvely hopeful. The same tightening of the throat accompanied each reading. He related the endless misfortunes that they suffered. She tucked the images of unhappiness away in the back of her mind.

In the spring, she hung around in the garden, asking for pots, soil, plants, and took pleasure out of plunging her fingers into the earth. Geraniums grew on the windowsill and on the bedside table.

Laurence saw there were nursing-school students, young women from good families. One night, before falling asleep, it suddenly occurred to her she could become a nurse. It was a moment of illumination, a state of grace, a mystical vocation that called out to the isolated girl. The very idea filled her simultaneously with hope and despair. She had been removed from school after grade five. It was something she forgot so long as she could rely on her physical capacity for work, her plucky tolerance of endless repetitive tasks.

Convent life was akin to family life in many respects. Women had a strong sense of duty. She took the world of women seriously, except when it proved to be narrow-minded. She thought before she spoke, never forgot that the sisters were taking note, and told herself that her dream would be judged on its merit.

With Sister Agnès, it was agreed that she would do housework in the nuns' pavilion in exchange for French lessons. Laurence no longer had a day off. Her solitude took on a more positive hue. She wrote home that she was getting French lessons, without mentioning the extra workload. The news was met with silence.

To the burden of endless work was added a feeling of insignificance. For weeks on end she never thought of herself. Then her cheeks suddenly burned with what she had repressed: the desire to confide in someone. Sadness and rage about doing nothing but work welled up in her. She swallowed her disappointment.

One day, when the tyranny of everyday life was winning out over her faith in the future, she received an angry letter from the father. He demanded an explanation about why she had subtracted a dollar and fifty cents from her last envelope. He was adamant, telling her in curt solemn terms to remember her duty and her promise. The daughter's reply was simple. The money was used to buy herself underwear, yellow cotton panties.

In autumn, 1925, enrollment at the nursing school was low, and the sisters needed to fill the empty places. Sister Agnès's influence played in her favour. Laurence was given the less demanding night shift. She watched over the sleep of the patients. Some moaned late into the night, despite sedatives. Disturbing ravings, nightmares and cries— suffering that never slept was agonizing to watch. Mental illness destroyed the body.

Towards four or five in the morning, when all was calm, she learned by rote, nibbling crackers and sipping milk to keep awake. She took apart the scientific terms, syllable by syllable, to be sure of the spelling and pronunciation.

Laurence slept after the evening meal. Within a month, the advantages of her special schedule became obvious. She began to think of herself as independent, rather than lonely. The young woman had taken charge of her existence, was bursting with new hope. She wrote to her family about the door of opportunity the nuns were opening to her. The father urged her to be grateful. She was grateful, but refused to behave obsequiously or with servility. On the contrary, she studied during the night at a desk she fitted out for her convenience. Except for Sunday mass, she was no longer seen at chapel. Step by careful step, she led her life on the fringes of the community.

Misleading rumours surged near examination time. Seated early in the morning before her notes and her physiology textbook, her scribbling seemed a hopeless confusion of letters, broken parcels of words. Her pencil wobbled in her grasp. She had put down vowels and consonants, one after the other, without considering their relationship to the memorized text, nor even to the sounds of the words. She was confronted with pages of graffiti, aligned symbols that simulated sentences, and, in the midst of the mumble-jumble, an occasional underlined word, correctly spelled.

Realizing the notebook was useless, she took up the textbook and memorized the terms by rote, tapping them out countless times on the tips of her fingers, closing her eyes and repeating them in their exact order. When she had a spare moment, she repeated the litanies to herself.

Laurence went off with the textbook, forgetting her notes in the ward. Sister Eugène, on the morning shift, saw it sitting there with Laurence's name on the cover, and opened it. The writing was indecipherable! She put it in her files.

The notebook was proof that Sister Agnès had not evaluated Laurence according to the norms. The student was getting unwarranted protection. Sister Eugène herself was going to see that order was restored. She would have a talk with the nun in question, which did not preclude her going right to the hospital director. Sister Eugène, frustrated with her inferior rank, had coveted Sister Agnès's post for a long time. She demanded to meet Sister Agnès, waving the notebook and the nurses' register. The lines of Sister Agnès's face froze. Her features were severe under her starched cornet as she tried to read an indecipherable phrase. Sister Eugène read aloud from the register that the young student left a trail of dirty glasses and crumbs of stolen food, that her irregular schedule prevented her from attending chapel. She had even noted the last time Laurence had appeared at morning mass.

Sister Agnès took in every word of Sister Eugène's charges. The notebook in the nun's possession distressed her. Laurence understood that both as student and as employee, she had failed to comply with hospital regulations. She insisted she should be given a second chance, that she would prove herself at examination time.

Alternately furious and upset, she was determined to better her lot, and refused to get bogged down in the trap of the present. Her boldness, her intuition drove her forward. At bedtime, she wept over her ignorance of the written language, which appeared to her, for the first time, as a sign of ignorance, period.

She refrained from eating and drinking. The words of the physiology textbook danced before her eyes. She stood to read the last chapter, memorizing it. The women were waking up. Sister Eugène came into the ward earlier than usual to find Laurence changing the bed of an incontinent patient. The nun searched for signs of neglect in vain. Laurence, who knew she was being spied on, worked harder than ever. Raised to be dutiful, she understood that work well-done would win the confidence of her superior. Nothing doing. The ten days leading up to the exams were trying. Sister Eugène found disorder in the linen cupboard, insisted the patients be seated in the refectory at the exact time stated in the rules. The employee was reprimanded several times. One morning she did exactly as bid. The patients were screaming, swearing, distraught by the abrupt treatment.

During the exam, the student held on to the idea that failure did not mean disaster. She was telling herself the opposite of what she believed, in order to defuse her anxiety. The manifest nervousness of the other students calmed her. Her lead pencil raced as she wrote down lists of words in reply to the objective questions. She reread her pages until the end of the allotted time and handed them to the nun. She had never been so exhausted.

She passed her exams. This didn't stop Sister Eugène. Convinced that Laurence was getting special treatment, her inquiries at the hospital office turned up a grade five diploma from a rural school. The nun, comparing her to the other students, well-born girls from respectable milieus, found her wanting. She was an ambitious girl with little talent, manifestly not called to the profession.

Sister Eugène made spiteful comments about the employee. The latter was afraid people would believe them. Her behaviour had to be above reproach in the eyes of the nun. She repeated this simple homily to herself. The veiled threats escalated, implying that Laurence lacked piety. The resident employees went to mass when their schedule permitted. Laurence was reprimanded for setting a bad example.

She was called before the hospital director. The interview was brief and ended on a kindly note. The director reminded her of her Christian duties, which, given her special schedule, required particular vigilance, using the analogy of evening prayers practised in families as a way of thanking God for the blessing of life. Laurence learned that she had been admitted to the school because of lack of students. The director wished her success. Thomas came to mind. He was protecting her.

The father wrote her on the occasion of Amanda's final vows. He asked her to join her voice to that of her sisters and brothers in prayer. The elder sister needed the prayers of each to help her give up worldly things. An ironic laugh bubbled up, vicious, disturbing. The idea of leaving behind the things of the world seemed to her a joke, a lie one tells oneself in order lord it over others. Even at a distance Amanda was conning them. She disapproved of her sister's high-falluting attitude, and at Sunday mass ignored the father's letter.

After the June examinations, she was returned to the day shift. Had the number of regulations increased or had the scales fallen from her eyes? The privileges of being on the night shift were a thing of the past, and Sister Eugène was in charge, the tasks defined to the last detail so that order might prevail, even in the soul, said the nun. The patients suffered more than the employees. No excuse was good enough for not following the routine. Without exception, the women were led like sheep towards the refectory, the recreation room and the walled courtyard.

Sister Eugène bristled with satisfaction at the sight of the cleaned and tidied dormitory. She kept a watch on it, making sure no one entered before the evening rest period. The older women whined and begged, drowsy in the torrid mid-afternoon heat. Some howled and swore when threatened with isolation. They tried to find pretexts and sneak chances to get back to their own little corners, and quarrels broke out. Laurence led the oldest women, those who slept lightly and woke with the light of dawn, to their beds.

The sister's zeal approached sadism. Warnings were accompanied by threats of punishment in the form of deprivations. The patients cried, moaned, their mania becoming more marked. The employees separated the aggressive women. The patients' discomfort was there for all to see.

During the second year of her studies, Laurence became friendly with Estelle Haley, the only other student not from the city of Québec. Very blonde with blue eyes, the girl resembled a doll. It was she who approached Laurence. Estelle was staying with a widowed aunt and missed "to death," as she put, her father, mother and village of Saint-Marie-de-Beauce. They had little in common. Laurence became the confidante to whom the girl told the story of her life as an only child, pampered, spoiled by her family. Laurence thought her likely the most well-to-do of the students.

The courses were comprised mainly of practical instruction that took place in the hospital's various pavilions. They worked as a team, learning the techniques and reciting their lists of terms to each other. Two good girls, one could say. The means did not count, only the end.

Months passed, oscillating between her double task, punctuated by a visit from the father, who neither encouraged her nor discouraged her. He was somewhat taken aback that instruction was being offered for nothing. He urged her to be grateful for this unheard-of chance at improving her social status. He was polite to the point of obsequiousness with the nuns, to show he set a good example.

The cold winter finally gave way to spring. An American circus was coming. The students described it as unique. There would be sideshows of human monsters never before seen. The Barnum Circus's reputation was based on the variety of shows it offered, of which the most popular, the one that caused the greatest excitement, was the array of extraordinary characters. The public hurried to see hunchbacks, enlarged craniums, dwarfs accompanied by giants, the bearded woman, the stork man, the fat couple, wider than they were tall, the Siamese sisters, the limbless man, the girl with rickets whose hair reached the ground, the hermaphrodite with women's breasts, people with one eye and a Cyclops. Bare-breasted women fought each other. A strong man with long hair lifted weights, pulled loaded carts so the public could throw pennies at him. The young girls were looking forward to the event. For them the hermaphrodite was a monstrosity that medicine could not explain. Soon they talked about nothing except the coming American circus.

Exam times were approaching and life became correspondingly more hectic. The nuns had a meeting. According to Sister Agnès, the sideshow was likely anti-Christian. She compared the Americans to the ancient Romans, materialists who would lead civilization to ruin. In Rome, circus games featured early Christians thrown to the lions, who devoured them before blood-thirsty audiences. Pagan decadence was invading the city. Sister Agnès waxed lyric in her opinion that their souls were in danger. She called for prayers. Sister Eugène sputtered, her face red in her white cornet. Would the hermaphrodite bare his chest? She was met with dead silence. They acknowledged they had no power over the municipal authorities. But the sideshow was forbidden to the nursing students.

Laurence learned of the decision before her companions. Sister Eugène told her they would not be allowed to go to the circus: we're not in Rome, she added. The Romans would invade the city; the blood of new martyrs would flow. She reddened with zeal. Their professor made known the director's decision. It was formally forbidden to attend the freak show, under threat of expulsion. The young girls grumbled. Laurence told Estelle that she thought the nuns were serious.

The American circus arrived in Québec a week before the exams. The nuns found out that the students had defied them. Certain students admitted it. A heavy suspense, a gloomy silence, reigned in the classroom. The last exam was to take place Friday. The director herself announced the expulsion. The third-year course would be cancelled. If the students wished to continue their studies, they would join their first-year colleagues, who had not disobeyed the rule. She dismissed them, telling them to take a year off to think.

Laurence's lot was that of her companions. There was no more talk of the circus. There was no scandal beyond the walls of the convent. The hospital hushed up the dismissal of the young girls from good families. The nuns used their power of discretion.

Estelle said goodbye to her, unsure if she would return. Being so far from her family caused her sleepless nights. The green-eyed student wept about leaving her friend, whom she praised in affectionate terms.

Sister Agnès gave Laurence the job of admissions clerk. On the final morning, Sister Eugène was persnickety and quarrelsome. While Laurence was washing the floor of the laundry room— which she didn't have to do— the nun followed her, telling her to hurry, to wash the baseboards. With a kick, the employee knocked over the pail and handed her the washrag. The floor was covered with dirty water. The next day, in the admissions office, still reeling from her angry gesture, she realized that an unselfish act doesn't oblige anyone to respond in kind.

In the train taking her to her father's house, Laurence evoked the sound of her foot hitting the metal pail. The water spread over the floor while she ran to take refuge among the madwomen. Now she felt like laughing at her abruptness, her famous impulsiveness. She couldn't explain her rage, even if provoked by a woman like Sister Eugène, whose punctilious manner was fairly typical. Laurence was not reprimanded.

Was it intuition or clear thinking? Fate guided her in the direction of Dr. Fournier's. Sister Agnès had protested. "You will never finish your studies. You won't come back." Laurence promised she would, but circumstances had changed and she never returned. The sister had been right. September rolled around without the least thought of studying, or of her disgraced companions. The memory lapse was perhaps a bad sign, but she didn't try to figure it out.

The adaptation to Beaupré seemed so fast. She had free time, evening hours when nothing was required of her. Having time on her hands threw her. She experienced the emptiness Estelle Haley spoke of. In the heavy silence, the clock in the corridor made fun of her. A cuckoo counted the passing hours and half hours. Her idle mind was a trap, and she went to bed early. The days grew longer. She felt like breathing in the very pure air along the river's banks. It was such a long time since she had heard the sound of running water, had let the cold run-off slide through her fingers. The bare fields were flooded with melting ice. The rapid thaw north of the forty-fifth parallel followed its course. Any pretext for going out was valid. Time grew short again. She was the country girl, once more, with her feet on the ground, breathing in the great outdoors.

She caught up with the summers spent indoors. Had it not been for her new social status, she would have tramped through the fields dressed any old way. She missed the presence of farm animals, their odours, the gestures of caring for them. The sight of any dog delighted her. She modelled herself on others, gravely miming their well-considered manners. In fact, the spirited young woman kept herself in check, uncertain of who she was when she wasn't on duty.

3

The evening would be cold, the maple forest reddened by frost. As Broughton approached, her excitement grew. Her mother's health dampened Laurence's joy. But she would fight the illness and Rosalie would recover. Her presence would free her mother from worry. No doubt it was exhaustion that kept her bed-ridden. Fatigue was something you recovered from. The mother's genes were as good as the father's. From the grandparents, who lived to a ripe old age, one could surmise she had a strong constitution. There had been one child after another, premature aging after the tenth, slowness of movement, shortness of breath, the dropped uterus after the fourteenth and fifteenth pregnancy. Rosalie was on her feet the day after giving birth. Lack of sleep, never caught up on, wore her out. The daughter, distressed, repressed her fear of mortal illness.

For sure the father was already waiting at the station and her impatience increased proportionately. He was a man who always came through in tight moments. They all counted on him, herself included. Even Edouard sought his approval.

Laurence admired Edouard. She had great respect for his good points. At the age of fourteen, he knew what he wanted and had started planning for it. During winter, he would work in lumber camps. Summers, he would help on the farm, and in slack times, work for others. The new agricultural machinery often needed to be repaired, and he understood how to do basic repairs from reading the manuals, in English, and from tinkering with the spare parts his father sold. He would buy some land with his savings. His goal was an efficient farm that earned returns. A business.

Laurence was eleven when he spoke to her of his plans. He convinced the father to let him put aside part of the money he earned. This happened in her presence, so that she was witness to the father's acquiescence. She was impressed with Edouard's sense of responsibility, his steadiness, his determination. Stage by stage, he let her in on his plans. She was part of the process, her approval was indispensable. At eighteen, he bought the land he wanted. He avowed he would not marry before the business was established. Sturdy and serious, he attracted the older girls already worried about becoming old maids.

His success thrilled her. At the age of twenty, no major obstacles had been encountered. He reckoned out time and money, planned in advance for what needed to be done, factored in a loan he intended to ask for as soon as he came of age. The father didn't agree. For him a mortgage was a debt, that would put him in risk of losing his land. His son was wagering his house, barely standing, and the barn, under construction. Léon flared up, calling credit the devil's invention. The neutral façades of banks concealed foreign financiers accumulating capital to finance wars. The son lowered his head. The father's ideas introduced God, and more often, the devil, into the economic picture, while the son added and subtracted numbers. Still, a shiver ran up his spine during the family prayers, and he smelled danger.

The construction of the barn, with its silo for fodder, was put off for a year. When he had men working for him, Laurence looked after the animals and made the noonday meal for the workers. She fetched water from the well, lit the huge wood stove with the two-tiered oven, and cooked a copious meal for ten men up since dawn. With her, he calculated their salaries and the cost of materials. Laurence developed a taste for itemizing and for imagining the final result, took pleasure in watching the work progress. She saw in the totally mechanized farm the guarantee of a future for the Naud family, safe in Edouard's hands. They were inseparable. She was his associate and companion. Edouard, who was quite pig-headed despite his thoughtful air, was always counting. He was embarrassed by Laurence's opinionated fervour. One day, she went so far as to suggest she replace the man hired for the harvest, to increase the profits from the sale.

He brother gave her advice, had enlightened opinions. She told him of her ambivalence regarding continuing her studies. A diploma would cost her a year.

The train slowed down and stopped. The door opened and she saw Léon Naud stepping forward. She said: good evening, Father, her voice rising with elation. He greeted her, erect, hatless, and taller than he, with a casual look. It was customary to greet without touching. They shared news in an animated fashion, mutually cordial. They were alike, both thriving on talk. He found her grown up, an adult. His daughter rekindled his spirit. The mother said a doctor was unnecessary. She had complained of fatigue, dizziness. She had attacks of vertigo, was eating almost nothing, and had been in bed for a week. He did not mention her shock at seeing an old horse killed, then vomiting blood. The sleepless nights started shortly after. Rosalie's silence bothered him. Her pallor, her weakness made him decide to call for help.

Along the road, she recognized houses lit by lamplight. Laurence knew them all. They had so often served as landmarks as she trekked to the village, or beyond. In the dark, a hillside, a bridge on the Palmer River, a crossroads sufficed for her to identify them. The air they breathed out in the country was suffused with the odours of the woods, of the crops, of animals. Back in Beaupré, the river dispersed the smells. The familiar childhood places felt foreign to her. She knew, intuitively, that whatever happened, she would never live here again.

Léon Naud's eyes, when the cart slowed down, fell on the bare right knee revealed under a short skirt. He reprimanded her as they disembarked. Laurence didn't understand at once what he was referring to. For the father, modesty was serious business. She would have liked her skirt to be longer. He made it into a question of propriety.

She was received in high spirits. The young ones jumped up and down for joy in the middle of the big kitchen, opening their arms. She kissed them. She was pelted with questions without time to answer. They wanted her to confirm her new position. Was she a nurse?

The small children giggled. Babies get nursed. Calves and lambs get nursed. But the idea of big people getting nursed seemed funny. They thought it silly. It was a doctor who looked after sick people. And a doctor was not a woman. The mother would not see the doctor, but accepted the nurse. Laurence was familiar with the kind of logic that took things literally. She removed her black kit from her suitcase and hurried to Rosalie's bedside.

The odour of sour sheets took Laurence by surprise. The mother smiled. The girl took her by the hands, deeply touched, and whispered that she would make her better. With her simple words and her direct gaze, she captured Rosalie's attention. On duty, her bedside manner gave patients the will to live.

Laurence functioned intuitively, the nurse's instinct overtaking the daughter's compassion. In addition to the fact that Rosalie was her mother, her obstinate refusal to see the doctor made it all the more important she do it right. They talked a little.

The next day she looked for clean sheets and found none. She sorted the wash, brought in wood from the shed, scoured the pails, cut the soap, stripped the straw mattresses. Laurence enveloped her mother in a blanket, sat her in the rocking chair, a hot water bottle on her stomach and a cup of tea to drink.

Her hair looked very white. She had brought all her pregnancies to term, well aware that she needed to eat properly for the sake of the unborn child.

The parents had got through the Spanish flu epidemic without losing any family members. A week-old baby died due to an erroneous medical diagnosis, and an ordinary infection took the fifteenth child. In her sadness, the mother became twice as careful. The last-born seemed fragile to her. Older cows or mares gave birth to fragile calves or colts. Anaemic females were at greater risk of falling ill. They were butchered. In her panic, the mother confused cows, mares and women. She let her sadness surface, talked at last of her fears. They concerned the children.

She was not as strong as before, and two of the girls and a boy, though a good weight at birth, were fidgety, high-strung. She compensated by giving them extra food, which they refused. Their rate of growth worried her for a long time. Now, at the ages of seven, eight and ten, they weren't yet doing their share of the work, as the older ones had at the same ages. Even the father acknowledged they weren't strong and did not consider their contribution necessary. They could take life easy. The two youngest spoke early, mimed the words of the elder children who took care of them. Odette, who was so pretty with her curls, was the despondent one. The little girl, silent, inscrutable, liked housework but was easily discouraged by any difficulty. Rosalie no longer had the patience to teach them. Odette spent hours watching her spin, knit, weave, sew, and when night fell, she couldn't sleep. Her brothers crept up on her, pulled her hair, amused by her moodiness and her reproachful cries. The youngest ones were not being well-raised. Rosalie said she had lost control of her household.

Laurence put her to bed. It was suffocating in the bedroom adjoining the kitchen, with its stained armoire, potbellied chest of drawers, battered table on which Rosalie had changed the babies, and two low chairs. They crowded the room.

The stove had heated for the washing, and the heat made it hard to breathe. The window wouldn't open and Laurence forced it with a piece of wood. The mother made an effort to break through her reticence, to express the fears that choked her. She had suffered from anaemia since the birth of the youngest. The doctor treated her, but she never got better. Since she had stopped doing the garden, she was limited to the house and the dairy. She no longer went to the stable. In June, she felt recovered. At her bidding, Isidore dug up the ground. The illness returned, but she didn't give in. She tired herself cultivating lettuce, tomatoes, cucumbers, beans, carrots, turnips, beets, and various kinds of onions and herbs. It was a good harvest, and she had made jam and pickles. Rosalie was being defensive, for the doctor had forbidden gardening.

She had no choice but to help, the father's affairs were in a disastrous state. Laurence whispered to her tenderly until she slept.

After her day of teaching at the village school, Aline prepared the usual omelette with lard, accompanied by vegetables. Rosalie refused her share. Around the big table, they ate with lowered heads. Aline took their sullenness as a rebuke.

The young girl prepared crêpes, buckwheat waffles, omelettes to which she added the traditional lard, for the men, not taking any herself. The father disliked her cooking, which was like having Lent every day. The tall secretive girl with the halting voice and subdued personality could not bear the extra workload occasioned by the mother's illness. She was overwhelmed by everything.

On account of her fragility, she was never asked to look after the animals or work in the fields. She hid her revulsion for butchering, and took refuge in sewing. She spent a day a month in bed, a sure sign of frailty. They neither condemned her, nor rallied to her. She made herself scarce, like a guest you wait for to leave. Even-tempered, unopinionated, she was like a young girl in an old-fashioned picture book. Her desire to enter the convent surprised no one, given she'd been thinking of it since childhood. Who would have imagined marriage for this girl, lacking in personality, easily disgusted and nauseated? To think of Aline as a mother was to think of a slow torture, a gross error. The father had granted her a year of studies as a boarder. Laurence's money provided for it. Aline studied, memorized the course material, neither questioning nor doubting its pertinence. Her results were good enough and interested no one. Was she pretty? She was, but her thinness was not considered attractive by boys her age. Her shyness, coupled with a fear of men, isolated her.

Because she was a teacher, she was obliged to impose her authority, which made her both suffer and feel certain she was called to her profession.

Rosalie had got a shock, was deeply distressed by the death of the old horse. As soon as they found themselves alone, Aline described the event to Laurence, relating it— and her mother's reaction— in detail.

They were waiting for the father, gone to Leeds that morning. The moon was up, with the sun still blazing. Time seemed stopped. The horse appeared, pulling a load of scrap metal, the wagon raising a cloud of dust. It looked like the devil smoking between the sun and the moon. Like always, the father gave the horse reign as soon as it entered the drive, trusting the animal's instinct to know where it was going. The animal was not wearing blinkers, affecting its sight. Blinded by the bright sunset and the waves of dust, it moved towards the right, stepped into the ditch and fell, pieces of metal landing on its flank. They heard a dry crack, followed by a deathly silence. It remained on its knees. Its head was down in a sign of defeat.

The horse was in pain from the torn knee, the broken bone. Abundant mucus flowed from its mouth. The father, with his sons, examined the animal. They decided to put it down right then and there. Isidore loaded the hunting rifle. The father aimed above the eye, near the temple. The sun had just set. The horse started, doubled by its moving shadow. The mother had not moved from the gallery. She wept silently, the young children leaning on her. The father said to bring around the tip-cart. Despite his fatigue, he and his sons hoisted up the horse. Isidore was told to take it to Edouard's farm. His wife vomited. How often had she reminded him of the animal's age? He obstinately persisted in overloading the wagon.

Léon maintained a stubborn silence. His wife's unspoken reproaches weighed on him.

He sorted out the metal, made a list of the spare parts purchased in bulk at the auction. He hadn't adequately examined the goods, ending up with an oddly assorted mix. He wouldn't be able to sell them as a batch for the good price anticipated. Nobody would want such a pile of scrap: most of it was useless.

Léon Naud explained his financial situation to Laurence: he'd had a very bad year. He reminded her of his famous prudence in business. A sheep buyer had shown up with a witness, who had endorsed the promissory note. He gave his word he would pay on delivery. He advanced part of the amount, plus the delivery costs, which the seller normally assumes. Léon believed he was dealing with a man as trustworthy as he was himself. To his questions regarding the balance of payment, the endorser maintained that the creditor had money in the bank, as well as rhyming off a list of goods, lands and properties in his name. They made an excellent impression.

Despite their terms of agreement, the farmer asked for credit when the livestock was delivered. This was against Léon's principles. He was afraid of being tricked, something that might entail a lawsuit, dug in and demanded a contract on his conditions. The wording specified that credit was granted for sixty days, with a fixed rate of interest on the balance of payment, and that he remained owner of the one hundred sheep until the bill was settled.

At the due date, feeling mistrustful of the debtor, he went to Leeds with the wagon. Morally, he disapproved of loans with interest. Though the practice was spreading, religious teaching forbade usury, money made with money, which encouraged perfidy and destroyed the social fabric. Léon Naud, a man who took comfort in his high morals, had betrayed his principles. He expected failure, for no one can serve two masters.

Anticipating what might happen, he would make a deal, would settle for bartering bundles of wool, bags of grain in exchange for the livestock. He reached the farm in a state of confusion, convinced he was dealing with someone dishonest. He forgot the possibility of concessions. Voices rose. The farmer pretended the sheep were sick. For half the troop he had got only the price of the hides. The fellow was lying. He had disposed of the meat to hotel owners, a bonus in return for political favours, for patronage. The father had not been careful enough. At the town council, it was rumoured the farmer was well-connected, the proof being that his son had been promoted to foreman in highway construction.

The debtor's refusal to pay led him to the endorser, an unsavoury type who worked for the farmer now and then. The father realized he was talking to somebody with a better-than-average education, who drank. The gin bottle on the table, though it was only noon, proved it. He was a stooge, and a fast talker.

Hooves kicked up the dust and the noise of the wheels drowned out his confused thoughts. The old horse went slower on account of the bad roads. He stopped at the village auction, managing to look at the lots at the last possible moment. The auctioneer mounted the platform and the sale started. Léon's tumultuous feelings kept him there. Ordinarily, he didn't permit himself to spend everything he had, but it would be a bargain to get a hold of spare agricultural machinery parts. The voice of reason warned him he was already in over his head. He had learned from experience not to rush things. He turned a deaf ear to the voice of his conscience, coveting the lot as if his future depended on acquiring it. The auctioneer opened the bidding for exactly what he had in his pocket, and with no other bid, it was his.

The father confided his worries to the daughter. For a long time he blamed his setbacks on his outdated farm equipment. The strong market put him even farther out of the loop, so that he could only obtain risky sales. Now he had tied up his nest-egg in a deal that ruined the season. He was still selling parts to farmers, sending for them to mail order catalogues, at a lower profit. He had to stay both in livestock and spare parts to keep afloat.

Laurence appreciated the father's talking to her. Even if it was the story of a failure, it was in the realm of commerce, which fascinated her. Despite possible setbacks, the possibilities seemed promising. He poured out his feelings without fear of disapproval, without asking her opinion, so certain he was of his daughter's esteem. As confidante in time of misfortune, a daughter was a better listener than a son. The father had spoken to Edouard, who responded impatiently, keeping his opinion to himself. Edouard had his own problems and was forgiven. The father interpreted his daughter's interest as a sign he was understood. He wasn't as stupid as he thought, because Laurence, sitting at the end of the table, didn't flinch.

She entered the girls' bedroom very late, not wondering why the father had omitted the episode with the horse. The exalted image of the clear sky with the moon risen and the sun burning above the maple wood from Aline's story of the incident came back to her. She fell asleep.

The next morning, Laurence proffered the money. The father tucked it in his vest pocket without thanking her. He took her cooperation for granted and never thanked her. Her compliance reassured him. He no doubt thought his daughter was acting out of duty. Laurence anticipated the request. She kept back the amount necessary for the return ticket.

4

Laurence soon realized the mother's illness was not fatal. With menopause, an ailment that had not been taken care of resurfaced. The monotonous sound of heavy rain falling penetrated the bedroom. Sitting near Rosalie, who was propped up by feather pillows drinking tea, she was reminded of a person who always kept in the background. Moving slowly, Rosalie distributed her energy, every gesture measured to avoid abruptness. It was her mother's way to be up before everyone, to see to her tasks, each dispatched with care and attention. Constant deprivation ushered in a state of mind that focused on essentials. Her apparent calm masked inner terrors and her impatience increased when food lacked. She felt degraded, and struggled to be forbearing. The interminable winters ended in difficult months when everyone suffered penury in silence. Rosalie asked nothing of Léon who, for his part, suited himself with what she served him. She respected him to the point of forgetting herself.

Laurence prepared a vegetable soup and a pot-au-feu in the Beaupré manner, which Rosalie picked at. In mid-afternoon the girl brought her some broth. The mother complained of overwork. Pathetic, aged, with emaciated arms and a sagging belly, she was the vision of a woman consumed by life, sacrificed.

With her sweet voice, Rosalie recounted the changes that had taken place since Laurence left. They had stopped growing flax the following year. As she no longer went to the sheep pen, it was not properly cleaned, resulting in sick sheep. They killed the ewes. The rest were put out to pasture for a time and then driven to the auction, where they fetched a reduced price. The second year, there wasn't a single one left.

The eldest, a boy little given to talking, went up to Abitibi. He helped out the family until he got married. Such was Joseph's silence that they noticed the lack of money more than his absence. Like his father, he did not enjoy farming. The growing northern town needed men to work. He adopted a frontier spirit, not minding the lack of conveniences in the new town. They thought of Joseph as being exiled in Rouyn. Laurence shared this notion of the meaning of the word exile.

The aging Rosalie now considered a daughter more useful to the family than a son. A son brought in money, a daughter organized things and saw to the general well-being. Aline's future was the convent, if they accepted her despite her poor health. Laurence had no vocation, and would marry. The father and mother had talked it over before she arrived. Rosalie was given the job of putting their proposition to Laurence. At twenty-three, a girl was no longer young. They would give her shelter, clothing, and a trousseau. The mother realized that she was not strong. With no help, the younger ones were running wild and would end up with neither the health nor the moral fibre of the elder.

Out of politeness, Laurence said nothing. It was customary to take time to think when one had a decision to make. Her mother's words put her in a state of confusion. Laurence knew that the educated daughters entered the convent and the dummies got married. As long as this state of affairs persisted, sanctioned by the clergy, people were destined to be poor. She would not participate in what she considered the servitude of women, the bearing of children raised in miserable conditions, possibly to go to war. The idea of marrying a village boy revolted her. Once more, she was thinking things she couldn't say. She checked her desire to argue, to reason with them. Her judgement of the village boys excluded her brothers, whom she perceived as different, as strong, strapping boys. Like Edouard. Her rebellious character predisposed her to refuse.

Her mother's condition moved her to pity. She'd left on impulse, abandoned her, and had got the best of the deal. Now her mother was imploring her, in a roundabout way, for the well-being of all. Laurence had to face the consequences of her flight.

The cold, hard precariousness of their situation rose before her eyes. They lived on the farthest concession road from the village, on sterile land in a nearly square house built by the father. A well provided water for the kitchen pump, but otherwise they lived as of old, with neither toilet nor bathroom. They used spirit lamps for light. The stove was used for heating the kitchen, cooking, boiling water, making soap, dyeing. Rosalie didn't make boots any more, but she still used flax and wool to make sheets, towels, table cloths, most of the clothing and underwear, all hand-sewn.

Under her guidance, Laurence had become very good with her hands. But unlike her sisters, as soon as there was a moment, she left the common room, the kitchen. Each day she slipped outside, regardless of the season. Her time was given over to the collective's efforts to survive. The rhythm of her lithesome, precipitous youth, when she ran, marked faster time, gripped by a muted exasperation that urged her on. Sometimes, for fun, she gave herself the challenge of seeing how fast she could go, testing her mettle and endurance. Bettering her self mattered only to her, for no one was watching. What was this voice that teased her, egged her on, made her breathless, open to change?

She was tormented by doubt. Her rebellion without a cause was replaced by a dutiful conscience. She didn't understand herself: her heart beat compassionately, but her spontaneous reaction was to flee.

Laurence held it against Amanda that her father threw good money after bad for the benefit of the religious community alone. The eldest was gaining in influence. The mother handed her her letters, as she had to each of the children. The nun wrote the same letter every month to the very dear father— Rosalie was called the beloved mother— and to the entire family united in Jesus and Mary through prayer. So her missive began. She drew attention to a date on the liturgical calendar, noted the feast days, made sure to mention the rank of the officiating priest and her own participation in the rites. Before the closing paragraph, signing off with a request to God the Father to bless the family, she wrote one paragraph that varied from letter to letter. This time it regarded Rosalie's recovery, for which she was fervently praying and of which Laurence was the privileged caretaker. She signed the letter Sister Léon-des-Anges.

Laurence discerned the overweening egotism in these letters, and a baleful, involuntary anger brewed within her. Amanda's influence was such that her epistles filled each of them with pride. Even at a distance the eldest daughter exercised her spell over them. Laurence was less troubled by being told what to do than by Amanda's blowing off about herself in each paragraph. Could she say so to anyone? Once more, she realized that her moral solitude was a consequence of her heretic inner thoughts.

Aline, seated next to her, pointed out Amanda's almost perfect handwriting, a sure sign of intelligence. The carefully formed letters emphasized the learned quality of her missives. Apparently impersonal, Amanda's certitudes paraded the role she had forged for herself.

In one letter, about Aline's vocation, the nun declared that the family was blessed when one of its members was called by God. The next letter insisted on the importance of choosing the right community. Léon played intermediary between his daughters and asked Aline to reply. In timid, deferential tones, she wrote that she would be happy in the ranks of the community, if she was admitted.

Between Laurence and Aline there was no rivalry. Her sister's daring shocked the timid Aline, who was pursued by her nightmares all day long. In the stable, after nightfall, the sight of the lamp's dancing shadows struck terror into her heart, and she wouldn't go in. Mentioning Edouard's old house was enough to give her bad dreams.

Aline confided her fears to Laurence about the house, in a bad location, too far from any neighbours, situated at a bend in the road that did not appear to go any farther. Edouard had boarded the second-floor windows and those of the unused rooms on the ground floor. A beam in the attic had buckled and the chimney seemed to hang miraculously onto the sunken roof. In the village, it was referred to as the falling-down house.

Edouard lived in the kitchen, where he had installed a water pump. The inside of the house frightened Aline even more. The closed-off stairway behind the stove, the padlocked doors of the living room and bedroom, made her think of a prison, of ghosts. The brother kept a hunting gun and some blunt objects by his bed. The room was cluttered with sundry belongings, including underwear and shirts on a clothesline. According to Aline, their brother must be a little out of his mind, for no member of the family would live like a vagrant. She grew silent, tormented by images she had seen in literature about the suffering of the martyrs, sliced up with various sharp instruments. As soon as she could read, Amanda had held her rapt with stories about the lives of the martyred saints. But Aline relived their sufferings as if they were her own, and interpreted this as a call to saintliness. She always woke from dreams about Edouard's dump without knowing who the victim was, and who the executioner.

Edouard welcomed Laurence, hugged her tightly. Albeit in a talkative mood, anxious to make up for lost time, and as usual, impatient, Laurence said nothing, letting him speak first, as was customary. They visited the stable and the building sheltering the farm machinery. He was occupied year-round by his machine-run farm, and no longer hired himself out, except for the slaughter of animals for meat in November and December.

A new truck was essential for a well-run enterprise, made it easier to do business. Both of them loved cars, speed, long trips. The automobile is the most marvellous invention of our time, Laurence exclaimed. Edouard was benefiting from modern innovations.

They looked at the plans for the new house, to be built close to the road. The front door would be on the side, the verandah covered by the overhanging second floor. There would be less snow-shovelling. The old houses, such as the father's house, were built several hundred feet back from the road, so time was lost in driveway maintenance. His house would offer its flank to the scrutiny of passersby, but he would put in a door and rough steps for safety and appearance. Laurence wasn't sure she liked the sensible but unusual notion of a house that did not turn its face to the road.

They would dig a new well with an oil-fired pump and a septic tank, as specified in a document in English on new technology, which he showed her. They discussed the diagrams for the future installations. Laurence understood the principles of physics as well as her brother.

Regarding placing the bathroom under the staircase, she suggested a room that could be aired. He said she was right. As usual, she threw herself entirely into Edouard's life project, forgetting her own. Edouard was now less reserved than usual, and they felt the old pleasure of being together. Their feelings for each other were obvious. She said she was so happy. The dark well-built man, who never said what he felt, got a lump in his throat. He was beginning to realize how much he missed her. Words failed him.

She described her life at Beaupré, her sense of accomplishment. On the subject of her mother's illness, her only worry, Edouard told her that after the death of the horse, Rosalie had stopped sleeping. Her chagrin seemed to involve some secret with the father.

Rosalie was repressing her anger. Léon, when he lost his temper, got far too carried away. When frustrated, he became odious, did not live up to the standards he himself set. They all knew this. Their father ruled over the household like a lord, his daughters and sons lowering their voices as soon as he appeared. Their politeness bore the mark of fear. And Rosalie cultivated her equanimity to keep peace. Laurence closed her eyes, her head bowed. Edouard added some lines to the plans lying in the middle of the table. The brother and the sister rejected the possibility of a serious disagreement between their parents. It was taboo to even think of a rift. There could be no question of it.

On the fourth day of her visit, Laurence began showing Odette and Cécile how to prepare meals. Odette muttered something in an aside, her pretty curly head turned towards Cécile, who was peeling a potato. The little girl understood she would have to set the table, and feeling cornered, slipped through the door leading to the dairy. Laurence repressed a desire to smile at the child's protest. Leaning against the wall, a wry expression on her face, Odette's indecision was touching. Laurence softly reminded her why she must do it—which the child knew already. With a stoic, glum expression, she took her place again beside her younger sister.

Odette dragged her feet, and Cécile made a game of it, going faster, then slower. Laurence finished the child's task. Teaching the girls took more time than doing it yourself. Just the same, she told Rosalie they were helping her.

Laurence asked her father for pieces of meat and chicken. Bouillons, soups and stews would bring Rosalie's health back. Anaemia was treated by a rich diet. She took the initiative, expecting nothing from Aline, whose stomach turned at the sight of red meat and would only eat minuscule well-done portions. Léon admitted he lacked the means, but he would ask Edouard to help him out at butchering time in November.

Already Aline was slipping into the background, protected by her sister. Evenings, the teacher made woven rugs from fabric ends that her father brought home in huge sacks. He sold the rugs at the market. Laurence learned and went to bed late, having finished her first rug.

It was Sunday before mass. She again had the fleeting impression that she had never left home— except that to the old routines were added the new prerogatives that came with being an adult.

Laurence put on her suit and went down to the kitchen. Her father, furious, declared that she looked like a tart, that her indecent skirt would cause impure thoughts. He ordered her to change. His voice was severe, loud, his reprimand a forewarning to all the girls. She had ignored his first warning. An ironic inner voice, the one that was always ready to be defiant, jeered: no wonder the Naud household turned out so many nuns. She obeyed reluctantly. He made her feel humiliated.

Rosalie, who was getting up every day, put on a dress. Laurence combed her hair and sat her in the rocking chair where she fell asleep under a blanket. Her daughter could be heard walking about, looking after the household. She aired the room, made the bed like the nuns had taught her, washed the cup, emptied the pot. An odour of cleanliness filled the air when the mother lay down in the afternoon. Laurence planned her activities around the needs of her patient. Everybody understood. Léon took it for granted. Like them, she had a sense of priorities. She no longer thought of Beaupré, nor Gaston, nor her future. Her labours, extending well into the evening, made her sleep like a log.

She saw Edouard again in his messy den. He was being held up by red tape. The bank wanted guarantees from ordinary farmers. He was therefore postponing building his house. So far, he had taken twice as long as foreseen in setting up his operation, and the crops didn't look promising. He was gathering various construction materials and would start digging the foundations as soon as possible in the spring.

They agreed they were at the mercy of bureaucratic decisions. Laurence told him how the students had been expelled, and asked his opinion about whether she should return to nursing school. Edouard didn't see any point in it. He saw the future from a different angle. What good was an official title if she already had all the advantages it could offer? Even with a diploma, how many jobs like hers were around? Both of them were motivated by immediate considerations, provided they had a goal.

Edouard wasn't happy living alone, was neglecting his housekeeping, and ate every day from a pot prepared once a week. He knew his pile of junk stupefied Aline, who brought him his fresh bread. Now he wished he had a wife for that and other things.

In the spring, at Thetford Mines, he had met a pretty middle-aged widow. She insisted she wanted to taste the maple syrup. They both laughed because he had no little glasses. She teased him that his crude display proved he was single. The woman wore a pastel straw summer hat, and he noticed the crystal drop hanging from her earlobe, and the dimple in her cheek. She bought two gallons and murmured her address. The whole morning, he couldn't get the ray of white light projected by the earring out of his head.

Dusk fell, and he got to her place later than foreseen. He stepped into the living room, dazzled by his hostess's tight lace bodice and the shining jewel on her throat. She was smiling. She had no longer expected him to come. He apologized. On a little round table, a bottle and two glasses stood ready. Face to face, they drank porto. She asked him if he had ever made love to a woman. He said he would be happy to if she wanted. The widow had set the scene. Edouard felt himself get hard even before touching her. Later, on the doorstep, she asked if he had enjoyed himself. He assured her that he had enjoyed himself very much.

What he told Laurence was that he had had the opportunity of meeting a widow whom he intended to see again. He hesitated, raised his voice, and declared that a man needs sex. The sister remembered his words. A sensible man who only spoke when necessary saw things clearly. She did not cast judgement on the widow.

Tenderhearted Aline sought to be comforted by her sister. They chatted while they worked. Laurence made her laugh and she let her reserve fall. A weight seemed to have lifted from her shoulders. On those nights, her sleep was free of dreams. But as soon as her sister alluded to the periods that kept her confined to her bed, Aline stiffened and clammed up. Laurence didn't notice her discomfiture. When she said this would continue as long as she menstruated, Aline thought she was putting a curse on her.

It had rained for days. The bare trees opened up the horizon. Rosalie baked. A wave of relief that the mother did not have an incurable illness flooded the household. In the happy atmosphere, the little girls applied themselves more willingly to learning their tasks.

Laurence received a letter from Dr. Fournier. The time to leave was approaching. The letter gave the father a pretext to preach at her. Her sisters had set good examples, decided already at the age of fourteen to become nuns, while she, at her age, was satisfied with a temporary job. When she left the hospital, she should have come home rather than running around the countryside with an unknown doctor. He insinuated that the mother's total exhaustion was her fault. He went on, sitting at the end of the table where she was working, making a rug. His every word damned her. He spoke acerbically, a man of principles. He expected her to give in, not to try and explain herself, which he would take as defiance on her part. Their rare past confrontations, their differences came rushing back to her. She told the naked truth: marriage didn't interest her. He grew intimidating, warned her that she couldn't always have her own way.

The next day, with her mother's agreement, she wrote to the doctor, postponing her return for a week. Rosalie had slept abundantly, freed of domestic concerns, letting herself be cared for by her daughter. Laurence, never idle, started a rug double the usual size in the afternoon. In the little sitting room, she counted the bags of fabric ends, calculated that she could make it all into rugs before leaving.

Apart from Aline, who was sorry she was going, her siblings considered her a visitor, were distancing from her. The young teacher knit her a hat and scarf of fine wool. Laurence worked, testing herself, a game of patience that she called going somewhere in life. She repressed the father's impassive coldness, no longer felt anything but the numbness in her fingers and wrists. The eve of her departure, the father enjoined her to reflect on her situation. He doubted she was making the right choice, reminded her he had taught her to put duty first. Next summer, once he was back on his feet financially, she could let him know what she had decided. For now, he needed her salary. She received no thanks. She put on her pale grey suit and Edouard drove her to the station.

With a heavy heart and her head in a fog, she dozed, inexplicably exhausted, in the large smoothly upholstered train seat. She relaxed, arms dangling, head nodding forward. The bare November landscape out the coach window was uniform grey, beautiful, flattening out the day.

She forgot the happiness she had felt in the same train bringing her to Broughton, her desire to see them all, her confidence in them, her belief that each was treated fairly, equitably. If she had let herself, she would, at this moment, have felt opposite feelings taking root in her, feelings she wouldn't have admitted were the result of a visit home, feelings of conflict that she was suppressing. Powerful ties bound them together, and to pursue her thoughts any farther on this score was to torment herself, to become unbearably anxious.

5

A memory roused her. Once the father beat her so severely she had to stay in bed for four days. There was heavy snowfall that winter. The shovelled laneway had such high snowbanks that the children could no longer see the fields. The flat-roofed school was almost buried. After wolfing down their food, the children squabbled, screamed and pelted each other with snowballs while the teacher finished her lunch. Their outdoor garments were of roughly woven material, mittens, scarves, thick wool hats that pricked if you stood still. The fields were inaccessible, lakes of snow where you lost your footing as soon as you stepped onto them. They piled snow against the side of the school. Every day they made the snow slide a little higher. They got the idea that a slide as high as the school would be really sensational. They worked and worked. Tomorrow, each one would get a turn to climb up. Cheered on by the little ones, the boys shovelled faster. They would go up first, would help those who were afraid. When lunchtime came, the teacher forbade them to go on the slide. Her warning was clear. They would be punished if they climbed up to the roof. The children knew they would pay for their disobedience. Laurence and Rosé no longer felt like playing. The boys wanted to anyway and taunted the ones who were chicken to join in. The teacher held firm and said all of them deserved to be punished. They filed up to the desk and received smacks on their hands with the ruler. Laurence looked directly at her and said that she and Rosé had not gone on the roof. She got smacked anyway. Rosé said the same thing with the same result. Laurence thought it over and decided that since she had received punishment for something she hadn't done, she would go on the slide after school.

She used this line of reasoning on Rosé, who refused to follow her. She wouldn't have it said she was being punished for nothing. Her act of defiance irked the teacher. At nightfall, the schoolmistress's displeasure with the strong-willed girl took her to the farm. Laurence witnessed the scene. The teacher told the mother her version of the story. Rosalie apologized profusely and ordered Edouard to walk the teacher back.

The mother pronounced only one dreaded phrase: your father will hear about this. The threat weighed on the little girl. The teacher had come all the way there to inform the parents. Laurence wasn't given a chance to tell her side of the story. The father returned home on a Friday after a week of peregrinations from city to town in his job as a travelling salesman. Rosalie told Léon of his daughter's misdeed, and said the teacher had come to the house.

The father opened the door of the little living room, usually closed, dragged Laurence in, and slapped her. His blows fell about the child's face, head and shoulders, but she didn't cry. He took this for a provocation, asked her if she would climb up on the roof again. She said she would. He became twice as violent, battering her harder, until, head bent, blood dripped from her nose and tears from her eyes. She fell down, dizzy, and he kept hitting. She hid under the love seat.

Rosalie stood in the doorway, now terrified at Léon's anger. She had dramatized the teacher's coming all the way to their house, but the real drama was taking place before her eyes. She thought he was going to kill her. The father didn't let up, asking again if she was going to climb up on the roof and she said yes through her tears and her pain. The girl clung to the bottom of the sofa. He pulled her by the arm, beating her black and blue with his feet and his fists.

The mother called the sons to pull the father off. They came, and led him, unresisting, out of the room. Laurence lay on the floor. They carried her up to bed. It was Joseph, the eldest of the sons, who warned the father never to try that again, or he would have them to deal with. The mother reacted in a cowardly manner, saying nothing, crushed by guilt.

Rosalie and Léon had been blessed by the birth of several sons. The help they would get from them in the fields and with the farm animals would free Léon. If he still wore roughly woven pants, he was also in the habit of donning a white shirt and a suit to drive the wagon or buggy that his sons hitched and unhitched. The smaller number of daughters to help out Rosalie was something the parents were starting to regret, especially with Amanda's departure that autumn.

Léon thought of Laurence as being bigger than she was. The parents barely discussed it. With the consent of his wife, he removed her from school. The girl neither acquiesced nor resisted. She was eleven years old. Amanda's departure necessitated her full-time help around the house. To the younger fell the lot that was normally the elder's. This switching of roles increased their rivalry.

When Amanda came home from the convent, she paraded her new manners and scolded and groused at Laurence for the spots on her shirt, and her tomboyish ways. The gap between them was widening. The younger naïvely tolerated the elder's comments, and didn't retaliate, relegating her confused feelings to the back of her mind.

In 1917, the mother was expecting her twelfth child. Rosalie taught Laurence to shear the sheep and to get rid of the lice that jumped from the fleece. She taught her the long labour of transforming fleece and flax into wool and linen, old traditions that died hard in the back country. In the barn, they looked after the chickens, pigs, cows, the bull and two or three horses, depending on the year. A large playful mongrel had the run of the farm.

Rosalie's ample dress hid her pregnancy. One morning when they were getting the butter ready to sell in the village, the mother was nervous about keeping the father waiting, the wagon hitched up in front of the door. Laurence was cutting the butter, filling the mould, which overflowed so that the rectangular brick lost its shape. The father slapped her face. This time, Rosalie intervened, interposing herself between them, and forbidding the father to touch her, now or ever again.

He had hit her for no good reason and Laurence never forgot it. She lost interest in the kitchen, preferred working in the stable. This division of labour suited Rosalie.

The daughter felt closer to her father when he and visitors to the farm talked about the conscription crisis, about sending Canadian troops to Europe. They were against the Borden government who had voted in conscription over the objections of former prime minister Laurier. The war, so far away, deprived families of their sons. The country's leaders were impoverishing the population. It was the majority opinion. The defence of England under the British flag was not their affair. They felt that the elites and even Wilfrid Laurier had betrayed the French Canadians. Laurence lent an ear, eager to listen in. Political events influenced the men's state of mind. Their conversations interested her.

The day faded. The November light fused the different shades of grey, and cooler air blew through the partly opened window. As the conductor passed to collect tickets, they were approaching Tring-Jonction, the village with the singing name. Gaston asked about you and wanted to know when you were returning, the doctor had written. She wasn't sure about the word love. She was no sentimental dreamer-type, dwelling on memories of tender moments, or pining for the next meeting. To her father she had said what she meant, that marriage did not interest her. The idea of seeing Gaston, as much as she looked forward to it, did not free her of the things weighing on her mind. She kept herself from trembling at the idea that she would be putting on her uniform tomorrow.

Among those boarding, a young woman who held her head unusually high attracted her attention. She was travelling alone. Her cloth coat revealed the lines of her body. Laurence had never seen such an outfit before, and its exceptional elegance astonished her. A fur hat set off her features to advantage. The new traveller removed the coat and folded it. Eyeing the woman's cinched dress of finely textured wool, Laurence thought she must be a bourgeoise from Sillery. Her modern refinement was a contrast to the Sunday best of the other passengers. Laurence noticed she wore no wedding ring, though she must have been thirty. If the traveller who boarded the Québec-bound train at Tring-Jonction had sat down beside her, she would have talked to her. She couldn't possibly imagine the woman trekking, for family reasons, from the back country to yet another small village, as she herself was. Did she buy her expensive clothes with inherited or earned money? She guessed the woman was a nurse who had decided not to get married.

She presumed the woman was single rather than widowed, an employee rather than an heiress, but certainly from a bourgeois family. She liked the idea that the woman had no husband. The idea that she might live alone was unthinkable. Laurence perceived a solitary life as necessarily wanting. The woman was the picture of serenity. Laurence banished the troubling doubt by telling herself there must be social milieux where one is never alone.

Laurence went to fix her hair, pull up her cotton stockings, smooth out her skirt. They were two women travelling alone. One of them wore a suit that was too pale for the season.

The odour of fuel, the noise of the train which was slowing down, the dim blinking railway signals, the blackened underground passage, indicated they were slowly drawing into the Québec station, snapping her back to reality. She was expected, of course, and that being all she needed, she smiled to herself.

The river air stung her face. Sitting in the buggy with a blanket over her knees, she listened to the doctor. He was enumerating the visits he had been unable to make, recapitulating in precise phrases the main events of the month. He inquired after Rosalie's health. At the mention of anaemia, he lowered his head. There was a long silence. The air was losing its scent of humus, the cold foretold snow. In front of the big house, he said supper was served.

It was snowing. As good as his word, the doctor resumed home visits to patients who lived at some distance from the village, to elderly people. His silences allowed Laurence to take in her surroundings. Women were no longer wearing hand-woven, hand-sewn woollen clothing. The men kept on wearing rough trousers, a second skin, an old habit they didn't give up easily. Many villagers had done over their kitchens, adding cupboards, installing lighter woodstoves of coloured enamel, complete with nickel-plated handles and hinges.

The prosperous years the father talked about when he returned from selling his wares meant more comforts for people. Down home they got only an echo of this. Laurence noticed the latest modern conveniences in modest homes.

They, back there, had not been touched by the economic recovery. They eked out a subsistence living in that remote place, at the mercy of every adversity.

Madame Fournier made her the gift of a coat with a fur collar, under the pretext that it took up closet space and was belted, therefore not attractive on a woman of her age. Laurence's brown eyes filled with tears. Her brownish homemade coat was abandoned. She thanked her, said she was overjoyed. The following day, the gift-giving scene came back to her, the happy feeling it gave her. Before the mirror, she stroked the fur collar, put on Aline's hat. The red wool framed her dark curls, made her black eyes look bigger. She was grateful to the future nun who had chosen red for her, rather than something neutral. Red suits people who like the great outdoors, said Aline.

She was back— with a throng of memories in tow! Despite the extra-long work hours, she did not feel quite in the present. On the roads, during the evenings, no sooner had she a spare moment than it filled with an image from her visit to Broughton. She had trouble identifying with the tender family scenes she conjured up. She felt guilty about her mother, and might well have become despondent had she not had the cold to struggle against. She grew sluggish under the covers at night, enjoyed the feeling of coming sleep that progressively erased memory.

To help her mother like she used to, or to send her her salary: the answer was becoming clearer. Laurence had not mulled over her decision, hadn't concluded that money was more useful than being at home helping. She was in the process of acknowledging she was responsible for her choice— which was basically to escape. She already knew she would give no reply to the father. There was no future back there.

Gaston caught sight of her in the village on the Saturday and exhibited a joking camaraderie, shrouding a shyness she didn't notice. For her part, Laurence, with a casual air, bubbled affably, her liveliness a sign of unfeigned confidence, the same as she felt with Edouard.

At the agricultural fair, he had told her you have to experience everything once. The phrase resonated in her, excited her curiosity, kept running through her mind. It was sensational. The young woman threw ironic glances at the young man, was teased in return. Now that she was around again, he was busy, taken up with the beginning of the hockey season. He invited her to go out with him to the Coliseum, where he refereed matches. She liked the idea, and found herself the same afternoon on the way to Québec.

One might wonder about Laurence's forthrightness, her natural self-confidence. She held men in high regard, attributed to them the same spirit of initiative that she saw in herself and that remained underdeveloped in most women. Some men possessed a self-control that she emulated. She stepped in time to the doctor's ponderous movements, reproduced his mannerisms, fought against her own impetuousness. As for Gaston, she got to know his sportsman's spirit in the following weeks. He won and lost with elegance. Games became a metaphor for life. The young man said nothing about the neurotic relationship he maintained with his mother. Laurence wouldn't have guessed he changed as soon as he crossed the threshold of the mother's house. She imitated men and was not in the least embarrassed about it. Her instinct told her it was the fastest way of adapting to reality.

Gaston took her to new places, teaching her things he knew along the way. Above all, she watched how he was with the youth whose matches he refereed.

The sportsman-like spirit was a model for human relations, bestowed a physical and moral well-being which she idealized. Laurence thought the years were coming when all young people, girls and boys, would practise sports. Those who were coming up now would be relieved of drudgery, not dragged down by heavy obligations. Her hope was rooted in changing customs, a new progressiveness, and in the fact that she herself was part of the change. She was catching up, a little out of step, a little behind, with the changing times. When, in the village, people referred to Gaston as the *sportsman*, she had a secret smile. The nickname implied not only a man of action, but also someone who was loyal and did not bear grudges.

The father's letter said that Aline had fractured her collarbone and they needed money. Her sister could end up with a disability. Dr. Fournier suspected she sent money to her family, but didn't realize she was sending her whole salary. She told him so frankly, and read him part of the letter about Aline's fall when she approached him about a loan or an advance. He gave her what she needed in recognition of her kindness and helpfulness. He said he would give her more, on condition that she reserve it for personal use. The doctor thought the family's demands on her unjust.

He knew that Laurence's dedication and meticulousness permitted him to run his practice like he used to before the absurd accident caused by a moment of distraction on the road to Montmagny. His long convalescence, abusing morphine to kill the pain, his visceral fear of icy roads, the kind of part-time help to which he occasionally had recourse, had made his situation precarious. He was coming out of a dark period, was doing home visits again, hitting the road without fear of falling asleep. The nurse's attentive presence improved his efficiency. His year-end accounting made that clear.

Laurence wrote back the same day, slipping the bills into the envelope and sealing it. She felt less anxious once it was mailed. She pondered the doctor's generosity. She couldn't have avoided asking. He appreciated her being there constantly at his side, he'd said as much. She thought it was normal. Lots of people weren't paid by the hour, and her job required flexibility, adaptability. When there was a delivery during the night, Rachel packed a generous hamper of food and hot drinks. The hearty lunches made hunger and thirst a thing of the past, and their excursion seemed like an adventure. Laurence knew he was generous, not ruled by financial considerations. A patient's ability to pay was a matter of discretion, and he treated each with the same consideration, the same courteous manner. With her, he was kindness itself. What motivated him? She couldn't say.

The doctor did as he said he would, and she got her salary on the first Saturday of the month, after he had finished doing the books. He put it on her desk, and placed two more one-dollar bills a little apart. His gesture was accompanied by the words: for you.

Gaston found some skates that fit her and took her to Beaupré's skating rink. He held her by the hands as she stepped on the ice. Laurence tried to get her balance, took strides that were too long or too short, fell down, got up again. He never ridiculed her. They laughed and he remained patient, steadying her by the arm. They were touching, but she concentrated on her movements. At the end of an hour, she felt exhausted. The very cold day made it harder to breathe. Gaston acknowledged this.

They tried again the following Sunday, under a white sky that promised snow. In their skates, very tall and slender, from a distance they cut a fine figure. People noticed them. It was whispered abroad that the *sportsman* and the nurse were in love. They paid no attention to the looks they were getting, nor got wind of the rumours. They were both independent spirits.

People became, once more, curious about Laurence. They wanted to know her age, her background, her place of birth, reasons for coming to

Beaupré. She lost the immunity to gossip that her status of nurse afforded her as soon as she started going out with a boy from the village.

In the doctor's waiting room, certain women had the temerity to question her. Laurence was not at all inclined toward chit-chat. The doctor, with his laconic manner, his attentive way of listening, served as an example that she easily followed. The village women had noticed the thick ribbed stockings, and hadn't forgotten the rough brown coat. Her reserve increased their curiosity. They were informed, who knows how, that she had not terminated her studies, and that she had worked for several years at Saint-Michel-Archange Hospital in Québec. She was losing her halo. The gossips knew the doctor's household was above reproach. Confronted with Laurence's lack of sociability, one of them asked the question outright: was she going to marry the Ramsay boy? Laurence told them that to find out they should get their cards read.

It was the village way to spy, to dig up information, to spread gossip. Love stories were as appreciated as accidents and fires. It also glowed in the dark and smoked.

Gaston wanted her to meet his mother. Laurence could tell she had been the subject of gossip. Madame Ramsay received her in the living room. Laurence's spontaneity evaporated. She adopted an affected manner, an exaggerated politeness, out of a desire to be accepted. The young man saw nothing amiss, thought, on the contrary, she was behaving in a suitable fashion. The mother inquired about her background, family, schooling, work. Gaston knew practically nothing about her. That she was a nurse was what counted for him; the rest didn't matter. His attraction was due, precisely, to her hailing from elsewhere. Chance had permitted them to meet and this made him happy. Out of respect, he kept silent during the questions, didn't intervene.

Laurence was observed, passed in review, studied. She had hoped to meet a woman she could be fond of. She found a widow who missed her past life, spoke little of herself but a great deal about her deceased husband, and her son in Holland. Madame Ramsay was more interested in her absent men than in her daughters, whose footsteps could be heard in the quiet house. She said nothing about Gaston. The meeting resembled an interview. Laurence was disappointed. It was so cool, distant.

That evening, Laurence examined herself in the mirror, madame Ramsay's face looking over her shoulder. She had come through what seemed like an inquisition. Her face was a nuisance. She no longer saw her large expressive brown eyes, only the beauty marks, two spots marring her features. Despite her efforts, she was thrown off-balance by Gaston's mother, felt unsure of herself.

The roads were dangerous. The last of the winter snow melted under the hot sun, the night cold froze the puddles. Patches of hard snow still covered the ground, not melting, particularly in wooded areas.

April reminded the doctor of the accident. He berated himself, as he took out his cart, for not having a car. In the old days, the idea of driving a car intimidated him; these days he justified his fears by saying he was too old to learn. Though he knew the roads by heart, their ups and downs, their twists and turns and their treacherous stretches— at this time of year the thaw altered the terrain, and the landmarks disappeared. Two pairs of eyes were better than one. It was a difficult week. The doctor went on about the risks, and relied on Laurence's good eyes, fixed on the road.

On a clear day they went to Québec. Gaston took her to meet the rink manager. The men talked for three hours. She who had acquired a taste for hockey was bored, grew weary sitting in her straight-backed chair. She waited for the men to finish their interminable discussing and arguing. The afternoon dragged on and on, as dull as could be.

Near Montmorency Falls, Gaston spun out of control when he stepped on the brake. They slid on the ice for about ten feet, the car choking and skidding to a stop on the lower side of the road, on an incline. The jolt left them in a state of shock, shaken but not hurt. In vain they tried to push the sportscar, their efforts impeded by the steep slope. The only alternative was to stand by the roadside and wait for a passing car. Gaston flagged the first one that came along, and asked them to send a man from the garage. They waited some more. Laurence said she had been waiting all afternoon. He agreed it had been useless and it was too bad to have spoiled a Sunday. He didn't draw out his apology. He warmed up her hands, threw her a small forced smile. They said nothing, worry increasing with the inordinately long wait. No car had passed for an hour. Daylight was fading. He held her against him. They didn't dare move. The least shift would loosen their embrace. In the distance they heard a truck approaching.

The driver had difficulty manoeuvering on the icy slope, finally succeeding after several tries. The young people arrived home chilled to the bone. Gaston went in with her and told madame Fournier what happened. He said it was his fault. The next day Laurence awoke with blue thighs from frostbite. The cold had numbed the pain.

Gaston, so handsome, attractive, had what she liked in a man, an independence that set him apart from others. People liked his affability, but at the same time he was the butt of gossip. Some said he was a phoney, spoke ill of him. His imposing presence ruffled feathers. She liked him for his sense of freedom. So many young people lost their spontaneity, took on sober airs, became taciturn, worrying for nothing and simulating maturity in the manner of their parents. Gaston's frank gaiety made him incredibly charming.

For Laurence, this way of being was a sign of self-control. It was okay for women to complain, and she sympathized with their lot, brought on by too many pregnancies. She expected of a man that he rise above the irritations of everyday life.

It was a happy summer. Laurence recounted the events of the day to madame Fournier and Rachel. Madame Fournier was on the qui-vive for possible indiscretions regarding patient confidentiality, but the former convent girl was able to distinguish between an anecdote and a medical record. Laurence's descriptions of the way people were, a judicious mix of country expressions and medical vocabulary, were hilarious. Rachel never went out. The very thought of roaming the roads at any hour of the day or night made her positively queasy. Sheltered, she took pleasure in the stories of others. She was able to predict coming storms and rainfall, and informed them.

On duty, fifty-hour weeks were normal. Trips out into the country for delivering babies made the day even longer, upset schedules, turned night into day. The nurse's vitality was a comfort to the doctor.

The young woman, accustomed to her task, found that its calm rituals kept her balanced. She no longer escaped to the fields. Evenings, sitting by the window near her potted geraniums, she knitted for Odette and Cécile. Sometimes a family thanked her for her services by giving her wool.

She was at ease with herself. This, coupled with her love for Gaston, was changing her, placating her edginess. The young man invited her to the Château Frontenac, taught her to dance. Learning the new steps in the midst of the luxurious tapestries, paintings and chandeliers that surrounded them, made her feel unreal, as if she were another Laurence Naud. She understood the importance of these rare moments. She memorized details, nuances of colour and shape, stored away for later contemplation. Gaston thought it was a game and played along, pointing out the waiters' uniforms, the silver trays, the glasses embossed with the hotel logo. There were waltzes, polkas, slow dances, fox trots. They left when the orchestra played the charleston. The dance evenings attracted two types of clientele. The first was couples, men and women of all ages, and the second, well-off youth, journalists, writers, and tourists who arrived around ten p.m., and who didn't mix with the country couples in their Sunday best.

A village woman approached Laurence after Sunday mass to say someone had seen them dance modern dances forbidden by the priest at the big hotel. A young girl was responsible for triggering evil thoughts in a man. A woman had to spare the man opportunities for sinning. The woman saw it as her duty to warn her.

Such a speech made Laurence angry. All puritanical grown-ups thought they had some kind of moralizing mission to fulfil. Gaston took her back to the big hotel where she defiantly drank cocktails.

She was reassured by the father's letters, which said Aline would start teaching in the village again. Her convalescence had permitted her to take time off and her help at home had made things easier for Rosalie.

Laurence and Gaston were in love. They didn't use words like going steady or being serious about the future. They displayed both the modesty of the young and inexperienced, and the boldness of a love fanned by casual encounters that made people gossip. Every time he came near her, she felt a raw sensual charge completely new to her. He sparked a desire in her that left her wordless. Her vivacity kept it in check. Gaston was getting to know and love her emancipated spirit, what he called her independence. She saw him as being so different from her. He considered her his other self, and wouldn't have it otherwise. When Gaston laughed with his deep voice, he breathed life into the present.

The end of the summer was euphoric. He dropped into the Fourniers' with or without pretext. She wasn't always there. Seeing her in uniform made him swell with pride.

Evenings, in her room, it seemed to her she could say anything to Gaston. As soon as he was beside her, she forgot, lost all desire to talk, the better to savour the moment, calmed by their togetherness. The longing to talk evaporated in an overwhelming inexhaustible abundance of sensuality and well-being.

He didn't know she gave her salary to her family. She encouraged him to look after his when he complained about his mother's demands. She reasoned it was the parents' right and privilege to make claims on their offspring, contrary to religious communities who siphoned money from families unfairly, especially considering that their daughters were going to enrich the community with their work. For once she said what she thought, with an abruptness that astonished him. Words freed her. Whether he shared her viewpoint mattered less than having the opportunity to speak her mind.

Formulating an opinion on something gave her a sense of moral satisfaction. An adult woman who enjoyed discussions didn't keep quiet for fear of putting off her companion.

A woman from île au Canot came to Beaupré to deliver her baby. It was a difficult birth. The premature baby required special care.

In the archipelago situated downstream from Québec, the island was inhabited by a single family who lived in a farmhouse. They were the island caretakers for the French Canadian who came to hunt in the autumn. They received an annual pension in return for small services.

The owner had loaned money to the doctor, immobilized for several months following his accident. The owner went to the doctor's office, and they agreed Laurence would be hired to go to the island. She would leave right away, look after the mother and child, and see to the family needs. Laurence grasped at the chance for adventure. The idea of going to an island in the middle of the river thrilled her. She longed for raw air, wind and the noise of waves. She packed her warmest clothing.

The father and son loaded the market produce into the large sturdy wooden boat. The nurse, mother, and newborn took their place in the middle. It was a clear October day and the trajectory was calm, although the farther they got from shore, the tinier the boat seemed in the middle of the waves. Laurence, chilly, shivered. She sized up the father and sixteen-year-old son, solid men who rowed in silence. Their skill reassured her.

Five children welcomed them, happy to see their parents. The family lived in a low dwelling with a minimum of furniture, dating from the last century. Nothing had changed for decades. Laurence slept under the slope of the garret roof in the children's room.

The first days went slowly. She took over the household, organizing it around the mother and baby's needs. The children did not attend school, followed her everywhere. She grew attached to them. The family said their evening prayers, and, Sunday mornings, the father read the Bible in front of the black wooden cross. A simple clock ticked in the low-roofed kitchen. A calendar hung near the rocker marked the date. Early on the first Saturday of November, the men left for the market to get winter provisions. The first wave of cold was accompanied by falling snow swept by the wind from the open sea. The sound of wind gusting combined with the boom of the waves.

The mother was recuperating. Pregnancy is not an illness. After six weeks, they both knew that the baby would live. He had gained enough weight to put him out of danger. The earth grew hard under the cold. Ice formed along the shore. The roof cracked at night, waking Laurence, with a start, to the sound of wind swelling the waves. Her isolation was getting to her. She worried about the possibility of being stuck on the island for the winter, which they said would be early. There would be intense cold with the full moon.

When the father and his sons killed and carved up a steer, using pulley and primitive cutting instruments, it felt like she was living as they had in isolated farms at the beginning of the colony. Her adventure was a return to the past, to a time when the absence of tools obliged a great expenditure of physical energy. The couple was old at forty, and already looked forward to the time when their children could take over.

The storm broke out. They had agreed on a Saturday. They waited for better weather, which took five days to come. Day broke, grey, foretelling snow. Small waves battered the shore. The father took along his two sons. Their feet sank in the wet clay river bank, helping Laurence to embark.

The three men rowed in silence. The wind blew, the water turned grey and they rocked with the rapid regular rhythm of the waves. Laurence, sitting in the middle of the boat, watched the house grow small. The men, standing, pushed as hard as they could, accustomed to rowing against the wind. The air stung, penetrated her clothing, and Laurence grew tense as the boat lurched into the current coming from the open sea. The low house was lost in the greyness and she felt a prisoner of the river, no longer knowing, as she watched the father, the sixteen-year-old son, and the fourteen-year-old, if they were strong or weak. The craft made dry resonant sounds as the waves slapped it about. The wind blew and, under the low sky, the waves swelled.

No one spoke. Apprehension increased. The more frightened she felt, the faster her heart beat— and the slower the minutes ticked by. She thought about how deep the cold water was, a shiver running up her spine. Firmly, she forbade herself to imagine the worst, fixed her eyes on the muscled bodies of the men, and gripped the bench.

The waves heaved the boat along faster than they could row. The crest of a wave hurled towards them and splashed over them. The father and sons bailed. They could see other waves approaching on the rolling sea, rising higher. The men, trying to avoid taking them head-on, were soon surrounded. The oars slid against the side of the rocking boat. The wind groaned, and they knew that they would soon be rowing through the storm's final wallop.

Laurence, sick to her stomach, sensed her fragility, and huddled up. She thought her time had come when an enormously large wave smashed over the bow. A huge crack could be heard. The boat reeled and nearly capsized. The noise was followed by several jolts. The men fought against the swells. The boat was being engulfed. They did everything at once, using powerful strokes to row while they bailed out the water washed in with the waves. The father checked the bottom of the craft. He saw that some of the wooden planks were damaged, said nothing. He was of the opinion they had seen the worst and ordered his sons to go faster. The adolescents, soaking wet, paddled with frenzy and gained speed. The high waves were disappearing. One of the sons broke an oar under the swaying boat. They took turns, heading straight into the current. When the boat reached the shore, each kept the fear he had had to himself. Laurence thanked them. The soft snow signalled that the wind was falling.

Laurence told her tale to madame Fournier and Rachel, praised the men for their courage. The two women, who dreaded the calmest crossings, listened to her with admiration. They imagined themselves in a similar situation and weren't sure they would have kept their cool. The three spoke a long time about the dangers of the river. The nurse gave the doctor a report of her visit, and, for the first time, permitted herself to recount something personal, her trip back from île au Canot. He concluded that they had risked their lives.

Gaston was shaken by her story. Born near the river, he had turned away from it and had never even swum in it. To her family, she wrote that she had been to île au Canot to look after a mother and her child. She had mentioned in an earlier letter that she was going, and now she was back. She didn't think it necessary to worry them.

II
EMIGRATING INWARD

6

Gaston had missed her. He bought a box of candy, some eau de cologne, and a mirror with a silver handle. The week before she returned, he had inquired at the Fourniers' every day. Madame Fournier opened up the living room for them. They were quite stiff, sitting on the love seat, speaking in low voices, and restraining themselves. The fashionably furnished parlour bespoke the Fourniers' material comfort. Laurence wasn't bothered by her rumpled clothing. The important thing was to act like a lady. The young woman believed that distinguished manners were proof of a certain savoir-vivre. Her studied way of holding her head high went well with her frank gaze. She pulled herself up erectly, making her waist even tinier. Gaston wrapped his long fingers around it.

They spoke of happiness, of marriage. They believed in happiness, in having a house with children who would sing, play music, and sports. They spoke their feelings prudishly, keeping sexual desire cloaked in talk about babies: they would have children. Gaston raised the possibility of getting the wooden house that an estate was trying to sell. She was ready to live anywhere with him. Home would be wherever he was. She'd never felt like this before. Love projected her into the future. Between the very living presence of the handsome, open-minded young man beside her, and the future towards which her desire pulled her, there seemed a strange gap or abyss to cross.

Near the coat tree, they kissed, embracing, beside themselves with desire. She felt the warmth of his male body. They lost their balance and fell down, bringing the hanging coats with them.

Laurence went again to madame Ramsay's, who invited her and watched her closely. Gaston was twenty-six, she could not object to his marriage. On the third visit, she couldn't help it, she told Gaston, in front of Laurence, that his future wife's waist was too small for her to have children. This hurt the young woman, and Gaston lowered his eyes. He said nothing. The phrase evoked the distant echo of Sarah, who could not give Abraham heirs. God heard the prayers of the sterile woman who gave birth to a son at an advanced age, the son that God had ordered sacrificed. Once grace was obtained, God's will required subordination.

Madame Ramsay wanted the family name to go on. She'd had a hard life with an alcoholic husband who'd died deeply in debt. The eldest son worked in a shipyard in Holland. He would marry a foreigner and settle over there. She had one son left, who, despite his freewheeling reputation in the village, was, she knew, if no one else did, very attached to his family.

The lovers ignored the mother's words, and Gaston asked Laurence if she wanted to have a son or a daughter first. She replied: a son called Gaston. A second child? A son called Gaston. A third? Another son called Gaston. A fourth? He would still be called Gaston. They laughed heartily. They were using their sense of play to get over the mother's harshness.

Gaston grasped her waist with his hands. She trembled. This, his first intimate gesture— expressing in so many words how much her slenderness charmed him— had now lost its spontaneity. He thought of plump young women, with padded waistlines, who were thought of as healthy girls of promising fertility. Country people held onto the old notion that a person with flesh on her bones ate well. Gaston had seen the Québec city women, and had been bedazzled, enraptured by their slender beauty. He bought Laurence fine shoes and light flowered dresses. She looked like one of those city women who danced into the night.

Laurence no longer had the unfortunate beauty mark, the raised growth at the end of her nose. There was still a scar that was slowly fading. When Gaston touched her nose, she told him that, every day at île au Canot, she had picked at the dark mass until she could loosen and take it off with a drop of caustic soda. He took that as a proof of her love, touched the other mole near her nose that he asked her to keep. He liked her with this distinctive trait, which set her apart.

The crash of the stock market was felt immediately at Beaupré. That no economy was sufficient unto itself was now obvious, however much some tried to defend isolationism. The falling North American currencies had inexorable consequences. Everyone reckoned there would be widespread lowering of living standards.

Never had the city of Québec seemed so close to New York. The newspapers reported the suicides of speculators. Journalists declared it was the beginning of a Depression, jobs were being lost. The unemployed and their families had nothing to fall back on.

At Beaupré, some said the farmers, at least those who used traditional methods, would manage. Farmers with modernized operations presumed they would lose their investments if the banks foreclosed their loans, or if produce markets fell. The sawmill employees waited. Uncertainty led to confusion. The bosses would tell them nothing. The workers delegated a group to inquire about what lay in store for them. They met a wall of silence— the boss even maliciously threatened to fire them.

At the village council meeting, held right after mass, the men anticipated the possible effects of the market upheaval. They dreaded the loss of things they had worked so hard to get. They had no faith in the government. Stories of embezzlement and graft of public funds made them wary. They latched on to vague rumours. They knew or they thought they knew— it amounted to the same thing— that someone had a brother, a brother-in-law, a son, a cousin, or an uncle who had benefited from favours, bribes, been overpaid for services. Now the grafters appeared to be sticking together in face of the disaster. Nobody said anything about their savings, their best-guarded secret. They all intended to be thrifty.

Everyone talked about the crash. Some were concerned about local impact, others opined there was nothing to worry about. The latter, the wait-and-see types, withdrew, refrained from spending, and considered that the talk of the former amounted to self-fulfilling prophecies, best ignored.

The general effervescence evaporated. People kept to themselves.

In January, 1930, the sawmill announced it was closing. It laid off the workers. The shock waves spread through the village. Now everyone was feeling insecure. The sawmill, which had brought them prosperity, was bankrupt. It was unbelievable that the crash in New York had repercussions as far away as Beaupré. The newspapers confirmed that the Canadian and American economies were linked. That capital had no borders. The much-touted model of liberal economy, based on supply and demand, was collapsing. Hard times were on the way.

The villagers were worried. They went to the doctor less often. He had fewer appointments.

Gaston was disoriented. He had worked at the sawmill for ten years. Like others, he found himself without a salary and without alternatives. He went to Québec, to Montmagny, trying to get hired in lumber camps. The supply exceeded the demand and woodcutters were being dismissed. Try as he might, the young man got nothing but no for an answer.

Dr. Fournier kept his composure. He travelled less into the countryside.

It took the nurse several weeks to notice that home visits were on the decline. She realized, one February day when the doctor had not a single office appointment, that he would not be needing her any longer.

Gaston remained himself, despite his state of confusion. With Laurence, he fabricated possibilities, talked about going elsewhere. She said she was ready, would follow him. He listed cities, asked if she would like to live there. He named Montréal, Ottawa, Windsor, Toronto, Lowell, Boston. The names were the colour of the rainbow. He was the one who had pronounced the phrase that bound them together in the deepest part of themselves: you have to try everything once. Grave, dispassionate words, ringing so true to someone with Laurence's sense of curiosity. They speculated, planned itineraries to calm their apprehensions.

At the beginning of April, the doctor told her that he would pay her until May, but that he was obliged to let her go. She cried during the night at the thought of leaving the Fourniers', her peaceful haven. She had to tear herself away, face an uncertain future. She was losing her job, and Gaston's job-searching efforts were fruitless. They were victims of circumstances, had no control over the larger picture.

The lack of patients, the unpaid-for home visits, the handing out of free medication, had rendered the doctor's situation untenable. Though she saw it coming, the news was a shock. The Fourniers had accepted her as she was, never once criticizing her. On the contrary, she had introduced a breath of fresh air into the silent household, and they had grown attached to her. Under their roof, she had become a self-assured, poised woman. In secret, she fantasized about staying, working for nothing, and had to bite her pillow one night to keep from sobbing aloud. They were hostages of the times.

Laurence didn't know the doctor had debts, had put off dismissing her. He would take her back to Saint-Michel-Archange Hospital, where the nuns were still looking for young healthy women, capable of self-discipline and hard work. He expected her to ask him to take her, but she didn't. Rachel had been sent home in February.

Gaston wrote to his brother. The reply came two months later. Meanwhile, he went off at the slightest hint of a job. His efforts were in vain. Demoralized, lost, he grew silent or lashed out angrily. He had already scoffed that there was only work left for nurses, school teachers and servants. Women's work. When she, in turn, lost her job, and he had received the letter from his brother, he made a pact with her. He would sell his car and go to Holland. First he would write to a relative of his mother, a nun at the Caughnawaga Hospital south of Montréal. She would be near the big city when he came to fetch her. They had spoken so much about Montréal, about living there. They would move there as soon as possible, he hoped. Laurence agreed. They waited for a reply, banking on the long-term solution. It was positive. The nun expected her at the beginning of May. The kind of work would be determined upon her arrival. The community would board and lodge her.

She started the letter over three times, wrote her new address to her father. To write about why she was leaving, to talk of Gaston's getting in touch with the nuns and their reply, required a serenity she no longer possessed. She shortened it, gave the immediate cause of her departure, her new address, and mentioned the date.

With a broken heart, she left the big house. The doctor gave her a train ticket and the equivalent of a month's salary. Madame Fournier put a blouse, gloves and a leather bag on her bed.

Near the station, Gaston said he couldn't allow their separation. He begged her, tried to get her to decide immediately. They would get married. They cried. He used persuasion to wear down her resistance, wanted her to consent on the spot. She decided in the affirmative, and he submitted to her opinion. The marriage would take place in eight days. Laurence's heart beat rapidly. She was ready to do anything. For two hours they lived in torment, torn apart, until reason won the day. Gaston accompanied her to the station. They repeated word for word their pact to meet in Montréal. The words seemed empty. It was upsetting to be at the station already. He took her in his arms. When he kissed her, she felt like the sky was falling in. He found her beautiful, radiant. Gaston remained on the platform. Neither made any further attempt to justify the reasonable decision they had come to.

The train carried off a dazed Laurence who held her head high, her hands gripping the arms of the seat, the jacket of the grey suit unbuttoned, revealing a silky bodice. The noonday light lit up her dark eyes, the breeze stirred the fine material of her blouse. She fought against tears, her posture theatrically statuesque. She thought of nothing, her head filled with Gaston's image. Sometimes the pain of love increases a woman's beauty tenfold.

A man sat down beside her. He asked her, without expecting a reply: where are you from? Where are you going? What is a beautiful girl like you doing on the train? She told him to go away. He took her hand. She said she would call the conductor. He got up, simpering, muttering: depraved. Prostitute.

Laurence had changed. A year of happiness had given her a confident air. The mole on the end of her nose, a birthmark that marred her appearance, was gone. Love made her beautiful, more open to the world around her. Another man tried to flirt with her, aggressive, fat, coarse, like the first. She had no choice, went to the conductor, asked for a seat where she would not be disturbed. He told her to sit beside him. She knew it, the big city of Montréal had a bad reputation with many families.

At Viger Station, an employee from the religious community was waiting. The car took rue Notre Dame in the direction of the Wellington bridge, followed the street of the same name to the Highlands neighbourhood in the shadow of Mercier bridge. They drove through the industrial part of the city, passing old greystone buildings, port installations, the goods station warehouse, which bordered on some residential streets. Night was falling. They crossed Mercier Bridge. The river, a thin arm of calm water, slipped by the Caughnawaga Reserve.

Laurence took a nightgown from her suitcase, threw her clothes on the chair and slipped into bed with her eyes closed, barely looking at her room. In the early morning she was ashamed of the mess.

The room was narrow and white and looked like a nun's cell. The toilets were in the corridor. Meals were served in the refectory. Notices under glass, framed, in the bedroom, the bathroom, the refectory, the corridors, and the stairs, contained lists of rules. She didn't remember so many rules at Saint-Michel-Archange.

The director welcomed her, questioned her on her training and experience. Her lack of a diploma, her interrupted training, the fact that her experience was not in the hospital milieu, made it impossible to confer on her the status of nurse. She would be a nurse's aid, and was handed a document containing the statutes. There were, as well, rules about going out and having visitors. The director advised her to read them carefully, to keep them on her bedside table. Laurence held her tongue.

She met a nurse from Lachine, an older nurse with an independent spirit, whose intention it was to resign as soon as she could be sure of a job in Montréal. She affirmed that the nuns were as punctilious as their rules, and personally didn't agree with their norms. For the moment, she got around the rules and regulations as best she could. The nurse wanted to go to an anglophone Protestant hospital, directed by lay people.

Léon wrote a letter of disapproval, saying a single woman remained under her father's tutelage for the sake of her reputation and that of her family. She had gone to Beaupré against his will and he did not approve of her new move. Montréal was a city of evil, dangerous for the Christian soul. She should trust his experience in such matters. As for the Indians of Caughnawaga, they were shifty and dangerous. Her obstinacy was leading her down the wrong path.

The family was now also suffering under the economic crisis. The farm prevented total disaster. Edouard was bogged down with his debts. Aline would enter the convent the following autumn. Though her teaching salary had been reduced, the dowry demanded by the religious community remained the same. He wrote his litany of sorrows, and signed, as was his habit, your father, Léon Naud.

She almost sent the money she had received at Beaupré, then remembered the doctor's words, his thoughtful comments. A letter from Amanda followed. Her experience of the novitiate in Montréal had fanned her prejudices about the city. She believed her sister's faith was in danger. As far as the Indians, different from us, religion had never managed to civilize them. They remained children of nature, cruel and bellicose of spirit. Amanda said God's generosity blessed the family by calling their sister, a sign of hope in the midst of deprivation.

Laurence sat dumbfounded before the admirable handwriting of an educated woman, and the signature of Sister Léon-des-Anges. The nun's intimidating manner and her foolish pride annihilated Laurence's self-confidence, her capacity to think. She tore up the letter, muttering to herself, and during a fitful sleep dreamed that she was falling off a cliff. In her solitude, she summoned Gaston, who, she knew, was on a ship headed for Amsterdam.

Laurence read the sad letter from Estelle Haley that opened with the words: I don't know if you will remember me, and our friendship at nursing school. I heard you'd moved to Montréal from my doctor in Québec, a friend of Dr. Fournier's, the same doctor who gave me your news when you were living in

Beaupré. Laurence remembered Dr. Fournier had mentioned, offhandedly, that Estelle Haley had returned to nursing school. I got your address from Dr. Fournier, she wrote. The letter's pages told of a liaison.

About the time she was thinking of enrolling in third year, Estelle had fallen in love with a married man. She reminded Laurence that the nuns had expelled them after the American circus had come to town. While visiting her aunt, Estelle was still trying to decide whether to re-enroll, when she met Jean Chevrier on the boardwalk of the Château Frontenac one May afternoon. The son of a bourgeois family from Québec, he had the reputation of a Don Juan who didn't get along with his wife. He didn't hide his marriage from her, nor his romances with several married women, none of which had amounted to much, according to rumour.

They became lovers, met secretly, conspired, lied. Her widowed aunt, who was a little deaf, knew that Estelle was seeing him by the end of the summer, and threatened to tell her parents if she didn't break with him, but didn't follow through, believing that when the school year started, her niece would settle down. She loved her niece and didn't broach the question of sex. The young green-eyed blonde, naïve, clever, seemed so gay that summer. She acted as if sex was not an issue, and persuaded her aunt. Her youthful energy enlivened their conversations. They avoided discussing the awkward matter. Prudishness kept the taboo under a veil. All references to sex were easily skirted, well-trained as they were in the matter of avoiding bad words.

By September, Jean Chevrier wanted to break up. Playing down the importance of the sexual aspect of their relationship had had the effect of magnifying her emotional attachment. The young girl saw her lost virginity as a major blemish. The bored lover said that when she became a nurse at the end of the year, she would be a free woman, no longer under the tutelage of her parents. She didn't believe the rumour that he was involved with another married woman.

Her relationship with Jean Chevrier might have ended had not her parents insisted on seeing her so often. The constant trips home, her absences from Québec, made her want him all the more. Estelle thought of nothing but love. Studying was tiresome. After a year of doing nothing in her parents' house, then a summer of passion, she was headed towards failure.

She appealed to her lover in the name of love, made herself more desirable than ever. The idea of pursuing two secret liaisons at once excited him, and he invited her on a four-day holiday to Cacouna, where he had to go for business. She lied to her aunt that she was going to Sainte-Marie. Estelle came back with the vague intuition that she was pregnant. She didn't try to see Jean Chevrier. They met three weeks later, and he swore that he loved her. She soon knew for sure that she was pregnant, and was anything but happy about it.

Jean Chevrier made a scene. He had tried to break up with her. It was she who had insisted, had pursued him. It was all her fault, because a young girl kept her virginity and didn't beg men to make love to them. He insulted her by saying she had acted like one of those servants who get thrown out for getting knocked up.

Estelle told her aunt about her pregnancy, who advised her to tell her parents. It was possible that a country doctor could deliver the child at home, that it could be adopted immediately. Estelle did as she was bid. She was so obsessed by her state that she could hardly talk. Her words belied her despair. Her usual lightness of spirit deserted her, and she was caught in a vortex of confusion. Her mother and father reacted in chorus, united in their repudiation of her. They put her out and said not to bother coming back after she got rid of the bastard. Her bond with them, as old as she was herself, and so necessary for her emotional well-being, was severed.

In Québec, the aunt took pity on her and didn't turn her out. When the time came, she would go to Montréal to have the baby at Miséricorde Hospital. Estelle sought out Jean Chevrier. He met her near the old ramparts and handed her a wad of money. He behaved like a solid businessman whose reputation was threatened, and preached at her. He had never hidden his marriage and his mistresses, he said. Now, if she was patient, she would cope, because she was pretty.

Estelle asked Laurence to meet her at the station and accompany her to the Miséricorde Hospital, where the nuns expected her the first Sunday in June. She would be travelling alone, and didn't know the city. Laurence wrote back that she would take the first train into Montréal in the morning. Estelle's letter was disconcerting, shocking. It seemed impossible that parents would abandon their only child.

The overnight train from Québec arrived in Montréal before seven a.m. Laurence, travelling first by foot, then by train, and finally by tramway, arrived at around eight o'clock. Something made her slow her steps as she entered the nearly deserted station. She saw varnished wooden benches. On the farthest bench along the side wall, she saw a woman outstretched, her light coat falling open. People were gathering around her. Slowly, Laurence approached an employee in uniform, accompanied by two policemen, just ahead. She walked in the direction of the prostrate woman. As soon as the gawkers stepped back, she recognized the blonde hair, the oval face. The legs were spread open under the bulging dress. Estelle lay without moving, her shoes in a viscous puddle. On the bench, Laurence saw a detergent bottle that a policeman picked up. The bottle was half-empty. Horrified, her feet planted on the ground, she stared, distressed, at her friend's blue face. A strong intuition kept her glued to her spot. In order not to be noticed, she retreated towards the entrance, without taking her eyes off the policemen, who were attempting a cardiac massage.

Tears came to her eyes, and she felt nauseated as she stepped outside and vomited, sobbing. She screamed, threw up again. A man nearby told another that the woman had a dead baby hidden under her coat. This confirmed Estelle's death.

Laurence moved away, unnoticed. As soon as she had understood what was happening, she had retreated. The police would open an inquiry. Estelle had killed herself. Her oval face had already turned blue, and the poison was beside her. She couldn't reconcile the violent suicide with the sensitive, sweet young girl. She trembled.

Laurence was alone with her secret. She bore it painfully, asking herself over and over about her inability to approach Estelle, about the terror she felt. In the middle of her turmoil, a voice of reason had warned her not to get involved. Thinking about her hurried exit filled her with dull pain. She justified her rapid, instantaneous retreat in the face of disaster by reminding herself of her precarious situation in the big city. She was aware that her heart was broken, but also that her rational side had won out over her feelings.

The nurse from Lachine had left the hospital. Laurence would not have shared an incident so heavy with meaning with a mere acquaintance. She reread Estelle's letter. There was no allusion to the final months of her pregnancy. She said nothing about what had happened after December or January. The address was not that of her aunt's in Sillery, but one in Lower Town. The hypocritical moral standards of a Catholic, civilized society disgusted her. Her anger, her pain, magnified by guilt, ate away at her.

7

Framed rules on the walls of bedrooms, bathrooms, the refectory, the hallways, and the visitors' room pursued her wherever she went, whispering their desire to create order in the midst of an invisible disorder. Laurence put the sheets of regulations in the back of a drawer. A supervisor noticed when making her rounds. Her disappointment grew when she discovered this was not a training hospital. She grew bored. At Caughnawaga, the good weather returned and she was lonely and restless. Recent events had muddied her thinking. She couldn't think straight, but she refused to focus on the dark side of things, which would get her nowhere.

One Saturday, the golden light of dusk filled her room, and she did her hair, put on a pair of sheer stockings, her silky shirt, her pale grey suit, opened her cologne bottle, powdered her nose and painted her lips. She looked at herself in the mirror with the silver handle, ready for an evening out with an absent man. Night had just fallen. She marched back and forth in the small room, murmured to herself. Being shut in made her feel more helpless, and her nerves were on the verge of cracking. Hurriedly she undressed, throwing her clothes on the chair and the table, burying her head under her pillow, smearing the sheets and white pillowcase with her lips, mixing the flesh-coloured powder with the sweat of her anguish and her tears.

Her dissatisfaction increased, and she only wanted one thing: to flee. She needed a letter of recommendation to another hospital. She would ask the nurse from Lachine. She inquired about the ferry schedule with the intention of going to her place on her next day off.

On arriving in Lachine, Laurence asked the way, and arrived at the house later than foreseen. Nobody answered, and she sat on the outside stairs, sure the nurse would return some time this evening. She should have written her. A heavy feeling grew within her. What if the nurse didn't come back? She didn't budge from her spot, torn between worry and hope. What had earlier seemed certain now seemed less likely. It was after midnight and no one had come. In the clear night, she walked past façades whose lights had gone out some time ago, looking for someone who would show her the way to the nearest presbytery or police station. She would turn to the police for shelter.

On the main street, men passed, alone. When Laurence saw a young well-dressed man, she decided to approach him and find out where the police station was. The young man, who had spent the evening with his fiancée and was in no particular hurry, talked with her. He offered her the sofa in his room. The fact he was engaged reassured her. They tiptoed into his place. The sofa faced the bed, offered her no intimacy. He handed her a pillow and a blanket and wished her good night. He undressed, got into bed, and she followed suit, albeit remaining clothed. Behind a curtain that separated the two halves of the double room, shadows whispered to each other, and she slept badly, awakening at the slightest sound. The next day a couple got up. They protested but said not a word to her, throwing her disapproving glances. She went with the fiancé to have breakfast at a restaurant.

Laurence told him her story with a certain tact, with the naïveté of a countrywoman who recounts her whole life to the first person she meets. He was soon getting married, but he was ready to help her. There was nothing ambiguous about her request. The fiancé knew his boss was looking for a nurse to look after someone in his family. He had overheard a conversation through the open office door. She asked him to speak to his boss on her behalf, and handed him her telephone number. He was touched by her boldness and determination, without knowing why.

The phone call came. They needed someone immediately. The fiancé pretended she was a distant cousin. His boss needed a private nurse for an undetermined amount of time. Laurence's youth worked in her favour. The father believed the presence of a young female companion would hasten his daughter's recovery.

Once more, she thanked heaven or her lucky star, and wrote a note to the fiancé. She resigned in the good faith that she was on her way to a household like Dr. Fournier's.

Laurence's frank gaze made a good impression during the interview. The mother spoke of a sudden shock, later she called it a setback, and finally admitted it was a broken engagement. She said: mademoiselle our daughter, as if she were talking about some distant family member. The mother wanted her to wear two different outfits. In the morning and during the evening, Laurence would wear a white uniform. In the afternoon she would don pink or blue dresses to look after the children.

The nurse met the doctor the same day. Françoise suffered from neurasthenia, he said, and refused to eat. He gave instructions regarding medication, minimal required daily food intake, supplements— a detailed list to study. The doctor added that the parents would have nothing to do with a psychiatrist, and were absolutely against a diagnosis that would require hospitalization.

In her garret room on the fourth floor, Laurence thought about what the doctor had said, and the patients of the asylum, abandoned by their families, came to mind. A woman, even if young or rich, who walked through the gate of the asylum, lost her identity, became unrecognizable, cast away and forgotten, for the most part, by those close to her.

The mother introduced them, and Françoise held out her hand from where she was sitting on her bed. Once alone with her, Laurence spelled out the doctor's orders and said she was there to help Françoise see they were carried out. The young girl nodded, indifferent. Françoise looked strikingly like her mother. She swam in her embroidered nightshirt. Laurence was touched by her paleness and opened the curtains.

The cook gossiped, a one-sided conversation. Laurence didn't encourage her. Mr. Léopold had left mademoiselle Françoise for her best friend. Mademoiselle should have broken with such a false friend ages ago. They had nothing in common. Mademoiselle is like her mother, a homebody, not the emancipated sporty type that the other was. Laurence had her own opinion. Monsieur Léopold, like Jean Chevrier, didn't know what he wanted.

A stone stairway bordered with ornamental shrubs curved uphill toward the luxurious dwelling from Côte-Sainte-Catherine. The terraces, offering a view of the city, the English-style garden, the fountain, the paths bordered with trees, were remarkably beautiful. Few could dream of such a lifestyle. In her naïveté, Laurence called them the upper crust of the bourgeoisie. She preferred the grounds to being indoors, where she behaved in a reserved fashion, conscious of her place, though not intimidated, thanks to her uniform.

The opulence fascinated her. She compared the house at Beaupré with this one, and the former came out best. She concluded, without exactly putting it in words, that luxury and immense wealth are useless. Being moderately well-off was fine, beyond that, Laurence had no point of reference. The house had too many boudoirs, anterooms, dressing rooms, the expendable trappings of high society.

Françoise's noonday meals, elegantly prepared and presented, included parslied bouillons, chicken breasts, filets mignons, slices of roast veal or beef with gravy, grilled salmon with fresh vegetables appetizingly arranged in the dish. They baked a special eggbread for her, made up fruit salads. Custards, rice or semolina puddings in smooth caramel sauce were lovingly concocted by the cook. It was understood that the nurse would sit in the armchair at a discreet distance from the bed, and wait thirty minutes before taking away the tray. Françoise kept silent. Laurence, when on duty, spoke only if necessary. A ray of August light warmed the room. The nurse opened the window near the balcony door. The patient did not protest.

Laurence thought of all the people who would never taste such food, and her mother's face appeared before her. She took back the tray, noting what had been eaten on the medical chart. Now attired as a children's nurse, she took her own lunch in the kitchen, where she surprised the cook standing looking out the window, gobbling up dishes of custard or pudding.

Laurence took the children to the sports club, organized games for them at home, talked to them. She was more than a starched conventional babysitter, giving of herself, feeling nourished in return, throwing herself into their games. With Françoise, her duties were more set, required a slow even pace to which she was not accustomed.

Even bourgeois people from Outremont were losing their homes, she heard. She found the misfortunes of the rich scandalous, incomprehensible. The newspapers said that landlords were throwing large families into the streets. Unemployment was increasing. Charitable groups opened soup kitchens. September afternoons, with nothing to do before the children were brought to her, she went for a walk and ruminated on her future. The idea of living in residence again awoke such rage in her that she had to choke it back. Her recent hospital experience had opened old wounds. People, if indoctrinated to behave like machines, could not establish reasonable relations among themselves.

Françoise got up and dressed herself one morning, sat in the armchair, and called Laurence to take her to the garden. The nurse spread mohair blankets on the double swing, wrapped her convalescing patient in them and covered her legs. The warm September wind ruffled their hair. You could hear leaves rustling. Muffled city sounds floated up from somewhere below. Without warning Françoise asked her: have you ever been truly in love? She was trembling. Her eyes looked enormous. Words were not adequate to explain a thing as vast, as strong, as love. Love couldn't be talked about like any other event. Laurence lapsed into a way of speaking Françoise had never heard to sum up, in three sentences, their meeting, their falling in love, and their separation. Françoise was shocked by the vocabulary and a country lilt that Laurence never used on duty, where neutral medical terms were de rigueur. She was persuaded, believed her, especially since the man had a name, Gaston Ramsay. A name, in itself, demanded respect. It was impossible to invent a name instantaneously. Gaston Ramsay existed as surely as the passion that had devastated Françoise herself.

In the boudoir, the doctor read the medical reports filled out daily. The man, whose allusion to psychiatric care had not impressed the nurse, turned out to be approachable, and she took him aside. The fact that he was a doctor for rich people didn't prevent her from telling him that she was looking for work in a hospital where she could finish her training. The doctor spoke of the continuing crisis. He had contacts at Miséricorde Hospital and promised to recommend her.

Laurence believed that to get a job, you had to have a contact. She thought that everybody knew somebody, that family relations or neighbours or professional connections were links of a chain connecting workers to society. It was fate that brought her the doctor to help out of her impasse. She had tempted fate and it had been good to her. She acted without knowing the rules, took initiatives in the good faith that society was an extended family that responded when you needed something. Consequently, she saw the economic crisis as being manoeuvered by high international finance, causing various degrees of helplessness, and destroying solidarity among people. When she heard talk of high finance, she imagined a secret government that lorded it over politicians.

In November, she was dismissed. The colour was returning to Françoise's cheeks, and the mother was already organizing balls and receptions for the winter season.

On rue Dorchester, Laurence found a large square room, with shared bathroom. The single bed had a metal head and foot, the dresser was bulbous, and the thick flowered cotton hanging in the windows all gave it a familiar ring. The homemade rug reminded her of the long evenings with Aline, their whispered conversations as they wove. It was a room for reminiscing.

The nun at Miséricorde Hospital questioned her about her training. Laurence described the courses she had completed. It was an interrogation for which she was not prepared, and she replied carefully. Fear of making an error caused a lump in her throat that choked the possibility of inspired replies. An inner voice whispered that she should elaborate on her replies, but she didn't hear it. The interview lasted two hours. In the evening she couldn't remember a thing about it. The next day she remembered the things she should have said. She mixed up what she had said and what she should have said.

The nun accepted her into the training school, but declared, sitting on her high horse, that it would take a year and a half for her to get her diploma. The reason for the extra half-year was that her dossier lacked certain theory courses. Laurence didn't protest. She would be admitted in January. The director made no reference to her lack of schooling, the five years of elementary school. It is possible that the small number of second-year students was the reason for making her do the extra half-year. She said nothing and thanked her.

In the meantime, she was given various duties. Laurence expected to keep her job on the evening or night shift during her studies. The school was against this practice, for there was no lack of nurses' aides. The school and hospital had different administrations, formed two different entities.

The hospital, known for its obstetrics department, took in single mothers from Montréal and around the province. The religious community reserved a floor for married women, who got entirely different treatment. The segregation bothered Laurence, all the more so since single mothers were admitted under false names to preserve family reputations. The staff looked after anonymous faces and bodies. They were clothed identically, in uniforms. Hospital management did not allow them visitors. For the most part, families acted as if they had forgotten them, and many experienced the long months bracketed by conception and birth as an interminable period of atonement. The nuns refused to administer anaesthesia and sedatives during labour because they must feel, and never forget, their pain. The women were expecting children begotten in sin and it was only right they should suffer the consequences of illicit pleasure. Their hypocritical language sanctioned the moralizing posture of the institution. Furious, some women called the practices abusive.

The women gave up their children, signing adoption papers prior to giving birth. They were not spared the belt-tightening caused by the Depression. Their delivery and their stay in the hospital had to be paid for. They paid the same as married women, more if they had taken refuge in the hospital some months before giving birth. And if they couldn't pay, they worked in the kitchen, in the laundry, as chambermaids, until the debt was settled. They were not allowed into the nursery. This was stipulated in a legal contract. Laurence saw these women, for the most part young, scouring the big iron pots, removing bedpans from damp beds. They didn't treat their situation melodramatically or tragically.

It took concentration and effort to imagine the broader reality of their existence. Her gift of observation was helped along by her critical spirit. The nuns, backed by the clergy, behaved in ways behind the hospital walls that the public knew nothing of.

She kept ripping up her letter to her father. Trying to write it gave her a headache. She wrote the raw truth. The director wouldn't allow her evening or night duty, and she would be earning seven dollars a month. Laurence's determination to pursue her studies did not prevent her from dreading his reply. It was ambiguous. He was pleased she was living in residence again, though he disapproved of her choice of Montréal. The father seemed to believe she was paid to study. He wrote the oft-repeated phrase: no child of his had ever lied to him. Léon Naud didn't beat around the bush; he expected them to be straightforward. His daughter disconcerted him. Laurence had no religious calling and he presumed she would one day marry. The bachelor existence, if not directly helping out the family, was more suitable for a man. The moral discomfiture she caused him was irksome.

In February, the roads became impassable. The accumulated snow formed banks that reached the second floor of the hospital. You only went out if you had to. Laurence grew restless, her books open on her desk. Doing nothing made her nervous. The director's refusal to let her work weighed heavily, and she invoked her isolation, her distance from her family. Her loneliness was recognized as a valid reason and they let her work Saturday and Sunday. The thought of having got around the regulations excited her as much as the favour granted.

She had not entered the programme at the same time as the others. It was an already-established group who noticed that the new older student wore heavy cotton stockings under her shapeless skirt. They noticed her frank gaze, which they interpreted as a sign of insolence. They were twenty-year-olds from bourgeois families, conscious of their status, forbidden to socialize with people from inferior situations. Laurence's appearance did not jibe with their notion of the nursing profession. She was aware of their coolness, and attributed it to her clothing.

The young woman memorized the lessons in nursing theory by rote, repeated the lists of scientific terms out loud to herself. She pushed her notebook away, lost patience, hated writing because the pencil refused to go fast enough. She feared for her spelling, her handwriting, on the simplest medical reports. Laurence hadn't got over the wound inflicted on the gifted child who had been taken out of school. Her letters home remained matter-of-fact, the words coming easily. She knew what to say. Faced with words in any other context, she was gripped with terror. Outside the family circle, language sent back a mocking reflection.

Despite what the director said, the training focused on learning through doing. Her skill and self-possession came in handy. They saw that she paid close attention from the very first exercise. It was good to learn the terms by rote, for she could come up with the appropriate technical term for the appropriate gesture. The students appreciated her. Their uniforms put them on an even footing. It was she who kept her distance, for reasons not clear to her. The Montréal bourgeois girls seemed more out for themselves than those of Québec. Here, each led, alongside her training, the life of a young girl of a privileged family. There, the group spirit had helped her to get to know Estelle Haley. Their unabashed individualism dampened her desire for a class companion. She kept to herself.

In March, she mailed the money earned on weekends, happy to be able to add to the small amount earned as a student. She got an unpleasant letter in return. The father believed she was hiding money from him. In the name of respect and honesty, he ordered her to say what she earned, complained of their lack of money, said another son had gone away. Laurence was disconcerted. Her benevolence was misunderstood, earning her reproaches. He demanded and she gave. Caring as she did about their well-being, she didn't bother to explain. She felt she had shown good faith and that was proof enough. She remembered Dr. Fournier's words, didn't know yet how to strike a reasonable balance between heartfelt giving and looking after herself. Her generosity was not appreciated. The grim call to duty prevailed, when what she craved was a sign of appreciation.

8

Following exams, Laurence met Solange Roy while on duty as a nurses' aide at the hospital. They immediately made friends. Being certain, now, that she would pass left the space for a wave of nostalgia as large as her loneliness. She arranged her room so the red geraniums had the best spot for growing in the summer sun. A little bit of nature, a quiet whiff of the past.

Solange Roy appeared on one of the lonely days. The newcomer knew how to laugh, worked without sparing herself, unconcerned by soiled linen or strong smells. She guessed Laurence was not a Montrealer, broke the ice by mentioning that the Depression had forced her to leave Québec. The brunette with the transparent gaze said she lived with her brother. What a long time it had been since Laurence had known a woman of her age, someone she could really talk to.

Laurence seemed embarrassed about being back in residence. Solange made no disparaging remarks, only suggested that they take a walk along Sainte-Catherine.

In high heels, Solange was as tall as her companion. Arm in arm, they entered the first department store they came to. Solange wanted everything, and she commented loudly, excitedly, before the counter displays. Their behaviour attracted the attention of other women shoppers, who turned and looked at them disapprovingly. They went into raptures over scarves, handbags, fine sweaters. Bedazzled by the quantity of goods, the young women consistently found the next thing more desirable than the last, running from one thing to the next. They coveted several luxurious objects in turn, crying out loudly as they passed some well-dressed young girls buying gloves, and headed for the hat department. Solange and a saleswoman exchanged words in English as Solange tried on a pink straw hat with a little veil and burst out laughing. The saleswoman wouldn't let her try on a second one, cutting her with a scornful glare. Solange was oblivious to her tone and attitude. Now that she had met a young man, she needed a hat so as not to look like the wrong kind of girl. Smart women went out in hats and gloves, even in summer. They could see that just by looking around.

Laurence made her way to Viger Station. The tragic memory of Estelle Haley's lot was superimposed on the painful memory of the last time she saw Gaston.

She had been waiting for a year now, had sent her hospital address to Beaupré, being under the impression that news from Gaston would reach her via the Fourniers. It was the obvious way for him to get in touch with her.

In the station, the railway put a table with paper and ink at the disposition of travellers. She wrote him, called out to him, beseeched him to return. Her confidence in him persisted. She loved him. Seated a little apart from the crowd, she wept discreetly. The station's anonymity comforted her. They would come together again, in the middle of the crowd.

On her days off, tormented by melancholy, she would turn in the direction of the station, in a state of despair over their separation, whose reasons she had practically forgotten, and write to her darling Gaston that he was taking a long time to return, that being alone weighed heavily on her. When the letter was written, she invariably stuffed it in her pocket. She turned twenty-six that summer.

The economic situation was getting worse. Young pregnant girls took refuge earlier and earlier in the hospital, unable to subsist outside. Free labour abounded. The wards were packed to the brim. Laurence continued her courses but could no longer get extra work. The employees were losing their jobs. Solange was nearly fired after missing a shift.

She saw Solange, whose schedule was no longer the same as hers, three or four times. Solange was either laughing nervously or talking ceaselessly. The young girl said she was ready to make any concession to her young man. Her wanting to be married so much, her obvious vulnerability, disconcerted Laurence. Solange spoke neither of love, nor even of being in a couple, only of getting married.

When Solange, pregnant, lost her job, she asked Laurence for help and was loaned twenty-five dollars, all she had managed to save. The marriage would take place the following month.

Outside the hospital walls, chaos reigned, but Laurence felt less isolated within. The studied indifference of the other student nurses had given way to congeniality. During a training period in the psychiatric ward, Laurence told of her experiences working with the mentally ill. The students, for whom a women's asylum was unimaginable, a dark cave closed off from society, listened. Some admired her: it must have taken guts and tenacity to work in a place like that. In their eyes, there was a wall of stone between normal and crazy.

Laurence studied serenely for the final exams. Six years, instead of the usual three it would have taken her to get her diploma. Such was the course she had had to follow. Her path was different than that of others, a fact she shouldered with pride.

Solange phoned. Her voice crackled at the other end of the line. Laurence had to speak loudly to be heard. Solange gave her the address of her brother who would return the borrowed money. Laurence repeated the address as she wrote it down. Solange said that was right.

Laurence walked down rue Ontario in the direction of de Bullion. She turned south, couldn't find the street number, turned north. She walked to the top of the street without finding the number in question. The address didn't exist. She approached a man who was going by to ask for information. Did he know a monsieur Roy?

The misunderstanding seemed impossible. The money was to cover the expense of leaving the hospital and renting a room for the summer. She wandered towards the south and turned north again towards rue Sherbrooke. Evening cast shadows on the city. She persisted in asking people she met if they knew a monsieur Roy from Québec. Windows and doors were closed against the cool air. The façades were sinking into silence. For an hour she had been walking up and down, hoping someone would turn up. She was on the verge of turning homeward when a man in work clothes, undergarment visible under his open-necked shirt, stepped out on a balcony, the door open behind him. He addressed her in what she thought of as an Italian way of speaking French. She was looking for a man, a monsieur Roy who owed her money. He assured her he knew him and invited her to come in. He slammed the door behind her, used the familiar "tu": so you're looking for a man on rue de Bullion. She saw now that he was shifty, knew she had made an error, and grabbed the door handle to go back out. The man twisted her arm and turned her around, facing the stairs. He forced her to go up, shoving her. He pushed her towards a bald man standing on the landing. She screamed, they threw her on the bed. They hurled abuse at her, the Italian and the bald guy, a French Canadian. She quickly understood they were the sole occupants of the house. The Italian ordered the other to hold her. Me first, he cried, pulling down his pants. The bald man twisted her arms, pinned them behind her head. She looked at the long thick member and felt like vomiting. He jumped on the bed, which sagged, opened her coat, lifted her skirt and slip, tore her underpants and leaped on her. He was tearing her, battering her, burning her. They are going to kill me, she thought. She was in danger, and she was being tortured. She counted every interminable passing second. The man's groanings petered out and he got up. The bald one started undressing. The Italian beside the bed leaned over the lower part of his body, covered with blood, examining himself. She threw herself on the ground, grabbed her shoe, ran into the stairwell, drew back the bolt of the door, and fled, her heart in her mouth, up the hill towards rue Sherbrooke. She was trembling, touched her legs, and felt blood. She had run, terrified of being pursued, and slowing down, the next step hurt. Laurence realized it was painful to walk.

There was blood on her coat and her skirt. Her torn stockings hung down. She knew couldn't go into the residence without attracting attention. At eight o'clock in the evening, the outside door was locked. She hailed the first car that passed, told the stranger she needed medical treatment, that she had been attacked, called on him to help. The man told her to get in. She was still trembling, hesitating halfway through the car door, fearing he might not be trustworthy. He suggested, speaking with a European French accent, that he take her to the hospital. He introduced himself as a doctor, Dr. Lenoir. She noticed his black medical kit. The man was telling the truth. She finally sat down, one hand gripping the door handle. He questioned her, realized she had been raped.

The doctor changed his mind. He would take her to his place. Laurence wanted to get out, choking on her words, shaking with fear. He reassured her that his wife and daughter would be there. They lived on boulevard Saint-Joseph. The car headed off in the proper direction.

There was a light behind the glass door. She did up her coat, hiding her torn skirt. A middle-aged woman opened the door, and the doctor introduced the young woman, after asking her her name. The three of them went into his office, where he gave her a sedative and a glass of water. Despite her shame and confusion, Laurence managed to say what had happened, where she lived, why she couldn't return in this state. The choked rhythm of her words expressed her devastation. Her tight throat produced hoarse sounds.

The idea that she could be dismissed from the school crossed her mind. Students were sent away for much less. Rape was scandalous, ostracized you. Some mistakes were not pardoned, were punished immediately. Hypocrisy would protect her aggressors, she was sure of it.

Madame Lenoir mended her skirt, sponged off the stains, gave her some stockings. Laurence washed herself and waited, clothed in a hospital gown. The doctor told her that even if a virgin, she could become pregnant. He didn't examine her. The sedative started to work and she trembled less. She felt a nervous exhaustion that kept her alert. The daughter, who was Laurence's age, was kept at a distance. She could hear the comings and goings, but didn't know what had happened. The law of silence sheltered the rapists.

The doctor drove her to the school, advised her to stay in bed the next day. He handed her some sedatives and reassured her that he would be there for her. She curled into the fetal position, caught between wakefulness and sleep, stock still.

Dr. Lenoir had not forgotten the first day of final exams and came to see her the evening before. They discussed venereal illnesses in a low voice. She had no symptoms. He recommended she take a sleeping pill and wished her good luck.

Laurence practised her technical terms every night, recited litanies of words, ate little, sought more than ever to be alone, less concerned than ever about whether her class companions or nuns noticed her, indifferent to the festive atmosphere of the last day. In her pale grey suit, she didn't spoil the group photo. A student said her studiousness had served as an example. Laurence was moved.

The summer of 1932, a summer of waiting, made her restless. On sunny days she looked for shade and solitude. She walked, and would not speak to anyone who approached her. The unemployed, who where numerous, hung about. Many held out their hands for spare change. The director confirmed the hospital would not be hiring new nursing staff in the autumn. Laurence wrote to her family that she was looking for a job for September, describing what she saw on her walks about Montréal to illustrate the grim effects of the Depression.

When she entered the wide vault of Viger Station, a symbolic place, pain flooded through her. She sincerely felt she could no longer marry Gaston. She still loved the man who had respected her, her chastity, even in the most passionate moments. The young man who had asked her for nothing, had staked everything on the long term. He was far away and she was sure he would reject her. She felt unworthy, cursed the rapists of rue de Bullion and the fact she could confide in no one.

The doctor came back, reassured her she was not pregnant. They talked about her search for work. He was evasive, said he was not attached to a hospital. Like Laurence, everywhere he went he heard about people losing their jobs. He didn't commit himself to helping her.

She heard nothing from Solange Roy, and had to give up on the money she'd lent her. At the end of August, things started to move faster. Her father's letter announced he had found her a nursing job at Thetford Mines Hospital, thanks to connections made on his sales trips. All she had to do was show up with her diploma and the rest was paperwork. Laurence wasn't in a situation to wonder if she wanted to return to her family.

She no longer had any source of income as she studied for the final exam for the Order of Nurses. Renting a room meant she had to count every penny. She put aside the amount necessary for a train ticket and had fifty cents left over for food. She procured a large basket of apples.

Laurence ate raw and cooked apples. She studied, sitting at the table. From what she'd heard, the exams were not difficult. But her independence depended on her success. A nun who analyzed handwriting told her she was the type of person who went directly towards her goal, who achieved what she wanted regardless of the obstacles. On the fourth day, the apples tasted acidic, and she couldn't swallow. On the fifth day, back in her rented room, she made an effort to eat out of fear of fainting. She was used to heavy food. Hunger gnawed at her. On the sixth day, despite her completely empty stomach, she was about to throw the apples in the garbage, when the sight of the fruit made her realize how foolish she had been. A potato, a carrot, a turnip were one hundred times better for an empty stomach. Before and after eating apples, she felt hungry, because apples don't fill you up. How stupid she had been. The seventh day, after dreaming of the community dinner planned for the following day, she took herself to the examination with a clear head and the spurt of energy that runners have entering the final sprint.

Laurence had prepared herself with the same meticulousness as always. She swore never to eat another apple.

Her train left Montréal in the direction of Thetford Mines one morning near the end of summer. Thinner in her grey suit, she sat up close to the window, her eyes taking in the moving countryside. Her mind was a confusion of happiness and disappointment that she didn't seek to untangle. She had her diploma, and consequently a very legitimate feeling of self-esteem that buoyed her spirits. The thought of seeing her mother, her father, Edouard, her sisters, brothers, the expectation of a happy reunion, filled her with a spontaneous joy. She was so close to them, even when at a distance, and hoped so much they would be spared sickness, hunger, and the tragedies that tear families apart. They hadn't suffered, like others, the perfidy of mortal accidents, constant illness, loss of material goods from fire. Absence of catastrophe, of those sudden mishaps that ruined peace of mind, was how she defined happiness. Her brothers were tall, strapping fellows who put their worries behind them after a hard day's work, after shaking the dirt off their boots. They formed, together, a family whose name enjoyed a good reputation, and every face brought warmth to her heart.

The train rumbled through Granby, Sutton, Magog, skirted mountains, ran along lakeshores. She didn't wonder what the rules were like for a resident nurse at the new hospital. Rules varied from institution to institution. Her freshly acquired nurse's status guaranteed her a certain independence, and she intended to take advantage of it.

Her route required changing trains at Sherbrooke, and she spent the night in the station, nodding on a bench, fighting against falling asleep, her head leaning over her suitcase, the only woman in a station full of travellers without money for a hotel room. She was full of optimism. The next day the train chugged through undulating countryside, ringing with a familiar beauty, as did the names of villages like Disraeli, Coleraine, Black Lake. She breathed in the air she knew so well.

Léon Naud appeared in his suit, a black tie knotted under his starched collar. She wanted to throw her arms around his neck, she was so happy. Her father, who hated effusive behaviour, avoided her outstretched arms. Laurence looked at his face, embittered by endless disappointment. He comforted himself by taking credit for anything good that happened to his offspring. He praised the nuns at her new hospital, said she must express her thanks. Priests and nuns belonged to a separate sphere in society. If they showed any consideration toward Léon Naud, he became even more deferentially obsequious towards them. Laurence thought he overdid it and that nuns were not charitable. He took her off to the hospital to thank the director for doing Laurence a favour. She was absent. The assistant director said she would see the new nurse tomorrow. He was disappointed, but he didn't stop raving for a minute about the kindness he had received, about how advantageous it was for his daughter.

Laurence asked about each of them, and particularly about her mother.

The father took up his diatribe against Montréal again, a city of traps and dangers for a young girl, and said that he would sleep peacefully, knowing she was near home. She shared his desire for peace of mind.

Laurence was thrilled to see the family. Her mother took her hands, smiling. She had aged much more than the father. A spark of tenderness passed between them. The youngest siblings, now adolescents, didn't seem to remember her. She was mistaken. It was their shyness that kept them at a distance. Vincent, the thin high-strung boy, stared at her and said: your wart has disappeared, making everyone laugh. They had not been in the habit of mentioning the beauty mark on the end of her nose, which had always given her a comic air. Cécile moved closer to her while Odette, the eldest of the three, still seemed reserved. Cécile asked where she had been, and if it was so far away that she couldn't visit like her aunts, uncles, cousins. Cécile was still so lovable. Laurence hid the sadness she felt looking at the tall girl with her prominent jaw and lively eyes. Odette's prettiness, her dark brown curly hair, stood out by contrast. Then Odette opened her mouth, revealing protruding teeth that spoiled her appearance.

There were new marriages in the family. Isidore, the most secretive of the sons, had married a Thetford girl whose family was well off. His future was secure, only they wondered about the ideas of the new daughter-in-law who wanted to limit the number of children. Emilien's marriage to a young blonde with alabaster skin had surprised everyone. After keeping company for a very short time, they got married at the age of twenty. Emilien said he would live in the old house formerly inhabited by her parents, a mile away from Edouard's. Since the birth of their third child, the mother hadn't got back on her feet. Rosalie and Léon thought blonde hair and white skin indicated precarious health, a weak constitution.

Laurence asked about Aline, a novitiate in Montréal. The rules forbade her receiving visits from brothers and sisters. Distancing from worldly things and relations was proof of commitment to one's vocation. The young girl persevered despite her fragility. Aline was going to adopt Sister Rosalie as a name, in homage to her mother. Amanda, called Sister Léon-des-Anges, had given her the idea.

Laurence slept in Odette and Cécile's room. Her return to a family that had grown through the addition of sisters-in-law, nephews, nieces, made her dizzy, and she fell asleep with a parade of new names trotting through her head.

Rain whipped the windows and the wooden walls, fell heavily on the roof. Having grown used to thick stone walls that muted sounds, the cloudburst woke her, and she thought the wind had blown open the door. The voice of madame Fournier, grown old, whispered: how am I going to let you know when Gaston returns, since I am dead? Laurence murmured Gaston's name, and buried herself under the covers next to Cécile.

After mass, Léon showed her a newspaper clipping of a recent obituary of madame Fournier. She wasn't surprised.

The assistant director was awaiting her return. The fortyish woman with black facial hair, in charge of setting schedules and enforcing rules, questioned her about her absence. Where had she spent the night? Laurence felt like saying she'd gone to see some ghosts, but answered simply: my family. The uptight nun went on at length about the whys and wherefores of regulations, about why Laurence must be reasonable, finishing with: you understand. With each phrase her face twitched and she repeated: you understand. A verbal crutch! You needed permission to spend the night elsewhere. The nuns pretended they were responsible for the resident nurses, given they were single women with their futures before them. The nuns made bodies as well as souls their business. This didn't prevent a young girl from considering marriage. One of the residents had married a man who had showed much gratitude for finding, in their ranks, a well-ordered disciplined wife that he had searched in vain for elsewhere. You understand, one of the advantages of our institution is the opportunity to meet the right kind of people. The long-winded speech had a double meaning. Laurence had heard it all before. She let her finish.

The nun gave her the night shift. You understand you are new and your companions who have been here longer have priority over the day shift. It suited her to work at night. The sister made sure to point out the daily mass schedule for nurses and nuns.

Laurence understood that if she didn't carve out a personal space for herself, she would be devoured by rules. She repotted red geraniums, which the month of September always inspired her to do. They added a special touch to the cold room with its large black crucifix and framed images of the Virgin.

The mining town seemed to have been spared the economic crisis. Although they were hiring less at the mines, you didn't see homeless families in the street, or errant unemployed men. The municipality had cut back on spending, so the road paving was put off. The open-pit asbestos mine coughed its black, caustic dust into the atmosphere. The air smelled bad. Housewives opened windows and dust filtered in. They dusted, swept, washed; back came the black particles as soon as the wind came up. The people of Thetford Mines were working, had little time for leisure activities. Newcomers, mostly from neighbouring villages, didn't notice the filth of the place until they settled in. They put down roots in the hopes of a regular salary and relief from the fear of not eating tomorrow. They absorbed the gloominess of the place, said nothing, diffidently withdrawing into their shells. The old habits of conviviality disappeared.

Laurence sensed the alienation. She introduced herself to the patients and adapted to the situation, thanks to her independent spirit. From her superiors she sought neither praise nor reassurance that she had a nursing vocation. Like all newcomers, she made minor errors, but didn't get worked up about them. Mornings, she took great care to write a meticulous report.

She didn't go to daily mass. She was reproached for this by the assistant director who could find no fault with her nursing practice. Laurence had two sisters who were nuns, so she knew better. The nun had had a word with her father, a devoted Christian. You understand, she added, as the eldest of our resident nurses you must serve as an example.

On November 1, Léon Naud came in person to collect her salary, to the distress of his daughter. He couldn't wait one day. On the pretext of a ten-year-old commitment, he took the money without thanking her. Never was there a letter of gratitude, nor even an account of how her money was spent. Léon took comfort in the old commitment, his daughter's promise to give him every cent she earned. He congratulated himself for Laurence's reliability. On thinking of the promise, made and kept since that day in July of 1923, he swelled with pride. He had raised his family to respect him and this brought him inexpressible joy.

The money was all spent every month. There were fewer mouths to feed, but Rosalie's strength was decreasing as well. Store-bought things replaced what was no longer produced at the farm. Léon felt above the trivial matters of everyday life, and refused to face his chronic inability to provide the basics. He cultivated imperious airs and a mystical attitude. He preferred his daughters with religious vocations, for they conferred on him the promise of social esteem and eternal life. None of his sons had been called, like Amanda. None had, in their choices, compensated him for his sacrifices and failures.

Edouard had torn down the crumbling old house and recycled beams and timber. He lived in the incomplete replacement, for which the bank had refused to give him a loan. The support-wall beams were in place and covered with cardboard, the floors were of bare boards. It was smaller than planned. The thirty-year-old man walked with a heavy gait, his arms hanging stiffly at his sides. He appeared to be carved from a single straight piece of wood. They discussed business and the economy, which Laurence thrived on as much as ever. Talking with her brother was such a relief after listening to the worries of other family members. She was forever lending a sympathetic and understanding ear. Together, she and he focused on hard facts.

His voice dropped noticeably when he mentioned that single life was weighing on him. You women don't seem to suffer from it. Having no sex doesn't take away your taste for work or sleep, doesn't demoralize you. You keep functioning on all fronts. Men need sex. They would do anything for it. Women have a different nature. Edouard spoke alone. Between each sentence, seconds passed. He was repeating himself. Each of his statements spoke much about his life. Laurence agreed, shared his opinions on female sexuality. But the difficulty of putting things into the right words rendered their conversation awkward. Though not overly modest, they were trying to speak of things nobody spoke of, transgressing taboos. Their complicity increased, even if they spoke in circles.

In Leeds, he had noticed a young woman, tall, healthy, a woman of his age, used to hard work. As soon as the house was inhabitable, he was going to propose to her. For the first time, Laurence felt that Edouard was giving in, turning his energies towards a desire for creature comforts. He had been struggling for fifteen years to set up an efficient, machine-run farm such as they had around Montréal.

9

Barely a week passed without a visit from the family. Without warning, one of them would show up, clamouring for medical treatment, pills, or a sympathetic ear. Laurence's shift began in the late afternoon. They took pride in seeing her in uniform, admiring her cap and the gold pin on her chest, outward signs of her station in life. These impromptu visits embarrassed her.

One day, Odette showed up, and cried out in despair. She had run off, a male neighbour had helped her. She wanted Laurence to talk to the father, wanted to quit school, wanted to stay at the hospital in her room, wanted so many things through her tears, her frustration, that the elder didn't know whether to scold her or to laugh. The adolescent was playing her best card. She knew intuitively to go towards Laurence, who was understanding, who wouldn't rebuff her. I'll leave like you did when I grow up, she said, when she had grown calmer, adding she would never be a nun. At a distance, Amanda, Odette's godmother, was wielding the weighty influence of a perfect image. The adolescent suffered in the shadow of the role model, who, in everyone's eyes, had achieved mythological proportions. Amanda had never returned home, for convent regulations wouldn't permit it. Reduced to observing the progress of her goddaughter from a distance, she wrote letters to her that demanded answers. The father insisted. Odette said she felt cornered by all these requirements, and rebelled.

Odette turned heads with her curls, her charm. Her brothers teased her, irritated her. It took nothing to make her lose her temper and scream. They couldn't resist the temptation to prove that someone with her irascible, gullible character would never achieve that thing called grace.

Laurence was aware people talked about Cécile's ugliness. Everyone acknowledged that she was kind and amusing. The youngest had a quick tongue, could think on her feet, and was a good observer of character. Her natural spontaneity gait made her more popular than Odette. She overshadowed her. She laughed when her brothers said she was ugly but nice and would make a good nun. In her absence they agreed, lowering their heads in shame, that no man would marry her.

Laurence was furious with Amanda's authority over her sisters, the way she took over, encouraged by everyone, and the nurse keenly felt her lack of power. She no longer shared their moral values, their way of thinking. She had broken away. Cécile was not exceptionally ugly. She had seen her share of horsy mouths, pig-like faces, aquiline noses, bovine expressions, skeletal heads.

Laurence noticed the attempt to manipulate Odette from the time she was very young, the teasing, the bothering. They had to be ignorant to chastise a face for its beauty. No one told Odette that she was pretty— instead they concentrated on whetting her already sharp character. They made fun of her and babied her.

For Laurence, work and family came first. The other nurses were colleagues rather than friends. The engagement of one of them to a doctor was announced. Everyone had guessed something was going on, except reserved Laurence, whose eye was only on the doctors in the sense of observing how they practised medicine. She compared their respective approaches to surgery, and to delivering babies, singling out those who botched the last steps of an operation by using stitches that were too large, badly done. The nurse developed early on a critical attitude about medical practice, didn't mind giving her opinion on things, though others rarely agreed. The doctors enjoyed an authority which condoned their actions and protected them. Even the nuns closed their eyes to the over-use of forceps, did not question excessive medication.

The year-end festivities were elaborate, convivial, drawn out over two weeks' time despite the economic situation. Laurence met a great many people, those who remembered her and others she had not met before, sisters-in-law and their children and new cousins by marriage. The same question was asked over and over, an insistent collective refrain: you're not yet married? She naïvely wished Edouard or anyone would justify her single status by mentioning the years of training to be a nurse, or the help she gave her family. She didn't wish to be thought of with scorn. She mentally fled this kind of question, gleaned strength from the watching children. Surely they would grow up to have more progressive ideas. To her mind, the future depended on well-educated mothers, and an improved economic situation.

The family was asphyxiating, sucked her energy, left her empty. They thought she owed them everything. Having managed to adapt to the hospital, the thought of being there for a family that drowned its moments of pleasure in lamentations about misfortunes gagged her to the point of silence. They didn't know about the important events in her life, the people who had meant something to her, because she hadn't told them. One evening they were talking about Montréal and Léon told her about his wanderings around the city with an English fellow. They had walked up and down the streets between Saint-Laurent and Bleury, and the man had pointed out cabarets, gambling dens, brothels. They'd had a drink in a dive, full of gamblers and sexy women. The English guy got a little tipsy and went upstairs with one of them. Not knowing how to find their hotel on his own, Léon waited for him. The house of debauchery had no outdoor sign. He presumed that there were places like that all over the city, traps one entered by chance, destined to lead the best

Christian into temptation. Women lost their souls, their virtue, their reputations there.

Laurence became certain that Léon Naud had followed a prostitute up to her room, whence his visceral hate of Montréal. He moralized, almost raving. Thanks to the nuns, she had escaped the disastrous tricks of fate that left their mark on a young girl. She thought that the older she got, the more she would become distanced from him. The father's words were deeply rooted in hypocrisy. No one was allowed to have a different opinion, or make even the smallest, most careful allusion thereto.

She didn't feel sad. She felt weighed down, stifled, a feeling that wilted her generosity, her warmth. Following several days of self-searching, of ruminating on her increasing dissatisfaction, a letter arrived from Dr. Lenoir. She wrote back, asking for help, reiterating her desire to work in Montréal. As soon as it was mailed, she felt badly for having been too direct, took solace in the fact that he had explicitly promised help.

Spring was coming. The alternately windy mornings and sunny afternoons of the first days of April proved it. Rosalie was fluish and had a fever. Her condition worsened, turning into bronchitis. Laurence took some time off. The self-effacing woman was worried Laurence's absence from work might have consequences, but didn't complain. A new closeness grew between mother and daughter. Laurence's presence enveloped her, providing her with unstinting and reassuring care. As soon as the mother felt a little better, saw she would soon be on her feet, her old spirit returned. Rosalie begged her to go to Emilien, who needed Laurence to help his wife.

Lawrence did not feel kindly disposed toward the sickly, lethargic blonde sister-in-law, and she responded with a determined detachment from the latter's listlessness. Emilien had married a woman like himself and he loved her so much he couldn't bear the smallest separation. They passed hours with each other, to the exclusion of all else, doing nothing, unable to face everyday tasks, and neglecting the children.

Emilien, glued to his wife's bedside, was crying. A dense odour of excrement led the nurse to the cradle. The baby lay in its faeces and urine. It hadn't been changed for days. Laurence cried out in repugnance. Emilien emerged from his torpor. The baby moved, too weak to cry, clearly hungry.

Its body was a limp object whose scaling red skin she washed and swaddled. Its low weight indicated erratic feeding. Two children, half-clothed, gathered round her. The heat and the bad odours were suffocating. Laurence took pity on the boy and girl. The bed-ridden young woman's neck bulged in front. The nurse thought it was goitre and needed medical treatment.

There was a week of coming and going between Rosalie and little Jérôme. The seven-month-old exhibited an inertia from which he only emerged after several hours of constant attention. The mother could see the signs of improvement.

Laurence got permission to be absent from the hospital residence during the day, before she went on duty. Normally, the nuns objected to bending the rules for fear of setting a bad example for the other residents. She invoked the need of consistent care for Jérôme, and got permission. She was quite happy with the arrangement until her brother Rémi refused to drive her. No argument could change his mind. He was responsible for the horse and carriage, for it was he who would take over the farm. He was already acting like the owner. Edouard or her father took her once every other week to see Jérôme. She suffered from being closed in again.

She wrote again to Dr. Lenoir, insistent, and suddenly realized that, if the doctor kept his promise, she would need money to rent a room. She got permission to work seven days a week. Through sheer willfulness, she managed to stretch hospital rules without arousing the animosity of the nuns. They took her for an oddball and ignored her comings and goings because they she was reliable.

She grew increasingly impatient, a latent anger brewing within, against herself, against resident life, against a family that persisted in taking six days of her salary every week. She met no one new in Thetford Mines, kept running into a wall of astonishment that she was neither married nor a nun. It hurt her that they could only speak of what she was not, of what she ought to be. The mentality of the town was a village mentality. She was starting to think it was a hateful place, when Dr. Lenoir let her know he was coming to Thetford Mines at the beginning of August. Her suitcase packed, her resignation handed in, Laurence emptied her pots of earth on the floor in the middle of her room, took the cross off the wall and planted it in the middle of the pile, and closed the door. She threw her arms around his neck and kissed him as if he were a father, better than a father. She called him her saviour, her benefactor. Laurence was turning a page, breaking away from a family that did not return her affection, cutting the umbilical cord with the past.

A total of eight years of residence life had come to an end. She hadn't lost her spirit. Resident nurses were kept in ignorance of the real world. Behind hospital walls, obedience in the form of self-abnegation was considered de rigueur. Her sociability and her desire for real give-and-take relationships were thwarted by spitefulness, and even threats. One didn't grow behind the walls of the hospital, one regressed. Her years as a nurse-in-training had provided her best residence experience. Being initiated into the science of medicine was an improvement over routine work. She had oscillated between the joy of learning and the growing awareness of the gap in her education, spurred on by the conviction that learning would make up for her impoverished family background.

The flatness of residence life had tried her sorely the last year. She couldn't stand it another minute. Nor was travelling between the father's house and the hospital a solution. Instead of reinforcing family ties, it foregrounded their differences, increased opportunities for argument. Down there they spoke only of themselves, making her feel more alone. Laurence never got over the lack of consideration her dear ones showed her. It was her soft spot. She was perfectly able to see that her return had plunged her into a permanent state of sadness.

With Rosalie, a circumspect woman who seemed the paragon of sincerity, she felt cornered. Rosalie's admiration for Léon twisted the relations they had with their father. Her faith functioned as law, meaning she was quite capable of handing over a child to the father for punishment, while trying to influence the latter to cultivate patience and reserve. Laurence had deferred her own coolly reasoned indignation, the hidden side of her timidity, rather than turning it against herself.

The new nurse at Saint-Luc Hospital took a room on the corner of Sherbrooke and Saint-Denis. The sounds of the city calmed her. She breathed in an odour that reminded her of geraniums.

Dr. Lenoir enjoyed spending time with her. He told her about his arrival in Québec after the war, compared his practice in Montréal with the one he had had in Lyon. He preferred, he said, the hospitality of people here, and had grown more appreciative of the role priests played with the patients. For a long time he had considered that the men in black soutanes and white surplices, preceding or following him to bedsides, were at cross-purposes with him. He brought his science, his rational knowledge to his patients, while the priests, those fanatics, encouraged giving up. But religion is the opium of the people, he said. Families, torn between healthy bodies and saved souls, called both doctor and priest, to be on the safe side. Having been trained to observe scientifically, the ways of ordinary people had shocked him for a long time.

His way of reasoning was so new for Laurence, who wasn't a reader; her intellectual curiosity won out over her natural argumentativeness. Being a foreigner, he could judge people from a certain critical distance. She took advantage of the exceptional opportunity, reserved judgement until she'd had a chance to think. The man understood that she did not reject his ideas out of hand.

He spoke to her about no longer being a virgin, about the sexual freedom she could enjoy. It was her right to do what she wanted with her body. She was old enough and she was autonomous. Sex calmed mental tension, restored energy, if not overdone. The doctor was addressing adult women in general, the group to which she belonged. He went farther, spoke of a sexual practice without risk of procreation. He spoke so little of pleasure, emphasizing physiological needs, using the analogy of a good meal, which was even more satisfying and as regenerative of vital forces.

He talked in the first and third person, was persuasive, but there was no suggestion of seduction in what he was saying. He remedied that by commenting on how much he enjoyed Laurence's presence. Her youth and vivacity filled a lack in his dull existence, full of obligations. His wife wasn't interested in sex any more. She deprived him.

The vigorous man, almost sixty, seemed experienced to her in the ways of the world. It's not clear what made her decide, the opportunity or a sense of time passing. Curiosity took her to the room of a good hotel where they drank pastis. The sensations created by strong drink blended with physical sensation. Laurence enjoyed an evening of escape. He wasn't wrong, she found it relaxing.

He told her one day that pastis was a derivative of absinthe, a hallucinogenic from which big drinkers suffered devastating effects. In small doses, absinthe had relaxing, and even analgesic qualities. Its frequent abuse had led to its being banned in France, thus favouring home distilling of a bogus product. Laurence fantasized that she was drinking absinthe.

The doctor determined the rites of their clandestine meetings, where they felt no compunction in using the familiar "tu." They knew they would one day decide to end their liaison, or they would drift apart.

They spoke of social inequality, one of the doctor's favourite subjects. Like many poor people who have received a religious education, Laurence reduced the cause of poverty to the sole economic factor. In stable periods, most people lived quite well, and personal initiative increased one's chances for prosperity. The doctor confirmed that social stability and progress alternated with the economic depressions, wars and revolutions that reduced poor people to misery. The least well-off were encouraged by sustained periods of economic stability to believe that personal prosperity was just around the corner.

One winter evening, as they lingered in the hotel room, he recounted the key moments in the life of Jean Valjean, a story that began with the prodigious incident of Jean Valjean's getting caught stealing a loaf of bread, resulting in his being sentenced to hard labour. The injustice of the sentence, its precedent-setting role, seemed somewhere between make-believe and reality. She experienced the story of *Les Misérables* like a child deprived of fairy tales, an adolescent spared cheap romances, an adult thirsty for knowledge, struggling against prejudices and prevailing morality. She questioned the doctor at length. They spoke of Jean Valjean. The character became real.

Dr. Lenoir gave her the novel as a goodbye present. Laurence opened it, persisted, reading laboriously, now able to become familiar with the whole story, thanks to the gift of the book.

10

That Bishop Bienvenu belonged to the religious hierarchy didn't bother her. The character he represented was generosity personified, which was how Church people liked to think of themselves. That she had never met anyone like him made her believe in him all the more. Bishop Bienvenu acts according to his beliefs; his influence will be felt later. A positive example, he follows his own inner inclinations, rather than acting with an end in mind.

That Jean Valjean, hardened by prison, deprivation and bad treatment, could steal the bishop's silver when the latter gives him shelter, was, to her, entirely believable. Unhappiness warped a person's physical and moral fibre. The conflict between the two men, the symbolic meeting of good and evil, strengthened her conviction that a man in flight hardens himself even more when he encounters exemplary goodness. A troubled past opens the door to spite. The characters were believable people with whom she could discuss things impossible to discuss with real people. From the first pages of his novel, the author Victor Hugo proved to be a confessor, a psychologist and a master portraitist of traditional mores.

For the theft of some bread, the hero had been condemned, punished out of all proportion to the crime. He had been delivered into the clutches of justice. There was no Bishop Bienvenu among his judges: the arbitrariness of circumstances jettisoned him among convicts, a dubious lot whom honest citizens view maliciously, fearfully. It takes so little to terrorize people.

To whom could she talk about her rape? Her father? Edouard? Her mother? Who would have dared hear her out, when society protected rapists? The consequences were serious. She wouldn't get married without confiding what had happened. If the man turned away from her, withdrawing his commitment, his desertion would send the message that she was unmarriageable. The violence done to her warped her present life. She couldn't forget the rape. She wasn't the type to dwell endlessly on the negative. But the thought of really falling in love made her dizzy with anguish.

With some exceptions, men were less bigoted than women, but were unreliable when their pride was at stake. She was neither stigmatized nor infamous, but victim of a violent crime that had gone unpunished, a poisonous secret that deprived her of her spontaneity. She had been raped right before her exams. Those who called her ambitious, would, had they known, have said she was being punished, being made to atone for her sins. Religion coupled with superstition.

The misfortune was an unspeakable secret that hardened the heart, threw the emotions into a turmoil. It struck a sensitive spot in Laurence she didn't know she had, and she covered it with stoicism. It was better that Gaston should be afar. Thus, she had refrained from writing to Dr. Fournier on hearing of the death of his wife. She had disappeared without a trace, and no one at Beaupré knew how to reach her. A sound decision.

She recognized her kind among *Les Misérables*, people who had to rely on themselves, were at the mercy of random violence. You can lose your mind for less. An unforeseeable incident had happened for which there was no possibility of retribution. She swore that no man would have rights over her.

She read for several months. Victor Hugo seemed to her a giant, a genius. When reading, she felt like the world was new, a world she had never imagined. Victor Hugo's humanism was dear to her heart, opened her mind to a wide range of things upon which to reflect. The discussion on the letter and spirit of the law instructed her about the need for reward and punishment in the family, in institutions, in society. Those who possessed power and authority, were they judges, policemen, creditors, or family heads, stirred thoughts of revenge, brutality, revolt in the hearts of those terrorized into postures of obedience and servility. To look up to one's masters was to lose something, was to lower oneself proportionately. The best way to bolster one's self-esteem was to be scandalized by a master's shortcomings, by his improper behaviour or acts.

Victor Hugo offered an endless parade of people, great and small, of love and hate, of pleasure and meanness, of the vicissitudes of success and failure, proof of the essential solitude of each, and, not the least, her own. She hated the idea of being alone so much that she misread the novel's ending. After mourning Jean Valjean's death in the arms of Cosette and Marius, she decided that the hero would really live out his long days with them, that they would console him, help him redeem the past and past injustices.

The death of the hero exorcized her pain, was cathartic. She read it word for word, and since the book was coming to an end, it shouldn't end like that. The idea of enduring happiness, conquered through phenomenal struggle, seemed so legitimate that she corrected the author's error. There was no such thing as solitary happiness, nor even happiness between two people, if close family, friends, were excluded. Laurence dreamed of a vast and generous understanding between people that would remedy maliciousness and wrongdoing.

Victor Hugo was wrong: death offers no relief from the sting of life. If the novel had ended some other way, everything leads us to believe Laurence would have still changed the ending. Her way of reading was to maintain some control, no matter how intense her admiration, her passion. The end of the novel offered a fresh opportunity for a heart-to-heart with herself. It was no longer Victor Hugo who decided the outcome, but she herself who extended it beyond the end of the novel.

There was nothing worse, in Laurence's opinion, than to try and substitute a state of religious exaltation for evil. The reader believed in Jean Valjean, a plausible character with whom she could identify, an inspiration.

One's background, the doctor had said, determined one's destiny to a considerable extent. But origins are not everything. Many people think they have successfully camouflaged their roots, hidden them. In this respect, the religious habit was an interesting metaphor. If some were privileged at birth, most people had to count on themselves, whence the necessity of fundamental liberties, such as the freedom to make one's own life choices. Without it, social relations became twisted and perverse. Then, there were the poorest of all, those who were offered no way out. Totally at the mercy of others, they were sometimes thrown bread, sometimes stones. When stones were thrown at them, some became violent, some submissive. Each and every one dreamed of revenge.

Laurence's mind drifted, for a second, to the days of May, 1918, when the family fought against the Spanish flu that threatened the life of the frailer ones. It was the worst spring in memory. The usual end-of-winter shortages, the scarcity of meat and vegetables, made it harder to fight against illness. Fleas and lice invaded hair and straw mattresses. They had to de-lice, clean, defend themselves on all fronts at once. The little food available was given to the weakest. The beds were infested with vermin. With Rosalie, she washed, disinfected, nursed. Their diet was reduced to buckwheat waffles, bread and omelettes accompanied by lard, which made the men stolid and churlish with the women. Each kept his thoughts to himself, bowed down by the harshness of his lot. Each said his prayers in the evening, stomach half-full and self-esteem at a low ebb.

There were better times that year, when they shared soups, stews and pies. Never was there enough for them to have snacks. If a child ate jam or sugar, he had surely stolen it, and was denounced and punished. At mealtimes, they kept an eye on the big eaters. One or the other always felt they hadn't got their fair share of desserts, thought the next plate had a bigger piece than his. It sufficed to change plates for the neighbour's portion to grow smaller when it was in front of you.

The word poverty was taboo, never uttered. It was a word for those whom the village priest helped out, wards of charity.

Laurence was used to not thinking of herself. She accepted where she came from, thought life determined you as much as you determined it. This was the case of Jean Valjean, a hostage of destiny, forced to go into hiding under different names. To run is not cowardly, but a manifestation of the common survival instinct. One day he can't stand his double life any more, reveals his identity and gives himself up so that some poor miserable wretch will not be punished for the infamy borne by his name. He goes to face the judge, although he knows it means he will certainly be locked up.

Québec City, Beaupré, île au Canot, Broughton, Thetford Mines, Caugh-nawaga, Montréal, a geographic triangle, her itinerary of defiance, her path of flight. Her decision to move on was determined by circumstances as much as by her will. The exercise of free choice was only part, a small part, of the whole picture. Within her rose a strange desire to set her own course. She was already in a state of denial about the role her rebellious nature played in her leaving Thetford Mines for Montréal. Confronting identity and origins was painful, linked her more to the past than the future.

Among her favourite episodes in the novel, she was enraptured by the passages where Mr. Madeleine, a.k.a. Jean Valjean, invents a gadget facilitating the manufacture of glass objects, creating jobs and prosperity for himself and his community. She dreamed endlessly of good living situations, understood that technical inventions represented a high point in human and intellectual endeavour. That comfort and wealth could be conceived from an idea, imagined, made real, seemed to her an admirable individual and human achievement. Nothing seemed impossible, for, to become rich, you just had to dream up some new way of doing something.

She identified with Mr. Madeleine. Being in hiding, he didn't have much choice; either he stole, or he used what he had, his head, his hands, his observant eye, his mettle for trying the new. Jean Valjean is changed by his passionate quest, his fertile mind.

Legitimate aspirations breed success. Laurence, in her isolation, firmly held this conviction. It was Edouard who had taught her to think thus, and she had believed him. Mr. Madeleine's success got him out of old ruts, bad company. He requisitioned his identity. A convict gets no help, no support, must find mother, father, and companionship within himself. Is courage ever more than the ability to gather together one's dispersed forces?

Mr. Madeleine can't let on he has become rich, because his bogus identity obliges him to remain anonymous. Money comes with a price. She found the idea of non-ostentatious wealth comforting. She valued money for how it could improve people's lives. It was good to be generous towards the poor. Everyone in the community should have a share. Laurence believed in the equitable sharing of wealth.

The underground hero nobody wants to pardon, the ransom he had to pay in retribution for his misdeed, his erring ways, were proof of the harshness of justice. She felt, without actually putting it into words, as if she also were being monitored, as if some power without or within constantly bid her not to be herself. She followed her inclinations, but had no guiding hand. The father only rebuked, warned, reprimanded. No matter how much she told herself it was his narrowmindedness that made him do it, such treatment left its mark. He induced her to be submissive, obedient, notions he defined more arbitrarily with time. The father thought it was his obligation to look after her moral education, since neither a religious community nor a husband had taken her off his hands. Defiant, diffident, she slipped through his fingers. Her financial obligations to him twisted their relationship, and her family's hardships bothered her more than did her own.

The father's life was ruled by his moral code, a fact he concealed from his business associates. He made all the more sure that his rigid beliefs dominated family life.

Laurence, who didn't mind what others thought of her, seemed incapable of duplicity. Good or bad, her feelings were hers and hers alone. Approval of others was nice, but what made her feel good was the sense of accomplishment she got from doing something. When she asked strangers for help, told them her story, she didn't worry whether they thought her smart or stupid.

Mired in Thetford Mines, she had found herself at an impasse. Nobody understood her. The old Laurence, from the past, rose up beside the Laurence of the present, and she could see she was losing her sense of self-worth. Rather than resign herself to the situation, she faced the fact that she needed to move on. The hope of happy conviviality, nourished on the train taking her to them, had transmuted into unbearable distress. The only solution was to leave again.

She subscribed to Mr. Madeleine's hesitation when dying Fantine begs him to help her little Cosette. Generosity should not be a matter of sentiment. A disinterested act of kindness must not be impulsive, must not expect something in return. Pity is the stuff of dubious sentiments, the fruit of gregariousness. A clandestine life requires skill and prudence, and anonymity enhances one's sense of self. You have to act on the spot.

The character, a diamond in the rough, became a point of reference, reinforcing her confidence. To talk about oneself was an act expressing confidence in the future. She would have liked to talk of herself, a free woman, to her father. He wasn't interested. How she perceived herself— or how others perceived her— was not at issue: she sought neither an audience nor a stage.

Laurence's opinion of herself was not dependent on the opinion of others. She looked reality in the face, confronted her solitude, the most difficult aspect of single life, in a clear-eyed manner. Jean Valjean approached Cosette, Fantine's little girl, became her adoptive father, and learned it was possible to love. One day, someone would come for her.

Victor Hugo's writing is unbelievably generous in its discussion of the need for the equitable treatment of each. The father's appalling way of comparing Laurence and Amanda made enemies of the sisters. Léon thought the second daughter so unlike the first that he exaggerated their differences. Laurence brought to mind his Indian grandmother, married for love, whose sons had emigrated to New England. He found Amanda's blondness, her alabaster skin, and her desire to please gratifying. He contrasted Amanda's grace to Laurence's joy in life. He took the latter's troubling curiosity and liveliness as manifestations of an unacceptable penchant for excess. The angelic face of his eldest reassured him of his salvation. He refrained from calling the other's traits diabolical out of fear of punishment in the great hereafter. The devil's world, its perversions, existed beyond the walls of his household, and he made sure they didn't enter. Léon Naud thought endlessly of evil, and its hold on people. The blonde daughter was the repository of good. Thus he wished it, cultivating a preference for her to keep him from erring in the face of evil. He feared the materialization of a she-devil.

Laurence shut her eyes to the real reasons for the unflattering comparison. She never held it against her father, mistook his motives and believed that the antagonism between Amanda and her came from their different characters. Believing it so emphasized the ways in which they differed. Léon was exonerated of his adulation of one and distrust of the other, and Rosalie of her wilful blindness.

Léon constructed Laurence into a Cinderella figure for the benefit of Rosalie, who never thought about the future. The trials of every day life sufficed. Rosalie saw earthly existence as a valley of tears, an exercise in self-sacrifice. She taught her daughter everything she knew. Laurence became very good with her hands, but hated domestic work.

For Laurence, Léon was a man dominated by his moral code, and she pardoned him. It was important for her to have a tie with the father. She blamed her sister. The elder's prejudices against the younger sister were sanctioned by the father. None of the other brothers or sisters were subjected to such discriminatory treatment.

Among her classmates, she, who came from the back country and had only gone to grade five, was the only one to receive no support from her family. Her left arm and her hand shadowed her page; she hid her note book, her pale handwriting, separating vowels and consonants, not pressing on the pencil. The letters undid the words, the errors blended in, dissipated. This daily struggle to keep up with her classmates transformed social differences into abstract signs. They caused her no suffering, by default.

When Dr. Lenoir pointed out that discrimination and inequality were at the root of strife and misery, she imagined paternal disappointments, families thrown into the streets, unemployed men reduced to depending on the public purse, an accumulation of factors resulting from economic hard times.

Reading Victor Hugo awakened in her the notion that it was the masses who invested authority with power. The sound of chains when convicts march past terrifies people, getting them all worked up. The men in balls and chains are anathema and the curious, the strollers, are attracted by the desire to reassure themselves they number among the solid citizens. They boo, hiss at evil, safe in the conviction they are walking on the straight and narrow. The crowd loves to be horrified. They shudder in unison, and hate even more.

Each and every one of the convicts— the bread thieves, the murderers, the political prisoners, all mixed up together and branded with numbers, dressed in prison garb, chained— each and every one nursed the desire to get even with society. In Victor Hugo's crowd are several unpunished rapists wearing innocent faces.

The life of a fugitive is in the hands of a cop like Javert, for whom self-respect and respect for order are one and the same. He never tires of pursuing and harassing. Such a purist enforces the law to the letter, seeking out quarry who will serve as examples. A cop like Javet, a loner despite the crowd's sanctioning, never notices his servility. He identifies with what he believes, and the more his allegiance is confused with order and authority, the more certain he is of his beliefs.

Javert chases down evil in the person of Jean Valjean, hunts him in the name of an absurd notion of justice. He is not, like so many, a man of vacillating morality, but the servant, the meticulous facilitator of the rule of power. With his rigorous conscience and his lack of humour, he is the master settler of accounts.

Jean Valjean is wily, disappears, posing as a gardener, behind the walls of a convent, or behind the barricades when the revolutionary struggle momentarily levels class differences. He is a transient with a nose for taking the right turn. In flight, held hostage by the whims of he who hunts him, he has an idea, no better nor worse than anyone else's, of where he is headed.

Laurence felt at the mercy of circumstances. Moreover, she was acutely conscious of her lack of awareness of the consequences of her acts. She proceeded without inner confidence, without good reason, a woman raised to be dependent on others, to obey without questioning. Like Jean Valjean, she reacted when pushed to extremes, made decisions on the fly, driven by necessity. There was nothing sad about this. Sometimes she took on an air of defiance, and, often, she saw the humour in her situation.

She was becoming detached from a family who hung on to the past. Education was the key. She was learning things they, with their rigid morality and narrowmindedness, ignored. She resisted their way of thinking, but it still affected her actions.

She knew they were deeply biased towards her, down there. The father had written that he never went to Thetford Mines any more. It would embarrass him to run into somebody from the hospital from which she had so ungratefully resigned, and with no good reason. He said she was capricious, which would cause her trouble in the future.

As far as her generosity towards them, he considered it her obligation as a daughter. Had the parents ever wondered what their obligations were? As far as they were concerned, nurses were fed and sheltered like nuns, without having paid the dowry required by the community. Out of ignorance and selfishness, for ten years they had demanded she give them her entire salary. They didn't worry what consequences this might have for their daughter. Now she deducted what she needed and sent what was left. This new apportioning of her salary neither pleased nor saddened her. She was sharing, as it seemed only fair to do. Laurence's generosity was for the single purpose of helping them rise out of their state of economic insecurity, of perpetual deprivation. She persisted in her hope that the father would succeed, notwithstanding the unfavourable context. It comforted her to think how impressive he looked in his white shirt and citified suit: he would manage, and under his leadership, they would all arrive at better times. The father had promised this, and she was doing her bit.

The young woman, motivated by her optimism, had been told she was ambitious, a word with two meanings, of which she only knew the non-derogatory one. Both ambitious and generous— a rare combination that made a woman seem excessive— she was one of those who looked toward the future. Such an attitude was generally not acceptable. She resolutely fled those who failed to understand her, moved on— as she was in the habit of saying.

Her inclination to look toward the future came from afar, perhaps from before her birth, or after, it didn't matter, from some distant impulse that played a role increasingly in the context of her present life.

Les Misérables was a cult work that opened her eyes to a troubling new reality, that of the degree of destruction caused by moralism and prejudice. The attitude of the people of the community towards Mr. Madeleine is a patent example. A tale of success ending in failure, it taught her that one can be robbed of happiness. Thanks to Mr. Madeleine's invention, the community progressed rapidly, prospered so that there was work for everyone. Solicited from all sides, Mr. Madeleine is elected mayor, but Javert is watching, confirms his suspicions, and denounces him. Jean Valjean, disgraced, realizes that a Javert lies dormant in most people. Mr. Madeleine is thrown out of the community. It doesn't take many years before the community begins falling apart, becomes destitute once more.

This story of a man who devotes himself to a group of people who all turn against him makes her think about how blind human beings can be. That they can destroy he who has brought them much good proves there is no limit to people's covetousness. The man who has brought them an easier life has hidden his past and they call him infamous. The reputation of Jean Valjean, convict, takes precedence over that of Mr. Madeleine. The group, speaking in a united voice, brings unhappiness upon itself.

Laurence was among the vast number of readers who wanted the characters to represent the victory of good over evil. A book should be edifying, should feature solid values. She knew about the consequences of original sin, had heard repeatedly that to spare the rod at the first sign of defiance was to spoil the son or daughter. The cult book was a balm to the harm done by such punitive language, restored self-respect to those who lacked, who were maltreated. Victor Hugo's authoritative pen made his readers see that good things could come in life. Laurence's attitude had something of the scholar's about it, and at the same time an incommensurable desire that the human heart not be fundamentally evil. The novel sees to everything: a miserable wretch overcomes his origins, a hardened man achieves goodness, an illiterate learns to read, a lonely person is surrounded with affection. The book promises redemption, grants the wish that good will triumph over evil. The triumph of a life lived in harmony with others. Laurence would have it no other way.

11

Les Misérables was the book of books. Laurence, in the manner of people for whom reading is a trial demanding tremendous concentration, even studious effort, applied herself like a schoolgirl. Every page reverberates with Victor Hugo's humaneness, his refusal to stand in judgement. The author constantly iterates his pact with the disenfranchised. Laurence saw him as a father, an exemplary figure, the kind an adult woman needed, a man who fed her hunger for meaning, for a point of reference to counterbalance the meaninglessness of existence. The book does not damn people who steal bread, nor unwed mothers, nor prostitutes, yet praises a bishop's misunderstood generosity, and refuses to avenge the weak. It is about removing shackles, obstacles to a new future, about opening a door onto new possibilities, turning points. The poor are granted no respite, only passing triumphs. The story offers appeasement, and, for a reader like Laurence, hope of ultimate reconciliation with the world around her.

Hugo's fresco of symbols, myths, beliefs, attitudes, social movements, wars of conquest, insurrections, opened her mind wider to the idea of fighting against her own ignorance, instead of taking refuge in the irrational thinking, in airy-fairy notions, or even religious teachings. Victor Hugo seemed to her as knowledgeable as he was tolerant. She confronted her lack of learning without abjection, eager to understand. The novel became less a work of fiction than an amalgam of references to history, to philosophy, to the study of language, custom, attitudes, and political and legal structures. The author's wealth of wisdom was contained in his book. Her admiration for the novelist sustained her effort, and she finished what she had started, despite the book's lengthy digressions, its occasional erudition, its frequent historical parentheses, which added depth to the unravelling plot.

Her own experience in her own social milieu was the result of a background that placed her in a similar paradigm, rubbed her up against the same questions. Why are we complaisant? Why are we so suspicious of strangers? Why does the city inspire fear? Religion's promise of eternal punishment kept the sinner in a state of passivity. Women's sexuality, explicitly and implicitly an object of apprehension, caution and future malediction, denatured the body, cheapening it with gross childish terms. There was no correspondence between words regarding one's sexual practice and the terms she had learned in physiological textbooks. She was perfectly aware of how unwed mothers were discriminated against, of how they were punished allegedly to atone for their sins. She grew certain that prostitutes, unwed mothers, carefree delinquents like Gavroche and stealers of bread, did not upset the social order, were victims of a prevailing punitive moralism so entrenched that the troubling ideas of Victor Hugo were not transmittable to the majority.

Ignorance, prejudices, and attitudes that caused fear and suspicion made social peace impossible.

Victor Hugo's epic story embraces history. The universe of war, a totally male domain, caught Laurence's interest. She had heard Léon speak of war. The little girl did not have her head in the sand. A threat had hovered over the house as they spoke of the eldest boy who would soon reach the age of conscription. The father pointed out the names of boys in the canton, followed the reports in the newspaper. The war sucked up the vitality of the region, served up nameless youth as canon fodder. She grew interested in stories of older countries, in the history of Europe, riddled with wars.

Laurence ruminated over what caused wars. War, an absurdity presided over by men, had disastrous consequences for all. She focused on the economic aspects. Armed conflict was the surest way to impoverish people, to deprive a country of its sons, disorganize its material life for the gain of the few: politicians, generals, who grew rich on everyone's backs.

The father's words had a certain resonance in the social upheavals related by Victor Hugo. A crook gains the reputation of a hero, a former convict saves lives. Insurrectionists commit crimes and atrocities that have nothing to do with the ideals they are supposed to be defending. There follows a general chaos which affects the civilian population. It is held hostage, becomes the quarry from which taxes are extorted.

The love scenes, dominated by female characters, pointed to a gender distinction, implying that women and pathos were one and the same. What did she have in common with Fantine, a pretty orphan girl? She knew they existed, these girls kept by lovers, abandoned when they got pregnant so the men could marry girls of their own class. She knew all about the secret lives of young girls from the country, maids in bourgeois homes, promised jewels, money, the chance to climb the social ladder. When she went dancing at the Château Frontenac, she noticed girls from humble backgrounds mixing with the rich boys, being taken out by them, having a good time.

She knew nothing of fairy tales, romantic novels, melodramas, never read the hagiographies that had fascinated Aline. She never bothered to take a book from the nuns' shelves, for she was persuaded that their purpose was to indoctrinate readers, to make devout Christians of them.

Fantine's good times turned to bad. Laurence was reminded of Estelle Haley, her passionate love affair, her suicide. Estelle's constant solicitude for her parents was not commensurate with the family's rejection of her. A huge gap opened in Laurence's understanding. She could tell it was about the baseness of existence; instead of dwelling on it, she grew more determined. When wracked by a desire for intimacy, she glossed over it, using a prudish vocabulary. The isolation experienced by young girls appeared insurmountable.

Cosette's naïve happiness, her being adopted and cared for by Jean Valjean, makes innocence seem childish. He protects her, sparing her the secret of her origins and of the checkered past of her mentor. Laurence knew that being born a bastard was something people kept hidden. Victor Hugo waxed eloquent on their right to happiness, even if it offended prevailing morality. Cosette was the personification of the young well-protected girl, spared knowledge of her disgraced, mean beginnings. Marvellous things happen to her. Her and her mother's early misfortunes are made up for; the troubles of Jean Valjean, vindicated. True justice offers restitution for misery. Laurence believed such a justice would exist for future generations.

For women, well-being depended upon whether or not they were accompanied in life. Their dependent state didn't make them second-class citizens. Laurence did not cast judgement on women, did not see in the lot that befell them a sign of weakness.

Happiness requires the presence of the feminine, is made complete by the feminine's pleasing, soothing qualities. An unnatural woman like Cosette's wicked nurse, la Thénardier, seems uglier, more vile and dangerous than a man. A woman, whether angel, devil, or weak-willed slave of her feelings, never changes, is a creature of instinct, of her nature, which is immutable. La Thénardier knows how to lay snares, knows how to keep her eyes open, to take advantage of people. No woman makes empty gestures, except the prostitute, Fantine, who sells her hair and her teeth to support her child, but what she gives of herself is not enough. Dispossessed of her beauty, hunted down, weakened by illness, she dies. Her story is a melodrama, a sad tale to stir the imagination of girls. Victor Hugo does not believe in the emancipation of women. His humanism is of the paternalist variety.

Laurence's identification with Jean Valjean was not a comment on the female characters. He is a solitary figure trying to survive, and he succeeds. Jean Valjean is not ambitious, lives by no rule book. Because he is among society's outcasts, such things never occur to him.

The hero, like Laurence, is born poor. Guilty in the eyes of the law, he cannot avoid the consequences. It could have been otherwise. Poverty breeds crime. Misery wears an iron yoke, the cloak of servitude. There is no such thing as a needy person who lets a day go by without noting he is poor, even when he no longer is. Poverty is a state of mind. Jean Valjean cannot really deny who he is. Being a fugitive from justice serves as a constant reminder. During his years of wandering, he is confounded by his desire for revenge. Hardened by life, he takes advantage of everyone he can, even a child. Violence engenders fear from which one can't escape, except by committing more crimes. He learns, at last, to live with his lack of freedom, without bitterness, without envy, forever conscious of the need to be on his guard. He runs more than he walks, develops a sixth sense for danger. Since he must not draw attention to his person, to his cornered, shut-in self, he hones his talents, relies on his brains. He doesn't waste time polishing his personalality.

Laurence refused to conceive of herself as stymied, ensnared. She didn't obey rules she considered silly, was forever dissenting, and would do anything she had to to get out of an unpromising situation.

The hero was the personification of a solid man, capable of doing without, never wasting energy. She identified with the physical stamina that underscored his well-balanced mind, and helped him ride roughshod over fears and inhibitions.

She reflected that people are born with different degrees of energy. Energy was both a gift and a determining factor. She was born active and resourceful, as others were born passive and floundering. You couldn't change these things, they forged your destiny. In her opinion, very little was determined by the individual self. External factors were brought to bear on a variety of personal configurations. The absence of real freedom didn't prevent one from action. On the contrary, it was what one was born with that limited choices in life.

For a long time Laurence had copied, imitated, adopted the ideas and behaviours of others. There had been Edouard, who had involved her in the planning of his farm. He was her favourite for the simple reason that he had an ideal, a desire to better himself, was ambitious. Solid and consistent, Edouard had a nose for business. His desire to succeed buoyed her and for a long time she shared his dreams, with conviction.

One day while they were digging potatoes, Edouard was called on for help by a neighbour whose horse had become enmired, and she continued on her own, her bare hands feeling for the tubers that she tossed, one after the other, into baskets. Several nights of frost meant they had no time to lose, for the potatoes were the first crop from the land her brother had just bought. She was always ready to work for Edouard, for they were accomplices to the point that the land seemed to be hers as well as his. She worked there in a different way than on her father's land, propelled by a pact between two young people who owned something that represented a step towards freedom. The sun was setting and no sign of Edouard. Laurence felt her fatigue, her knees on the ground, back bent, hands moving with rapid perseverance. She went faster rather than letting her rhythm grow sluggish, her gestures mechanical, forgetting her body. The more numb her wrists felt, the harder she worked. The cracked skin on her finger joints was bleeding. Edouard still hadn't appeared. She finished her task: the whole field had yielded its harvest of potatoes. She was unable to straighten up entirely. Not having drunk anything, she was thirsty from eating dust, her lips chapped, her tongue thick in her mouth. Her face was black with earth, her throat covered in sweat. Spurred on by the idea that it was urgent to complete the job, she had pulled up every potato. She measured time by the five or six hours spent waiting for Edouard under the September sun. She was three miles from the house. She walked, dead beat, partly happy about what she had accomplished, partly put out by the brother whom she suddenly caught sight of chatting with the neighbour. She was so hurt she kept on walking, dazed at the thought he was taking advantage of her. She expected him to thank her. He did not. Edouard was like other men, taking one for granted when it suited him.

Laurence bore no grudge against him. One could always use her, for a time. The brother's selfishness was part and parcel of his masculinity. The necessity of believing in the future won out, and she continued to have a high opinion of him.

Dr. Fournier's memory evoked feeling cosy under a cold sky filled with wind and snow that obfuscated the roads. They took off in a clean sleigh, heated with hot bricks under their feet, covered with furs and rugs, a basket full of food stowed away, complete with a thermos of coffee, without knowing when they would return. She was never cold or hungry at Beaupré. The doctor drove carefully over packed snow, over new layers of heavy or soft snowfall, over ice. He enjoyed the meticulous rituals of his profession, identified with his art; his person and practice were one. Time didn't matter. He had learned the importance of comfort, the better to forget oneself on behalf of the patients. The nuns spoke of vocation, of devotion, but not the doctor. Though he devoted himself to his work, he referred to it as a practice, refusing to make of science a question of morals. When illness struck, social inequality was a non-issue. He went when he was called, ignored the religious edict to save the child rather than the mother. His medical practice had a human dimension compared to that of the nuns, who saw illness as divine intervention or a message from on high, and, who, in their practice, proclaimed the need for rules of conscience, self-sacrifice, abnegation. The yoke of sacrifice had no currency at Beaupré, thus removing a useless burden that only resulted in self-pity.

The uneven road grades along the banks of the river, the deep woods somewhere beyond which were little farms, made every expedition different. Duty obliged them to travel long hours. The precise pensive man found the young woman's exuberance and constant good humour touching. They influenced each other, reciprocally.

The Fournier household ran on a schedule adapted to the husband's professional needs. He was the centre of gravity around which the women turned. Laurence didn't imagine that it could be any other way. She idealized the peaceful harmony, the role women— including herself— played in the smooth running of things. Thus, she justified her autonomy.

Laurence had long copied the behaviour of certain men, using them as role models. Edouard had taught her how to think in terms of the future, avoiding the rigidity that led to defeatism, that kept one mired in the past. Edouard had toiled for fifteen years to establish a machine-run farm, and his gamble had paid off. The announcement that he would soon marry the woman who was the same age as he, the one from Leeds, a good housekeeper, proper, to say the least, did not particularly move her one way or the other. Love and marriage were not the same thing for Laurence. She had loved and his name was Gaston. Otherwise, people's marital pledges left her indifferent. In this, she mimed the father, who had never alluded outright to either sex or love. If Rosalie and Léon did not address each other as Papa and Maman, but persisted in using their Christian names, it was because it was natural for them to keep a respectful distance from one another. Rosalie did not take Léon's arm when she walked with him. In church they sat close, due to the crowded benches. Though the children saw animals coupling, human procreation remained a mystery to them. Marriage was what one spoke of, not suspect desire, not that deceitful hidden glint in the eye called love. There was a gap between the two. Two bodies side by side evoked sex, and Léon couldn't look at a young man and a young girl sitting close on a bench. He flew into a rage of irrational proportions, betrayed by his tormented expression, his agitation, his snarling.

Had Gaston influenced Laurence? In him she had found a kindred spirit. He had said: you have to try everything once, a little musical phrase that rocked her to sleep. Like herself, he was forever amazed. Even his sporty attitude, his frank, relaxed manner, was not unlike her own. She would have liked to somehow translate his masculinity into the feminine, to mime his debonair manner. This was not yet possible in relations between women.

Sometimes she adopted the male viewpoint, imitated their good sides. Those whom she respected became points of reference, but she didn't make a rule of it. Better than that, she took what she needed from the men who were her role models.

Her reading of *Les Misérables* broadened her mind, made her more principled. Jean Valjean struggles, protects his freedom, which freedom is granted by the author rather than by society at large. Victor Hugo's pen makes of him the archetype of men maltreated and misjudged by their peers. Unfortunate from the start, he is destined to wander for years, to be decisive, to think before he acts, and to fight for the right to a peaceful existence with his loved ones, a very legitimate desire. There were countless Jean Valjeans, men and women without means, kept down by religious and social mores, doomed to despair by the economic crisis.

For once and for all, Laurence saw through the father's lofty phrases, promising eternal life in exchange for suffering in silence, for not uttering a word, even to those around you. The power of his preaching had been such that no one was allowed to look reality in the face, a reality that he misrepresented for the sake of his own honour and moral standards. She gave herself permission to see things as she saw fit.

Had she had female role models, she who identified neither with Fantine nor Cosette? Her mother, in the shadow of the man she admired, cultivated the art of silence. Rosalie subdued the children out of respect for the father, ordered them to be quiet as soon as he entered the house. Amanda spread a white cloth on the table. The women fussed over Léon when he appeared, obeying tradition to the letter.

Rosalie's patience in the training of her daughter was invaluable. Laurence knew how to get things done without a thousand useless questions or pointless objections. She threw herself wholly into a task, mind focused on the movement of her hands. Patience comes from resignation, but also from perseverance, which is a kind of wisdom.

There had been Sister Agnès, who had taught her French, had got her into nursing school, a kind woman with a positive outlook. She had understood Laurence's aspirations, hadn't repudiated her on the grounds of suspect motives such as envy or small-mindedness. Women's qualities, due to their feminine natures, were considered weak compared to those of men, propelled by self-will. Laurence knew she had a strong character, even if she often went as the wind blew. In her opinion, prerogative was not the unique preserve of men. She adopted certain male behaviours, without bothering about whether they were suitable for a woman. She neither disdained nor rejected what she could learn from them. But though she felt no domain was closed to her as a woman, she would not have wanted, for anything in the world, to cause her father embarrassment. She was as proud as he, but was also humane in a way that he could never be.

She found in Jean Valjean, who was sensitive to others, to their way of being, a plausible model, a source of inspiration. She had fled her family a second time, and for good. She shouldn't hold their treatment of her against them, she told herself. She opened herself, heart and mind, to a book, had a private dialogue with it that helped her confront her own reality. The book's influence was powerful, direct, and filled her with an inexplicable desire to share it with others.

> *Will the future come? It seems that we may almost ask this question when we see such terrible shadow. Sullen face-to-face of the selfish and miserable. On the part of the selfish, prejudices, the darkness of the education of wealth, appetite increasing through intoxication, a stupefaction of prosperity which deafens, a dread of suffering which, with some, is carried even to aversion for sufferers, an implacable satisfaction, the me so puffed up that it closes the soul; on the part of the miserable, covetousness, envy, hatred of seeing others enjoy, the deep yearnings of the human animal towards the gratifications, hearts full of gloom, sadness, want, fatality, ignorance impure and simple.*

The meekness religion taught her in childhood made it impossible to conceive of the rich as people who committed all sorts of crimes. She dreamed of affluence come by honestly, so people wouldn't look down on her, as they did on those down in Broughton, whose moral precepts kept them in their place. She was unable to avoid the growing feeling, itself a kind of creed, that her own happiness was inconceivable as long as they remained destitute.

She remembered how isolated she had felt in the rich mansion on Côte-Sainte-Catherine, worse than when she was behind convent walls. The conflict awakened in her by Victor Hugo hadn't been resolved, seemed, on the contrary, more intense.

Laurence had started reading without any preconceived ideas, knowing nothing about novels, though sensitive to words. She gobbled up the words with the hunger of someone who had never read, had never entered a library or bookstore, tackling the mystery of language that leads one to one's self. For a Catholic, unfamiliar with fairy tales, romance novels, a book had something of the biblical, though she had never read the Bible either. The idea of the Book as something containing the sum total of human experience was always in the back of her mind. Laurence, who was looking for an oracle, a sage, a philosopher, found them all in the magician Victor Hugo. She admired him, he revealed the impenetrable truth of the human heart. His words were a subtle mix, exorcizing the cruelty of destiny and advocating the possibility of peace, in the end. A woman of her situation, no less than a man, could not bear the triumph of evil. His words consoled her, comforted her, and she believed in the progress of good, in the possibility of true communion between people.

Les Misérables opened one to the possibility of human mercy, tolerance instead of punitiveness: the novel was an anti–Bible. The authoritarianism, the rigid intransigence of her education were reframed, and she welcomed these words that redressed injustice and helped her justify her flights from the family.

The novel didn't awake a desire to read, it satisfied it. The effort expended in reading was rewarded, and she was convinced that evil could give birth to good. The narrow-mindedness of her origins no longer seemed like a moral blemish, but a matter of attitude. It's all they know... became her favourite phrase. She excused them.

It took common sense to see the relationship between the book and reality, to switch mentally from one to the other. She thought about how things were represented. It became a game to improve on the novel's ending, to plead in favour of the right to happiness. Words she didn't understand added depth to those she did. A reader who reads word by word grasps the poetry of a work. If she persisted to the end, which was her way with any undertaking, she saw the job of reading as comparable to other work.

Laurence had satisfied her curiosity as far as books were concerned. She intuited that no other book would teach her what *Les Misérables* had. She had read the Book that contained all other books.

12

Laurence walked home from the hospital, a worn leather handbag hanging from her arm. It was an impeccable July day in 1934, the sky blue, a little breeze blowing the light clouds. The clear light gave sharp outlines to the shadows, and the façades on the west side of the street were mostly shaded, while the east side glinted in the sun. It was a little after six. The young woman walked quickly. She was not in a rush. She always returned home with a brisk step.

From a distance, she perceived a female silhouette on the steps of her stairway. It happened that passersby paused there to rest, or that a roomer stepped out for a change of air. The wide stairway leading to the busy street was a place of choice for strollers.

The young girl sitting there turned her head from left to right, her arm tightly clamped around a little suitcase. Laurence didn't take her eyes off the girl, who appeared to be waiting. The curly hair was like Odette's. Having murmured the name to herself, she recognized her while still a hundred feet off. Surprised, she walked more quickly. Momentarily speechless, she finally spoke to her in neither a welcoming nor unwelcoming manner, asking her simply what she was doing here, to which Odette replied that she was waiting for her. That was all they said, displaying no warmth at seeing each other again. Laurence was as amazed as Odette was determined. The presence of her sister, clearly in no hurry to offer an explanation, flabbergasted the nurse.

Standing, the adolescent, who was much shorter than Laurence, seemed so young. The grave, shocked gaze of the elder, still stunned into silence, left no impression on the younger. They went up the stairs without another word.

Odette looked around, took stock of the size of the room, started to say something, stood with her mouth half-open. Laurence wanted to know how she got here. She had taken the train to Sherbrooke, changed for another going to Montréal, getting off at a station whose name she didn't know, and then asked for directions. The address was written on a torn piece of paper, the street name incorrectly spelled. She gave the ghost of a smile, revealing the protruding teeth that spoiled her pretty face. It was easy. Her satisfaction with herself bespoke a proud bearing that pleased Laurence.

The trip had taken twenty hours. Odette smiled. She'd done it and was now with her sister. The astonishment was mutual.

The sisters felt at ease with each other, though a little unfamiliar. Laurence welcomed the visitor, come from afar, without warning, like a hospitable hostess. Travellers usually speak of their trip and their reason for coming, but Odette said nothing, standing, her suitcase on the bed, holding her brown wool cardigan. Laurence tried to make her feel at home, inviting her to sit down and tell her what brought her here. Odette was here to see her. She added she wanted to live in Montréal like Laurence did, weighing her words. This laconic reply, accompanied by a smile, revealed a certain malaise, a certain awkwardness, despite her satisfaction at reaching her goal without any problem. Odette had put herself to the test and succeeded. She expected to be rewarded. The elder complimented her resourcefulness, treating her like an adult, like her parents treated visitors back home. The welcome constituted the reward for Odette's initiative.

Laurence asked endless questions about the family, for it was customary to ask news of mutual acquaintances. They spoke of family members, and in doing so, grew closer.

The youngest sister helped prepare supper, cooked potatoes and carrots in salted water. They shared a portion of boiled beef. Odette devoured her food, accompanied by buttered bread. They cleared away the plates before drinking tea with milk. Odette asked if she might live with her sister, stressing the verb in a determined manner.

She spoke of her boredom at the farm, of the lack of things to do. There had been problems at the village school, still others with the old maid with whom she was lodged. She never dreamed she wouldn't be allowed to go out. It was like a convent. She complained, enumerating past and present dissatisfactions, mixing last year's events with yesterday's, pell-mell. The sixteen-year-old girl was persuasive. Laurence, who never felt sorry for herself, was alternately embarrassed and troubled by her list of recriminations. She took her seriously, refrained from casting aspersions on her. Odette's miserable face was enough to convince her without further commentary.

Odette saw the opening, declared she wanted to stay in the city, never go back to Broughton. Still in a state of shock over the drama fate had dished up in the form of Odette, sitting there before her, Laurence asked what she would do in Montréal. The young girl detected a threat, and improvised, offering to cook and clean. She had been asking to stay repeatedly since her arrival, urgently, trying different tactics. Laurence wasn't against it. Odette, seeing she was not refused, breathed easier.

The old cardboard suitcase weighed hardly anything. The two cotton dresses were hung up. The greyish underwear and the less-than-clean night-gown exuded a fetid odour. When the thick stockings were removed, a dirty comb with teeth missing remained in the bottom of the suitcase. Laurence was taken aback by the light baggage and broken comb, signs of unspeakable negligence. She could not believe that was all her sister possessed, and felt as perturbed as she had at first sight of Odette. It both saddened and annoyed her that her sister had set out with such unkempt personal effects.

Her despair at the thought their parents had let her leave in that state was such that she gave free reign to her irritation, and made a disparaging comment.

Though she had slept alone for ten years, Odette's presence didn't bother her. The young girl was deaf to the noises of the city, sleeping soundly after her unusual day.

Two days later, without any explanation, Odette announced that her boyfriend would be coming around that evening. Laurence had a start, simultaneously repressing a smile and throwing her arms up in the air in a gesture of disapproval. She found out who the boy was, and how Odette had met him. She told her it was the delivery boy, the one who delivered groceries on a three-wheeler. They had gotten to know each other and she had invited him over for the evening.

Laurence refused categorically, telling Odette firmly that she wasn't going to bring home the first guy she laid eyes on. As two women roomers, they must behave with discretion; their safety depended on it. Furthermore, it was not acceptable for a young girl to entertain perfect strangers.

Odette pouted, but didn't insist. Her sister's firmness got the better of any arguments she could come up with. She didn't feel intimidated, but didn't talk back as she usually did. She didn't mind that much. When he knocked at the door, Odette did as she was told, saying she wasn't allowed to invite him in. It was, as she said, the pimply grocer's boy.

Laurence was under the impression that Léon and Rosalie had consented to Odette's departure. The girl told her she had been working for Edouard.

The idea of leaving came into her head the moment she was handed her first earned dollar. She was proud of herself for having made money. It was her money just as it was her idea to leave. Her fragmented story, vacillating between self-satisfaction and discontent, made sense.

Knowing her parents knew that Odette was with her, Laurence wasn't concerned, nor offended that no one had asked her opinion.

On her day off, they took an interminable walk, during which the newcomer was frequently beside herself with excitement. Laurence showed her the display windows along Sainte-Catherine. Odette coveted high-heeled shoes, thought the light cotton dresses marvellous, not to mention the pearl-encrusted angora sweaters, the silky blouses with embroidered collars. She laughed at the hats with little veils, pointing at the funniest ones. She was constantly pointing to things in shop windows and along the street that she found hilarious. She alternated endlessly between coveting things and giggling. Like Laurence, furniture, kitchen accessories, household linens did not interest Odette. They paused, speechless before a display of luxury jewellery. Real gold, gold plate, fake gold, it all looked the same. A very ordinary watch caught Laurence's eye. They passed a window of brassieres, corsets, panties, slips, nightgowns before which each maintained an embarrassed silence. Laurence wasn't against showcasing intimate items, but she couldn't look at them without flinching puritanically.

Odette was thrilled. The young girl wanted money to buy herself things, without knowing which things. There was something to satisfy every desire, and more. She fantasized aloud.

Laurence learned that she had run away in a letter from Léon. Odette had slipped off without telling anyone. He presumed she was with her and reprimanded her for her harmful influence. He demanded the return of his daughter, a minor for whom he was responsible. He reproached Laurence once more for leaving Thetford Mines, a city close by, for Montréal, a city where so many women went wrong, where there were dens of iniquity and where more crimes were committed than anywhere else in the country. He went on, haunted by the idea that evil was progressing in every place that had left behind rural moral standards.

The brutal, authoritarian letter left Odette distraught. Up until now, anything he said about the big city could be summed up in a sentence: women lost their virginity there. The word "debauchery" implied having fun was shameful. Pleasure unleashed dangerous passions in a Christian haunted by the devil and the fear of burning in hell. Always unsure of his own salvation, he was at risk of being damned himself if he threatened others with eternal damnation. As chief of the family, it was Léon Naud's duty to be beyond reproach in words and acts.

Odette screamed and cried that she would not return to Broughton. The scene was pathetic. The young girl didn't rant or complain or tentatively refuse. She dug in her heels. Her entire body manifested resistance. She was sincere, felt afraid, caught between the will of her father and whatever her sister decided.

Laurence had never grown accustomed to being rebuked and threatened. The current letter didn't concern her directly, and had little emotional impact. She knew he was counting on their obedience; it was unlikely he would show up. For the first time in her life, she made a decision as a responsible adult. She took it on, refusing to worry about the consequences for her own personal future.

She had to reply. Odette proved conciliatory, ready to make concessions if she had to. The sisters talked and talked— always and only about her. She had never been the subject of conversation before. She listened better. Odette had her grade nine diploma, and it was decided that she would study stenography and become an office girl. First off, she needed new teeth. She was pretty, but her teeth spoiled her appearance. Laurence told her how she had got hers extracted at the hospital, though they weren't too bad. For her, it was a way of avoiding problems and toothaches. The two sisters were sure that saying the teeth needed to be replaced would soften the father's determination. It was a matter of gaining time. Odette felt better. The idea that she could be pretty placated her. Laurence said nothing about her running away, and Odette, in a state of denial, forgot it.

Laurence wrote home using her usual respectful tone, and firmly stating that Odette needed new teeth. She could procure the dental care through the hospital. The image came back to her of the broken comb in the bottom of the suitcase, a sign of poverty, a reminder of destitution. She would not abandon her sister.

A letter from Amanda, addressed to Lawrence, followed. The nun dared to do what the father hadn't, declaring that in leaving the family circle, one's soul was at risk of eternal damnation. More than sure of her own salvation, it was on behalf of their father that she pronounced what amounted to a malediction. Her imperious phrases, far from setting an example, had the opposite of the effect intended. As Odette's godmother, it was her job to guide her. She was praying to God that her goddaughter would turn her steps homeward. Amanda's letter was a supplement to the father's, explicitly damning her. She made no mention of debauchery or sex. She used abstract references, generalizations, contenting herself with pointing a finger at the sinner, at the cause of the disruption of the good order of things.

Laurence's anger was huge, nameless, an icy fury she mostly managed to keep under check in front of Odette. The young sister was not aware of the conflict between her elders. Out of respect for the father, the rivalry between them had never been out in the open. Caught in a triangle, the first sister came out on top. With every victory she chalked up, the elder grew more statue-like. Laurence, the loser, struggled with everyday life. She overcame her awkwardness, her country manners and speech as best she could. To be admonished, damned, enraged her. Her family was taking sides against her, trying to make her live in the past. She came to this realization in her torment, and it altered her love for them.

Odette's presence toned down her reaction. Laurence showed her the letter, said that Amanda was talking nonsense. It was the first time she had dared speak critically of her elder. She got carried away, said Amanda was crazy, clapped her hand to her mouth, disconcerted by her outburst.

She suggested Odette reply as she saw fit, for she, herself, would not be writing back. The young girl received her own letter the next day, in which Amanda, as her godmother, asked her to return home. The worried adolescent held out the letter to Laurence, who said nothing. Odette, who had no intention of writing back, pretended it had never come. Rather than tear it up, she buried it in the bottom of her drawer.

Laurence thought a woman should look after her appearance. She therefore made sure Odette's hair was neat, that her clothes were clean and her shoes polished. Going out, even on a weekday, required dressing for the occasion. They went to Parc Lafontaine, sat near the pond, watching the rented boats go back and forth. There were many families, young people, people of every kind, some in their Sunday best, others who hadn't bothered to change before going out.

For Odette, the city offered an endless supply of potential pleasure. She wanted so much to go for a boat ride. She didn't ask— just blinked impatiently. A man walked toward Laurence. His relaxed smiling manner made a good impression. He reminded her that they had met at the hospital. She remembered, and introduced the handsome gentleman to Odette. Laurence was in a pleasant, flirtatious mood that day. The stranger's appearance cheered her, helped her forget her recent problems. They walked around the pond, talking between themselves, so that Odette couldn't get in a word. As they passed the boat rental hut, she blurted out they should take a boat ride, and he agreed. They sat opposite him, and he rowed, happy to have the company of two women. With Laurence, who was delighted the handsome stranger had recognized her, Odette had the feeling of living a special moment, where any wish might come true. The city enchanted her. She sat straight, and let them talk.

The conversation continued. They were walking towards rue Sherbrooke, the leaves rustling, the sun continuing its trajectory across the sky. He invited them to eat a spaghetti dinner on Sainte-Catherine. Odette was overjoyed, and Laurence, amusing herself with a vengeance after her recent worries, felt light of spirit, never thinking the fortuitous encounter might conceal an ulterior motive. He walked them home and asked the nurse if he might see her again, to which she, feeling light and happy, agreed.

It all seemed so simple and natural to Odette, who dreamed of meeting someone like that. The past few hours had offered one new experience after another. She fell asleep, pleased with her day.

He arrived ahead of time. Odette let him in. Laurence, rushing back from downtown, opened the door and saw, before her eyes, in the middle of the room, the man's back, his head bent, kissing her sister. It took Odette a minute to get hold of herself, troubled by the fugitive kiss. He was red in the face. Laurence exploded with anger, threw him out on the spot and ordered him to forget about both of them. He would never be welcome again, no matter what the pretext. He left without saying a word.

Her day off was spoiled. It was a lost chance to get to know a man of her age, but the jerk wasn't worth seeing again. She admonished Odette— didn't she know a respectable young girl didn't kiss any old man? The younger's naïvety did not prevent the elder from feeling a prick of jealousy. Laurence's attitude was more straightforward than Odette's, who kept silent out of resentment.

Later that evening, Odette articulated what had been brewing in her mind for several hours. She wasn't living in the city for her sister to keep her from doing what she wanted. She would study stenography, work and get married as soon as she met a man who was interested in her or who pleased her. Her words were bold and defiant. She wouldn't be an old maid, or a nun, either. For Odette, her sister was too old for love. Her assertion, full of the arrogance and naïveté of youth, took Laurence by surprise.

Odette wasn't curious about whether or not Laurence had been in love. It seemed unthinkable to her that her sister had had a romance. The adolescent treated love and marriage as one and the same. For her own part, the fleeting sensual moment had given her confidence. She was old enough to please.

A solitary woman, Laurence had suffered her share of trouble, and her gritty ambition to succeed kept her striving doggedly. She had acquired a resolve which left its mark, not only on her, but also on those around her in ways she didn't realize. Capable of making do without, she couldn't imagine that not everyone was. She knew how to submit to the demands of duty, practising self-denial to the point of excess. An inner voice warned her that she was overdoing it. The line between the demands of others and what she deemed reasonable to give of herself vacillated constantly. Odette's appearance did nothing to placate this inner struggle. She was thirteen years older than her sister, strong-willed, though little inclined to mothering.

Laurence dealt readily with unexpected events, reversals, the hazards of existence, over which one has no control. She picked herself up, looking straight ahead. Her confidence in the future kept her moving forward.

For one year, the sisters resisted family pressures. Laurence didn't abandon Odette to her worst fears. She supported the younger's desires, drew an analogy with her own life, and believed her sister would have a chance to make her own choices. As far as she was concerned, it was never too soon to start.

To get on in the city one had to look good, be well-spoken, raise one's voice a little and use clear pronunciation to avert errors, which, in the urban context, stuck out like sore thumbs. It took a confident bearing to command respect, Laurence said. Odette, wearing new clothes, was enrolled in a stenography course. Laurence would have liked her sister to show some enthusiasm for her studies, as she would have, had she been given such an opportunity. Her sister sulked, was in a rush to earn money, didn't know any more why she was going to school. They argued. Laurence was against her sister working in a textile factory, where the women laboured long hours in filthy conditions. She wanted to spare her from hard physical labour. It was a matter of pride that Odette not go to work in a factory. She taught her that social standing was important when it came to finding a husband. For a rosy future, you had to give up things in the present. They planned as if they were not in the middle of the Depression, because, otherwise, there was no good reason to have come to Montréal.

Odette turned seventeen in December. Laurence figured that her immaturity went with her young age. The elder sister regretted their isolation, that they had no social milieu, knew no one in the business world. She thought about her post as a private nurse looking after Françoise in Outremont, remembered the father whose office was on Phillips Square. She instructed Odette on how to present herself as a potential employee, on how to put her best foot forward. Odette lost her composure at the building's entrance, became shyer than ever before. Terrified, she didn't dare enter, felt like she was nobody, or a beggar, panicked and fled to their room.

They scrutinized the help-wanted column. Laurence grew suspicious at the sight of strange addresses and faceless bosses. Odette seemed so young to cope with things she'd never even heard of. The list of reputable enterprises was very limited. Odette grew discouraged after one failed attempt, which required knowledge of English and typing.

One March evening Odette had a fit. It wasn't fair that she had to sit around doing nothing. She wanted to work like her sister. Laurence gave in, on the grounds that she would gain experience in the working world. Odette had a contact for work in the textile industry, another roomer who was a seamstress in a men's clothing factory. She was hired and began on a Monday. The mid-town wokshop, on the third floor of a building, was a distillation of racket, dust, filth and cramped space, a microcosm of the city.

The bosses spoke English. The neighbour was patient with Odette, who was eager to learn and jittery. Her jerky hand motions broke the thread. The morning was spent threading the machine. The young girl was frantic by the time she got home from work and dreamed of thread and broken needles so that on waking, she felt she hadn't slept, had kept on working all night long.

On Saturday, she arrived at eleven o'clock with an excuse that the supervisor ignored and finished at five, too exhausted to eat. Her pay envelope contained two dollars. It was piece-work. She had received a warning. A machine had to produce a certain quota, otherwise it wasn't worth it. She slept through her day off, while Laurence worked.

Odette grew discouraged the following week when the supervisor refused to accept her work. Her impulse to protest was dampened by a second warning. The young girl was paid off on Friday.

Laurence consoled her, and thought, without saying so, that her sister did not have her stamina. She didn't blame her for what had happened. She was too young for such a hard job. Odette made no connection between her role in the firing, her proficiency as a worker, and the role of the supervisor, and concluded it was all the supervisor's fault. Laurence replied shortly that on no matter what job there are supervisors who make high demands of you. Odette didn't argue with her and refused to think about it. They went out for spaghetti on Sainte-Catherine, and felt lighthearted again.

There was the story of the brief out-of-character flirtation Laurence had with an insurance salesman she met in a bank line-up. She warmed to the idea that the bachelor had contacts that might be useful to Odette. The man spoke in a jovial tone about his business successes, boasting. Laurence agreed to go to the movies with him. Over a coffee, she dragged him off the subject of himself to talk about a job for Odette. He lied in order to see her again. A spring breeze was making the sap rise. Laurence made herself want a relationship with him, even though she found him only moderately attractive. His interest in her augured well: he held the solution to their impasse. She saw him again, and included Odette. In their room, Laurence introduced her sister and raved about her strong points. The insurance salesman diverted Laurence's hopes in a way she didn't notice, by playing up to Odette. He thought he would have both of them. He came back, one late afternoon, and came on to Odette, who laughed at his propositions. He tried to kiss her, held her hands loosely. She found him old, unattractive, marked time, played coy, the usual banter. They did not hear the key in the lock.

Her anger quickly won out over her surprise. Laurence was at no loss for words, and reprimanded him for causing trouble instead of helping. The man apologized, saying he would keep his word. He was lying, and she ushered him to the door. He had no excuse for coming into their place without an invitation. She threw him out as she had thrown out the handsome fellow last summer. This time it didn't bother her, he was a bore.

The sisters discussed the matter as soon as everyone calmed down. Odette was learning and had to know that you don't permit a man, even a man you know, to come into the rented room. Men who would behave respectfully towards the sisters if they lived with their family, got carried away at the thought of women living alone.

Odette alternated between high spirits and low, felt dissatisfied once more, and despaired. Laurence knew a decision had to be made. Odette's interest in office work was sliding. She hadn't applied herself at the stenography school, and at any rate stenography without typing wouldn't get her a job. She had no idea of what a secretary was. Laurence's work interested her, but the thought of three years of studying left her cold. Three years was an eternity, time stopped, a useless digression that had nothing to do with her real plans. Laurence suggested a course in paediatric nursing that took eighteen months. The thought of wearing a white uniform, which implied a certain social standing, persuaded her.

A letter arrived from Broughton shortly after. Rosalie, bed-ridden again, wanted Odette to come back. The father wrote that he was worried, a letter that was neither remonstrative nor condemning.

This shook up their plans. Odette was conciliatory, for the letter appealed to her as an adult. Laurence would go with her to the Youville orphanage, and she could enroll for September. It was thus a sure thing that Odette would come back. The nurse would ask for her vacation in July and would join the family for her time off, so they could come back to Montréal together. The young woman knew the father would concede in the face of Laurence's persistence, and her fears dissipated. The elder sister knew that Odette's living in at the orphanage would weaken the father's resistance. They celebrated their decision at the restaurant.

Laurence took her savings out of the bank, bought the train ticket, added ten dollars for the father. You didn't show up empty-handed from the city, she said. Odette left with a light heart. Laurence was ambivalent about having her space to herself, and thought that fate's tricks brought good as well as bad. The room seemed empty, the bed too large, the food less tasty. Re-experiencing solitude she found trying. Responsibility didn't bother her. On the contrary, it was normal for the elder to look after the younger. The family accepted that Odette would live in Montréal, which was what counted. She really felt her sister had no chance of happiness back home. Now that she knew her, Odette seemed to her a young girl even bolder than herself, and she deserved a chance. Laurence, generous to a fault, idealized the members of her family. She had never spoken to Odette about running away, and the thought of it made her smile. It wasn't a big deal, but it was proof of her mettle.

The two youngest, a boy and a girl who were now teenagers, used good humour to compensate for their lack of comeliness. Vincent's ugliness tended to be forgotten, while Cécile's obliged her to put up with disparaging remarks. They had all convinced her to become a nun, the habit would hide her unattractive face. It seemed to Laurence that she had seen faces like that in the city, that a plain face might make things difficult for a woman, but it didn't mean she had to end up in a convent. Her ideas clashed with their ideas, which were ignorant to the point of stupidity. Cécile was spirited and her fine intelligence shone forth. In Laurence's opinion, it was dreadful that young girls like her swelled convent ranks. Cécile was different than her sisters who were nuns. She was neither in the clouds like Amanda nor terrified of her shadow like Aline. She loved life, bore no bitterness for the harsh words aimed at fitting her into a mould, at convincing her of her destiny.

She would go to the convent the following year, like her sisters, would become a teacher like them, would enter the same community. Laurence promised she would pay the requisite year of teaching studies.

Despite the hard times, Edouard had finished his house, and a car parked out front elicited an exclamation of surprise from his sister. With greying hair and a bit of a stomach, he cut a thicker figure. His perpetually worried-looking countenance had never appeared young. Laurence, compared to Edouard, was slender and supple and appeared ten years younger. But the important thing was that the brother was succeeding. She didn't care about appearances, as long as her own didn't spoil the family portrait. Edouard's mature air exuded a certain well-being, assuring the awaited child of a good future. The new pregnant sister-in-law served the meal. The couple behaved as if they had been married forever. Laurence took this as a sign they got along, each assuming their role in an enterprise well-seasoned by force of tradition.

Edouard's asking why she wasn't married got on her nerves. She was hurt by the inevitable allusion to her age and single state. As soon as she was alone with him, she determined to speak of the rape. The memory was so painful, the words so unexpectedly charged with the violence of the event, that she didn't know what to say. Her frank eyes opened wider, her pupils trembling. She spoke simply, blurting out that a man had taken her by force. No further narration was possible. Edouard scowled, and said nothing, had no reaction whatsoever. The empty seconds ticked by. Troubled, despairing in face of the surfacing memory, she tried to say more. Edouard, a contented man, saw Laurence in a new light. He didn't reproach her, he simply refused to hear. The young woman wept into the night. The next day Edouard made not the slightest allusion to their discussion, as if he had forgotten.

With Rosalie, the same distant tenderness infused their conversations. The daughter grew calm in the presence of her mother, who said she had been a real help to the family. But what was almost an expression of gratitude was spoiled by her mother's adding that their hardships had exhausted her. Never a thank you, never in the past, and not now. These words: thank you, the children had been taught to say, an upbringing based on formal and social politeness, a one-way moral construct. The children owed the parents their lives, a debt that could never be paid. For the moment, the daughter contented herself with the mother's words, with her insidious language, aimed at propelling her into ever greater generosity. Coming generations would overcome poverty. Her serenity was recovered by letting her mind flee towards the future.

She went over to Emilien's to see little Jérôme, who neither walked nor talked. Even in summer, the house exuded an odour of excrement and sour milk. The blonde sister-in-law with her goitered throat was looking after the newborn in the cradle, while Jérôme was all alone upstairs, confined to his crib. Jérôme, not yet three, suffered from endless ear aches. They thought he was deaf, for he made incomprehensible sounds. The child was lying in a soiled bed. When Laurence raised him up, he let his head roll backwards, refusing to straighten. The mother admitted that she never got him up, that he had passed the winter in bed with her until the new baby arrived. They saw no cause to worry about Jérôme's gentle passivity. Unlike the others, overactive and demanding, feeding him kept him happy. His mother kept him in his bed, didn't sit him up. They had no money to consult a doctor. The sister-in-law summed up the situation by saying he was always sick. He slept most of the time, didn't cry, had trouble moving. They carried him to the table to feed him.

Laurence found the medicine that she had left for Jérôme two years earlier, unopened. Their negligence roused her to indignation. Emilien, exhausted from haying, complained of his fatigue. The sister-in-law served him tea in the rocking chair, and sat down beside him. Two children came in barefoot, and in torn clothes. Apart from the baby, it was a portrait of poverty. But the peaceful group disarmed Laurence. The husband and the wife, with their symbiotic love, were bringing up their children in another world. Were it not for Jérôme, Laurence would have enjoyed the calm family scene, where no one raised their voices in violence.

Her brother and sister-in-law did not understand her alarm. The mother's sickliness had isolated her. She consented to keep Jérôme up if he got over his ear aches, an affirmation she made in good faith, and with no sense of having done wrong.

Jérôme needed constant care and observation in the opinion of Laurence, who set no stock in the diagnosis of mental deficiency made a year earlier. The idea of taking him back with her to the city seemed a solution. The child would get better.

The mother was against a long separation, and they agreed on six months. A little bag was packed, insufficient for the length of the stay. Laurence appealed to the other sisters-in-law for blankets and warm clothes. Jérôme moaned when she and Odette, loaded down with bags and suitcases, carried him off. Laurence's sense of humour set the tone: Odette, loaded down like a vagabond, had lost her citified look.

The new arrival took up a lot of space. Laurence told the landlady she would be paying her rent late, and informed her their nephew would be living with them. The woman was understanding and loaned them a stroller stored in the shed. They made him a bed out of a huge dresser drawer, which they put on the floor. The child moved so little. Jérôme seemed like an abandoned child, lost deep within himself. He required constant attention.

Odette entered Youville nursery just as Jérôme was starting to walk again. Other children his age were walking and talking. He was also much less active than they. Laurence made babysitting arrangements with the landlady. Jérôme slept in the afternoon. She kept him awake in the evening, after the meal and the walk in the stroller or on foot, speaking to him, playing with him, urging him to run, washing him and putting him to bed with her around eleven o'clock. She brought him a teddy bear that he took with open arms and round eyes. He wasn't deaf, but took a very long time to say a word. He seemed to have no reflexes. The child took a lot of energy to look after. The six months were over. She felt as if she had accomplished a mission. Laurence had become attached to Jérôme, to his little accomplishments, his sweet face, and gave him up reluctantly. The little boy didn't protest. His now obvious mental deficiency was very painful to her. She thought of the future that awaited him, and was engulfed by sadness.

13

One cold, white February day, feeling a little blue, she entered, for the first time, the bar of a downtown hotel. She delicately sipped a pastis, listening to Gershwin's "Rhapsody in Blue" being played on the Steinway piano. The stolen moments were pregnant with a salutary emptiness. She examined the luxurious decor. The clients, men for the most part, saw her precisely as she saw them. Laurence wanted to amuse herself for a change.

A man at the next table ordered a whiskey and asked her if she would like a drink. She accepted, adding, after her thank you, that she was taking a break. The man said it was not necessary to thank him, that he rarely saw women alone in such a place. He hesitated before speaking. If a woman likes to relax as much as a man does, why do they not, as a rule, frequent bars? She replied that the prejudices of their milieu prevented it. Their silences were filled with the music. She drank slowly, the glass raised and held in the tips of her fingers.

Laurence stood up and said goodbye. He looked her in the eye, introduced himself in three sentences, asked if could see her and shook her hand. She gave the telephone number of the landlady. In the yellow light of the tramway, the effect of the alcohol increased her desire to sleep.

Two weeks later, Louis Brodeur, chemist and bachelor, sat down opposite her at Ben's. They ate New-York-style cheesecake, and drank coffee. They spoke of her work as a nurse and of the satisfaction it gave her. He could tell immediately by the way she spoke that she came neither from Montréal nor from the bourgeoisie, as he did, and from which, he said, he had broken. She told him of her studies, begun in Québec and finished in Montréal. Her lively stories moved him. He himself had worked for the same company for twenty years, little affected by the Depression. He remembered that when he was a student he had argued with his sisters, trying to get them to further their studies as well.

He shared her opinion that society did not encourage girls to stay in school. She spoke of her sisters who had studied to enter the convent. They agreed that the habit of shutting the most educated women in convents was peculiar to French-speaking Canada. There was a long comfortable silence.

Louis Brodeur interested her more than he attracted her. She loved his way of speaking, a cut above the usual platitudes. With his bourgeois manners and his dark shirt, worn without a tie, he seemed non-conformist.

Single men of his age had their little habits, a well-organized lifestyle, sometimes to the point of compulsion. He was getting older, a man used to his comforts, for whom the hard times were a moral issue even if he lacked nothing himself. A feminine presence in his life was refreshing. He wished to know Laurence better and invited her to his place.

They used "vous" when addressing each other. He entertained her in what he called the reading room, a room where bookcases with glass doors covered the wall opposite the window. An enormous globe on a tripod of varnished wood stood in the corner near the sofa, a family piece dating from the beginning of the century. Between two wing-backed armchairs, a cabinet contained a small bar with spirits and glasses.

Laurence, who had never seen so many books, was intimidated. The presence of the globe, which represented the earth, comforted her, kept her from using the shrill tone of voice that she adopted when feeling insecure. The globe protected her against her worst self. The brown drapes and the frosted glass shades lent a masculine air to the surroundings.

He said he had travelled alone, and that contrary to what people think, one is very alone when travelling. He had been influenced by people he met, people who knew how to think critically. He learned that in different places you encounter different mentalities, and felt, with a little distance, that this was the greatest discovery made on his voyages. Now he could discern society's biases, and appreciated his solitude.

Louis Brodeur rediscovered, with her, his taste for good conversation. They had a discussion on religion that excited Laurence. The narrow-mindedness of their peers was due to the overwhelming influence of the clergy, who encouraged gullible thinking. The Church, with its wealth and power, ruled. As a result, politicians were not free to make independent decisions regarding civil matters.

They were still building fabulous churches in an epoch when people living in dire straits received no aid. The politicians legislated no social programs, but the clergy continued to demand money. He knew bourgeois families who had given considerable amounts for twenty years to keep their daughters in convents, and families who had promised to leave money to religious communities. The money they extracted from poor families for daughters to enter the convent required huge sacrifices. Louis Brodeur said the Catholic clergy had too much influence over people in high places.

He informed her that Maurice Duplessis, the new chief of the Conservative Party, was promising his allegiance to the clergy if elected. The corruption of the Taschereau administration had to be overcome, Duplessis declared. The promised reforms would change nothing. Laurence didn't read the papers. Like all women, she did not have the right to vote. The power of the Church seemed palpable; that of the government, distant. That the Church manipulated politicians seemed credible, for the Church's influence was everywhere.

They talked gravely, enthusiastically, and came away invigorated. Louis Brodeur felt younger and she, more mature. He didn't want her to misunderstand— he did not lack faith. He stopped, for he had promised himself to no longer talk about his personal beliefs. Laurence looked suspicious, he noticed, took him for a fake, for a man who was not saying what he really thought. He said he dissociated his belief in God from Catholic ordinances, and rushed to explain, then interrupted himself mid-sentence. She respected his right not to say more than he saw fit, satisfied he was no hypocrite. Kindled by the passion of conversation, she kissed him. He took her in his arms, a rush of warmth prolonging the embrace. It was after midnight when he accompanied her home in a taxi.

Their discussion brought up things that she imagined could not be put into words. The meeting of Louis Brodeur was a major event in her life. It legitimized her ideas. The man had travelled, frequented different milieux, which permitted him to challenge social norms. She admired him.

During her monthly weekend off, Odette cooked copious meals under the pretext that the orphanage cooking was terrible. Laurence gave her consent, happy to have her supper served. Her sister's visits were extravagant moments that she enjoyed all the more because shared.

It suited the adolescent to be in training, to wear a uniform, to have a roommate. It was emancipating to earn and spend four dollars a month. She was not studious— the exams were largely of a practical nature. The students, working either the day or the night shift, did everything that a licensed children's nurse would. They looked after the infants, and learned as they went along. Laurence thought it was abusive of the institution to use them as cheap labour. This remark disconcerted Odette. She took it to mean there was competition between them, that her sister was putting her down, critical of her training.

Later Odette recounted how, at seven months, they started toilet-training, so that by a year the children were continent, and praised the method they used to teach the children to wait. Their first word was "caca" and they wore panties during the day. The girls, when scolded by Odette, restrained themselves better than the boys. For the latter, patience was required, keeping the child on the pot. She added that a slap on the bottom was not considered out of line.

Odette was in favour of order. The nuns taught them that a strict schedule developed good health and formed the character. The time to go to bed and to get up was strictly observed and the punctual routine taught them discipline. As soon as a baby appeared in the nursery, the paediatric nurses applied themselves to curbing their whims.

They isolated the stubborn ones who refused to be trained. The nurses didn't talk to them, except to reprimand them for the purpose of nipping strong wills in the bud. The nuns taught that, in a one-year-old, good health and toilet-training went hand in hand. They learned how to walk and knew how to ask for the pot as well as for food.

Odette used the words order and disorder, the first things she learned at the institution. Laurence's playful side was brought out by the presence of a child. She could see no problem with flexible schedules and told herself she would not make a good mother. She encouraged Odette to pursue her studies because even if there was no work, they would be useful someday in raising her own children.

Contrary to the training of regular nurses, the education of paediatric nurses seemed distressingly inadequate, saddened her. She kept her thoughts to herself.

Laurence said nothing about Louis Brodeur. Their meetings concerned her and her alone. To have stimulating intellectual discussions requires the right interlocutor. She who coveted these exchanges kept her trysts a secret.

She expressed her desire for a more intimate relation after he had spoken of the unhealthy way men were obsessed with finding a virgin. The deliriousness about virgins poisoned relations between men and women. He told her bluntly he wouldn't sleep with her if she were a virgin. His matter-of-fact words sent shivers up her spine, but had the merit of being clear, and of leaving it up to her. She desired and had come to trust Louis Brodeur. They made love. Laurence, appalled at the degree to which her body responded, did not let on that she was coming. Louis Brodeur, happy, showed off his sexual expertise. He thanked her, using the formal "vous." His gratitude added to her pleasure and her confused feelings of guilt dissipated.

Laurence recalled Edouard's words: he wasn't likely material for a husband, but a bachelor who needed a woman. Louis Brodeur did not look down on prostitutes nor did he eulogize them. He recognized the role they played in society, while deploring the poverty that forced them to sell their bodies for money. Society ostracized prostitutes, when it should be protecting them. He had paid for sex, provided the women had no procurer. If he had the impression that a pimp was taking their money, he refused to have relations with them.

He thought it unnatural that their relationship, entered into by mutual consent, had to be discreet. Vicious gossip would poison their encounters. How often they met was decided by him. They saw each other once a week, and made love every second time. He was a man of little passion who enjoyed his well-ordered existence and believed that moderation was a virtue. Unimpressed with prevailing values, he created for himself a peaceful, quiet way of life. Now, his forgotten youth surfaced and he was more voluble. Laurence's tenacity brought out his sense of loyalty. She found his rational language and behaviour stimulating. She felt she was learning things with Louis Brodeur, organizing hitherto unsharable thoughts by questioning him, challenging his retrenched ideas, making him clearly articulate his ideas.

Religious beliefs became a subject of conversation despite his resistance. He said all religions had the same God, whether one was Catholic, Protestant, Jewish, Buddhist or Moslem. The way of referring to God varied, depending on your religion, itself a product of man's imagination. It was human opportunism that created the multiplicity of religions. Though he practised no religion, he was a believer.

He said the authority claimed by influential people such as politicians, journalists, in the name of the Church, sanctioned judgemental attitudes; they perceived evil everywhere, feared pleasure, condemned sex, censored books, thwarted economic initiative, and advocated alienating rules of conduct which were all counter-productive. Religion is always seeking out the guilty party, he said. Before Laurence's eyes rose the image of Léon Naud. It was as if Louis Brodeur knew him. She was silent. Never had she confronted the father before in such a direct light.

Standing, holding his glass, he warmed to the discussion, lost his habitual restraint, got worked up. She was thinking of Léon, without saying so. They were no longer debating, but rather acknowledging facts. The conversation grew less animated. He thought he had shocked her, which he did not wish to do. She said, simply, that she was overwhelmed. He was only saying what he thought, without trying to influence her. She said his ideas were important to her and he felt better. They had drunk more than usual. He accompanied her home. When she awoke the next morning, the paternal image had disappeared.

They were lovers with no thought of the future, without romantic attachment. He had an expressive face that made him attractive, but an ordinary run-of-the-mill body. Laurence felt she was acting like a grown-up woman. When she went to see him on rue Drummond, a strange melody played in the back of her head.

It was summer. She had saved the money promised to Cécile, which she sent to the father, and managed to buy a red-flowered dress. For the first time, she allowed herself to buy a dress.

Louis Brodeur had spoken of the question of mind expansion in the occult sciences, of the study of the aura, and telepathy. He himself possessed the power to get rid of burning sensations caused by fire, he said. People had powers they weren't aware of, unplumbed spiritual resources, but he said couldn't reveal how he had discovered his gift.

His library had numerous books dealing with the occult, both ancient and modern, that he read during his solitary evenings. In fact, for him, several of these were textbooks. He had applied himself rigorously to learning about these things, a process that took years and modified the course of his life. It wasn't a matter of a hobby nor was it an escape mechanism. He integrated what he learned into his life, slowly transforming himself.

He believed it possible to avoid traumatism through use of psychic powers. The mind had sway over the body. He worked at developing these parts of himself for his own well-being. Contrary to what people thought, evil and superstition were not taught in the occult sciences, which were not of the devil, though he recognized they could be used to negative ends. Their goal was to strengthen the spirit and the autonomy of the individual, which posed a serious problem for people in power, because the more ignorant people were, the easier they were to govern.

The psychic powers of which he spoke could be seen in people for whom goodness, generosity and love counted. Since he had begun his studies, he had become convinced one's spirit lived on after death.

They perused certain books together several times. Laurence believed in the possibility of communicating with another world, and told him of the apparition of madame Fournier one stormy night at Broughton. Madame Fournier had told her that she could no longer pass on Laurence's messages to Gaston, because she was dead. The next day her father informed her of the woman's death. Laurence displayed a predisposition for understanding the occult, Louis Brodeur was certain.

Louis Brodeur's library included books on religious history that he had read a long time before as part of his apprenticeship. He had concluded that religions indoctrinated people and could lead to fundamentalism. He detested political and religious fanaticism, which mutually reinforced each other. If a religion did not make a fanatic of one, its sermons and dogmas taught one to debase oneself, to be content with suffering here on earth. Religion's fundamental concern was evil. There was more to life than hell-fire and damnation, he insisted. His interest in the occult was a search for physical and spiritual well-being.

14

In January, 1937, having completed her paediatric nursing course, Odette moved back into the room on rue Sherbrooke. She was lethargic, which was incomprehensible to Laurence, who had thrown herself into work the day after her exams. There were no jobs at Saint-Luc Hospital. Her fatigue turned out to be jaundice, and Odette took to her bed, to be cared for by her sister, who protected herself against the illness by taking great care with hygiene and sleeping on a folding cot.

Odette got her colour back, stopped vomiting, was able to eat again, although she was forbidden certain foods. Laurence decided she would take the time she need to convalesce. Odette slept away the month of March. She stayed in bed, was protected, fed, attended to without having to worry about the future. When she was on her feet again, only one loose dress fit her. She had gained thirty pounds, which made her laugh.

By the end of spring, she gave up looking for work. Odette didn't let it get her down because Laurence said it was still the Depression. Underpaid hospital employees didn't dare leave their jobs. The hard times were not favourable to worker mobility.

The two sisters moved into the largest room in the house. Since Odette's return, the visits to Louis Brodeur's place were becoming less frequent. They distanced from each other without minding or saying goodbye. Laurence's interruption of his comfortable solitude was an unusual event, for it had been a long time since he had had a lasting relationship with a woman. She saw no reason to try and tighten a bond that was loosening. They avoided an outright break-up. For a long time after, when she referred to Louis Brodeur, he had become monsieur Brodeur, an older man, an expression full of meaning.

The summer was full of little happenings. Laurence and Odette met two women from the Gaspé, two friends who were roomers like themselves, two young girls bursting with life, seamstresses in a downtown textile factory. Marthe enjoyed her work, while Lili, not so sure, toyed with the idea of becoming a waitress. Lili was twenty years old, talked non-stop, full of plans, with a tremendous zest for life no matter what. Marthe had just broken with her fiancé. Odette became friends with them, and Laurence grew to like them, sharing their good humour, their excitement, and serving on occasion as confidante. They took Odette off to the factory. The desire to earn money helped her triumph over the difficult learning process. Odette lost her extra weight and a new, sculpted body emerged.

The Gaspé women suggested they go skiing in the Laurentians the coming winter. Laurence exhibited as much enthusiasm as Odette, but had no intention of going. At thirty-two, she thought she was too old, but told them they should take advantage of their youth. Obligations and constraints would come soon enough.

The two sisters shopped for Odette. Laurence didn't back down when confronted with the high cost of the equipment and ski outfit. She knew skiing was an expensive sport, something bourgeois people did. They shared the costs, part of which were charged. Feeling gay, impulsive, Odette let on she coveted a raccoon coat in the window of a furrier. Laurence liked it too and promised she would have it the next year.

Odette had the nicest outfit. The hood, trimmed with fur the same colour as her curly hair, reached low down the back. She would ski bareheaded, despite being told not to. On Sundays, the three friends took the Train du Nord to Saint-Sauveur, carrying their lunch bags. They learned to ski and had fun. The season ended too soon.

Odette became shy with young men. She could now distinguish the "serious prospect," as she put it, from the guy "out for a good time." Laurence took care of her sexual education, referring to things in a roundabout way, or telling stories of cases she heard about at the hospital. They were sure Odette was better informed than many young girls. On this score, her training as a children's nurse hadn't helped much. The nuns never spoke of illegitimacy, prudishly concealed relevant birth information. Laurence did not know how to hide her discomfort regarding sex and she communicated embarrassment, facts, and fear, all at once. Though Odette didn't let on, she savoured these sometimes dramatic anecdotes recounting excessive behaviour, and could see no connection with true love.

Laurence, for some time, had been mentioning the idea of music lessons. Amateur musicians played on Dominion Square. The four of them went to listen, and learned to sing the popular tunes of the day. They were delighted by the accordion's rendering of popular songs. It was a modern instrument that could be brought out the minute a party started. Get-togethers between family members, between friends, were enlivened by music. The indelible memory of evenings of dancing accompanied by the violin and the harmonica was a crucial one for Laurence. Now she could hear music on the radio. They played French popular songs, and she savoured the words and the rhythms. Odette could carry a tune, had a good ear for music, and Laurence told her so.

Odette enrolled in music lessons. The sisters acquired a piano accordion, a quality instrument worthy of a professional. The young girl grew more keen as she learned how to read the notes, play a popular song, quit her lessons, practised on her own, learned songs by ear that she played for the group. They sang along and enjoyed themselves. They hummed popular tunes, encouraging Odette to get the sheet music for this one and that one. Traditional songs were added to her limited repertory.

Through her sister, Laurence was living her old dream of introducing music into a daily life full of obligations. She felt sorry for Odette, working at the factory, though she didn't let on. Apart from the demanding cadence of production, she had to put up with surveillance and inspections to which the young girl sometimes overreacted, threatening to quit the next time she was harassed. With the help of her friends, she kept herself in check, having understood she would get the same constraining treatment elsewhere.

Marthe told of her break-up. They had gone through with the engagement even though the young man had lost his job. The planned celebration took place, for the dress and ring were already purchased. Her fiancé became drunk, drank on though his friends tried to reason with him. He lost control of himself to the point that she no longer recognized him. He drank again, discouraged and jealous of her job as a seamstress. He was so different that she, seeing he had changed, decided to postpone the marriage. He pretended not to hear, kept trotting out the mantra: born for a crust of bread, saw himself as a victim of fate, defeated in advance. He refused to put off the marriage for a year, saying instead they should call it quits for good, and humiliating her with insults and swear words in the process.

Marthe's brown eyes filled with tears. The friends empathized with the sad story, with the young girl who was trying to forget. Marthe took the engagement dress, which she would not wear, out of the cupboard, and the ring, which was kept in its case. Both emerald green, their colour wakened a dormant memory for Laurence, a troubled reminiscence. She said nothing, tormented by a vision of the forest-green sofa at madame Ramsay's.

She slept badly, stirred by these sad tales of love. Laurence, who knew how to ward off fear, was overwhelmed by feelings of sombre foreboding, imagined the different events were somehow related, and concluded that green brought bad luck. A silly superstition occasioned by coincidence, or so it seemed.

Later, during an outing of all four, Laurence spoke in earnest about the colour green, and told how her love for Gaston was opposed by madame Ramsay. She declared that the colour green was mesmerizing and produced negative vibrations. Odette thus learned of the man Gaston, an old story that failed to move her. It didn't fit with the idea she had of Laurence, a self-willed woman.

Laurence was convincing. Marthe sold her ring and dress.

Lucien Desrosiers observed Odette for a long time before approaching her. Odette looked the young man over, torn between carrying her head high or bowing it in shyness. He got over his fear of rejection, behaved like a man, and asked her name. Lucien did not flirt, he was too awkward for that. Each day that he delivered Coca-Cola on rue Ontario, he hung around, certain that if she passed, she would say hello. She made the same wager. Odette, shy in the company of men, met one who was the same around a woman— if she was pretty.

The room was large enough to curtain off a space the sisters called their boudoir. The bed, the icebox, and the gas burner were concealed behind screens, while, near the table, a loveseat and an armchair were arranged in guise of a living room. The day Lucien came to visit, Laurence bought a floor-lamp with a parchment shade.

Odette refused to admit their tête-à-têtes were not amusing. The new experience, the presence of a man, the vague sense of having to project unmitigated good humour to get the relationship on the right footing, was a strain. It was the idea, rather than the fact of keeping company with a particular young man, that pleased her. On thinking about it, what she liked was that they saw each other often.

Lucien, neither ugly nor handsome, complained he was tired and shortwinded. A delivery-truck driver's job was exhausting, he said. Laurence had welcomed him into the household with sincere cordiality. By the time he mentioned his health problems to her, she had already noted the symptoms. She warned Odette that it was surely inherited, something genetic from which he would suffer all his life. Such blunt words, such frankness, went unheeded by Odette. She presumed her sister didn't like him, which convinced her that she was becoming attached, that it was time to fall in love.

What with Odette's little attentions and Laurence's discretion, Lucien soon felt at home. He started showing up in his delivery uniform, a lack of savoir-vivre the elder sister found off-putting. It indicated he was not well brought up. She compared country ways to city ways and found that in the city boys did things country boys wouldn't dream of doing. It wasn't her boyfriend, so she kept her thoughts to herself. If Odette didn't mind sloppiness, there was nothing Laurence could do about it.

She dealt with it in her own way, by encouraging her sister to buy the coveted raccoon coat. The thick shiny fur with a narrow collar and well-padded shoulders set off the way she carried her head. The coat required the hat of matching fur, to make her look taller. The outfit changed Odette: she looked more womanly, a veritable city woman, or an actress, said Laurence, with unstinting enthusiasm. Odette was transformed. The sisters were in debt, which didn't in the least spoil their pleasure.

With the girls from the Gaspé, they celebrated Odette's new coat. She tried it on for Lucien, who reacted with a vehement outburst: it looks like a smelly animal. Laurence's comeback was as heated as Lucien's comment had been impetuous. She reprimanded him for his lack of taste and sophistication. Lucien didn't apologize, but he understood that he had to wear his street clothes if he took Odette to the cinema or to dinner.

The expression "sowing wild oats" meant that young men had the right to a good time before getting married, within the parameters of the free time and economic resources available to them. The six-day work week limited them a little. Laurence spoke of the importance of taking advantage of one's youth, a nuance that distinguished between men and women. If a girl, it was best to remain a virgin. In a group situation, the word never came up except indirectly, in reference to pregnant young girls they heard about at the hospital or the factory.

Odette was taking advantage of her youth, in keeping with the adage. She skied, played the accordion, had her friends. Her restlessness vanished. She was never bored, but busy from morning 'til evening, happily going from one diversion to another. For several months, there were no untoward incidents at work. Her pastimes were having a beneficial effect.

Odette was discovering she was a woman of action. Stimulated by her social life, full of energy, she was gaining confidence in herself.

Laurence talked to the young girls about her desire to travel. As usual, she made it up as she went along, until desire became necessity. Though limited, financially speaking, they agreed it would be nice to travel outside the province. New York was too far and frightening. They didn't know any English. The thought of a city bigger than Montréal meant the threat of that much more violence. They needed a destination with meaning, a reason for visiting a place. They had all heard of the Dionne quintuplets, whose family put them on public display. It was a phenomenon well worth seeing. They reached a consensus immediately. The would go to Calendar, Ontario, for their vacation.

The trip happened. They rented the services of a chauffeur. Odette brought along the accordion and the sheet music. They stayed at a hotel, saw the quintuplets, argued about how much they looked alike and how much they differed. The fine weather made it into a real holiday. They came home contented and kept the snapshots taken by a travelling photographer.

The newspapers reported incidents in Europe. Rumours were circulating to the effect of a coming European war. They discussed the situation in conventional terms. What the politicians wanted would win out in the end over what people wanted. If war happened, it was the people who would pay for it. As far as that was concerned, Daladier, Chamberlain and Hitler were one as guilty as the other.

The Depression was over. Working conditions were improving, thanks to the unions. Odette learned that the work week ended at noon on Saturday in other factories, quit on the spot, and waited a month before getting rehired. Lili became a waitress in a restaurant. Marthe met René, a nice young man of a good height who won compliments from Laurence. She compared René to Lucien and ruminated to herself. She thought of provoking a break-up between Odette and Lucien, but worried about the consequences.

Laurence put aside a week's salary to outfit Odette from head to toe, and promised her the best. One Friday in May they scoured the stores. The young girl displayed an ostentatious gaiety, an unbridled feverishness. They strolled along Sainte-Catherine, went into several stores, picked out a dress, a slip, panties, stockings, shoes. Laurence insisted on quality. She had promised and she did as she had said. It was nearly closing time. Odette's frenzied volubility hadn't let up, and Laurence took it for an excess of good humour. The last purchase was a corset. Laurence had to admit that the best corset was too expensive. The saleswoman showed them another, less expensive, and Odette pouted. She tried it on and grumbled. Laurence added up the bills to show her they had spent all the money, but Odette muttered and sulked at the cash register. She yelled at Laurence as they stepped into the street, threw the shopping bags and the dress box on the ground, raged. Her body trembled, her eyes bulged and she threw a tantrum, denigrating her sister for lying about quality. Laurence tried to reason with her, saying she had spent her last dollar, had no more, promised she would have chosen the first had she had the money. Odette would not calm down. On the contrary, Laurence's attempts to reason with her increased her foot-stamping and she yelled at her sister again out on the sidewalk, in front of passersby.

She was used to her sister's sudden mood changes, but this frenzied behaviour was unacceptable. Beside herself, the elder withdrew, not understanding the degree of violence of this outburst. She was giving things to her sister that she had never had herself, out of the belief that one granted special treatment to the youngest, without expecting gratitude. The happiness or some expression of satisfaction on the part of the other sufficed. She thought of throwing Odette out, an idea so odious that she did not linger on it.

Odette kept quiet about the incident she had provoked and took refuge in silence. For the first time in her life she felt that her sister was bossing her, imposing her will to keep her in a submissive state. Though she had wanted the ski equipment and the accordion, the decision to acquire them was out of her control. She enjoyed her life as a young woman, when her sister wasn't around. Odette was twenty-one, the age of consent and she was gnawing at the bit, ready to take off. The thought of leaving Laurence made her so anxious she put it off. The young girl soon forgot the incident. Once more, there were so many things to do that peace returned.

The idea of participating in the amateur evenings at Dominion Square came from Lili and Marthe. If Odette played the accordion for the group, why wouldn't she play it in public? The suggestion amused them. One July evening, when the public was gathering around the amateur musicians, Odette got a case of nerves and fear despite the support of her friends and sister. The playing distracted her from reality, the audience disappeared from her line of vision, and she did fine. A heavy weariness followed the experience and she didn't do it again.

Laurence planned to rent a three-room apartment on rue Chambord, but Odette was reticent because Lucien was likely going talk to her about getting married. The elder said that Odette would be able to take any furniture she acquired when she left, and that it was time for Laurence to have a place of her own. They bought kitchen and bedroom furniture. Their loveseat and armchair would be fine for the living room. The two sisters moved at the beginning of October.

Odette and Lucien broke up occasionally, but not for long. Sometimes she told him to leave, then changed her mind, as if he were the only available man. Smitten, he submitted to being dismissed, begged to be allowed back. One evening Lucien was the recipient of a volley of angry words that he didn't understand, and he grew silent, mulish. She was humiliated that he was taking his time to commit himself, that he didn't take their getting married seriously enough. Regarding marriage, it was up to the man to take the initiative. She was so angry she couldn't say another word. He left, ashamed. His sadness bothered Laurence, who thought that Lucien was patient and tolerant of Odette's moodiness. Lucien did as her sister wished, gave in willingly to her demands.

Lucien had never spoken of the future. Odette bolstered her courage and stood waiting on rue Ontario at the time he delivered there. They reconciled. She decided to speak to him about making a commitment. He said he would marry her, that was his intention. Odette appeared to have regained her serenity. She felt belittled waiting, for no date had been fixed. She began to nurse a mute indifference. For a moment she saw him as a stranger with whom she was keeping company, a man neither ugly nor handsome, weighed down by a hard job, incapable of changing. She felt greatly cheated.

III
ODETTE AND THE GAMBLER

15

Winter's sullenness, evenings without music, without Lili and Marthe, with discontented Odette stuck in her rut, in a word, the lack of action, weighed on Laurence. You needn't let a situation get the best of you when you can do something about it. Laurence wanted to relax more in her free time. For years, her priority had been her responsibility towards Odette. She suggested they spend a summer in the country. City people, like city flowers, restricted to pots or minuscule and sickly courtyard gardens, couldn't breathe properly. She dreamed of a lake, a forest and a wooden cottage battered by wind, rain and storm. They would invite Marthe and Lili, and fix up a room for Lucien if he agreed to visit. Laurence said it explicitly: they would see new faces. It was easier to meet people in the summertime. Her project snapped Odette out of her passivity.

In April, the sisters visited a chalet at Duquette Beach on lac des Deux-Montagnes, which they travelled to by train. They rented for three months, enthusiastic about the idea of swimming, of fine blond sand and picnic tables. They would leave the apartment on rue Chambord at the beginning of June.

Lucien sulked and Odette grew impatient. He promised to help move the furniture and didn't turn up. They left their three rooms exhausted from loading the truck. They laughed nervously, the effort sharpening their enthusiasm. The day after moving in, the first train took them from the lake to downtown Montréal. An early evening train took them back. The signs around the little station, on the general store, the restaurant, the bakery, all bore the name Vidal. Laurence burst out laughing, Vidal being a name she had never seen. Since everyone was called Vidal, it must be common. She pronounced it with different accents and decided it sounded least ridiculous with a European French accent.

They subscribed to the popular notion that lake water is not clean enough to bathe in before June 20. The late thaw in the region introduced bacteria that sun and underwater currents eliminated.

The first swim made them hungry. Laurence put four pork chops and a piece of butter in the pan, but the flame of the gas burner ignited the paper meat wrapping, then the larded chops, running along the wall and spreading to the light curtains. They had to pump water, the pail being only partly full. The pump was hard to pump, and the sink was located at the end of the room—

they needed to call for help. They grabbed their handbags, the accordion, and the ski outfit. One of them ran towards the neighbours', the other to the village to alert the fire department. Some neighbours organized a chain with pails, the flames now blanketing the walls as high as the roof. The firemen appeared after the wooden chalet was already burning out of control.

People came to stare. Men, women and children came, young people from the vicinity, who had followed the water truck. A fire was a spectacle not to be missed. Rumour circulated that the gas tank had exploded.

Their clothes and furniture were gone, destroyed by the flames. Odette was trembling despite the intense heat. Laurence kept herself under control, her eyes bulging, watching the fire consume their belongings, reducing them to ashes.

The fire stripped them bare. Laurence perceived them as naked. Standing, her arms crossed over her blouse, it seemed to her that fate wanted to rob her of the clothes on her back, to leave her naked, isolated, in the midst of some fifty neighbours and observers. The catastrophe was like a war, a bomb aimed at a single house, the wooden chalet. She was mentally taking stock: Odette and she were losing all they possessed. Three hours before they had owned a bed, a sofa, a table, chairs, essentially all the recently acquired furniture, plus smaller household items. This sudden stroke of bad luck frightened her, but she got hold of herself. She still had a healthy body and mind. She refused pity and distinguished between sincere offers of help and superficial promises.

Both of them had strained faces, looked older. Odette cried, tossing back her tussled curly head. She freely displayed her grief amid the crowd, who in turn expressed their compassion. A young man, moved by the sight of the flames that the firemen were unable to squelch, and touched by the story of two women who had lost everything, came towards them. Two women had rented a summer cottage, which was unusual. He misunderstood Laurence's apparent cool reserve, but was moved by Odette's distress. The wavy chestnut hair made her suffering poignant. She was so young that the bad luck seemed even more unjust. He walked over with the air of someone wanting to help and asked how the fire started. She grew calmer. Despite a thick veil of confusion, a feeling of being lost among strangers, she said the flame had caught the cutlets in the pan and that the fire had spread from the wall to the curtain. It seemed true and yet also false. The shock made it everything unreal. And there before her was a well-dressed young man, in a fine shirt and impeccable trousers, black hair fashionably cut, who introduced himself: Paul Vidal.

Some neighbours took them in. Laurence decided they would go to work the following day, withdraw their remaining money from the bank, rent a room near Phillips Square, and return two days later. Odette agreed.

Laurence took control of the situation, carried out the plan. She fell into a deep sleep after the long day's work, the disruptions and displacements. Back at Duquette Beach, they borrowed boots and sifted through the calcinated remains of the cottage. There was nothing to save, a total loss. They were choked with grief and rage. Kind people had brought sheets, bed covers, and towels to the neighbours for them. A woman had ribboned two nightdresses. Real help was given anonymously. There were visitors who felt sorry for them, and others who wore them out, accusing them of being irresponsible, siding with the landlord. Laurence got the impression people were blathering about them.

Paul Vidal was trying to attract Odette's attention by his loquaciousness. The young woman looked up at him, not grasping what was going on. People with nothing to do, usually men, tended to run off at the mouth. While a neighbour was offering to accompany them back to town, Paul smiled at Odette, his gaze clear, serene. The well-dressed young man, tending to chubbiness, was a cut above the others, seemed to come from a good family, was well-spoken. He offered the neighbour and Laurence a lift. Paul did not misunderstand the nature of the relationship between the two sisters, addressed his offer to the elder. Laurence, despite her unhappiness, exercised her usual common sense. She pulled herself together, swallowed her tears, and accepted the help offered. Anyway, a handsome young man was worth more than a wrinkled face.

For weeks they talked about nothing but the fateful event. The lack of clothing obliged them to be painfully thrifty. The room on rue Mayor was inadequately equipped, so they couldn't cook properly. They managed the necessities, but their extreme poverty left a bitter taste. They had wanted a nice easygoing summer and got serious hardship instead. Laurence understood how much she influenced her sister when the latter repeated, word for word, things she'd said the night before. Odette was reproducing her gestures, her way of talking about things. This mirror-image of herself took the elder by surprise.

From then on, she refused to mention the fire, to go on about deprivations, about being tossed about on the winds of fate. She had said: a fire is like an accident; in one second your life can go from comfort to destitution. She never spoke of the pretty red dress, preferring instead to point out their presence of mind in rescuing the fur coat, the ski things and the accordion. Odette was getting over her sadness.

The presence of Paul Vidal kept them going. He sensed Laurence was secretly pleased that he found Odette attractive. When they sat at a café table, he was the centre of attention. Jovial, freshly clothed and perfumed, he charmed both sisters. The sparsely furnished room didn't seem to bother him. He liked to feel singled out, to be the object of their attentions. When the opportunity arose, Laurence got him to talk about himself, his family, about the village of Saint-Eustache. They knew far more about his background than he about theirs. He was easy to please. All you had to do was make him the topic of conversation. More than anything, Paul loved to talk. He provoked discussions and sought Laurence's opinion. He'd never met a woman who could hold up her end of a discussion, could contradict him, could argue with him.

He gazed longingly at Odette, while speaking volubly with Laurence about the land around lac des Deux-Montagnes, currently being divided into lots, about new construction, about road works. He knew the land speculators, could recount stories about sales, disagreements, fools' bargains and other manoeuvres that really made him chuckle. Paul got caught up in silly anecdotes. Sensible Laurence brought him back to the subject at hand. Property transactions were child's play, and though he did not speak in the first person, Laurence could see this was where his interest lay. The sisters had left lac des Deux-Montagnes in painful circumstances, but they'd grown attached to a region with so much to offer, and the idea one could become comfortably well-off by building houses or cottages awoke a new ambition in Laurence. To listen to Paul, you'd think people bought and sold property on whims. Laurence questioned him about the rudiments of speculation, and weeded facts from fancy.

Odette followed the conversation, without contributing. The idea of growing rich through speculation put her in a happy state of mind, titillated her. To become comfortably well-off, all you had to do was want it. She lapsed into a vague daydream. It no longer mattered if she had nothing to say. Paul promised to return.

Lucien was a thing of the past. Laurence had hoped that a summer by the lake would help Odette get over a love match that was wasn't working. The fire was the turning point. As Lucien faded into the background, Odette rebounded into the present.

Paul, in order to endear himself to the sisters, addressed Laurence during discussions. She understood, from questioning him, from the way the conversation bounced back and forth between them, that he was seeking her acceptance. Odette was no longer enjoying this, and, after several evenings over coffee, threatened to move out if Laurence didn't leave her alone with Paul.

She accused her sister of being an old maid who was trying to keep her from having a boyfriend, pretending one thing and doing another. Odette presumed she would hit a vulnerable spot by calling her an "old maid." The malicious expression was uttered with the intent to hurt. Odette knew exactly what she was doing when she used it. When she blew up, she lost all sense of proportion.

She swore she would leave. She felt at home in Montréal. She could very well organize her life on her own, and would not tolerate being bossed around by Laurence another minute. Her outburst was an expression of a remote desire for independence. She blamed her sister for making plans and decisions without asking her, said she was suffocating, then stopped, hesitant, her eyes glowing defiantly. The young woman was learning how to be like those who use intuition, coolly and shrewdly, to guess what makes others tick.

Laurence conjured up the worst possible dangers lurking in the big city, and refused to let go of Odette, to put her out. She was committed, had often reiterated her promise to herself to watch over her. The father's vindictive words, whose sting had diminished over time, transmuting into a delegation of authority, now resurfaced accompanied by Amanda's damning prophecies. Odette's impetuousness brought to her mind the July day when she found her sitting on her front stairs. Other reminiscences surfaced. For naïve people, Montréal was full of pitfalls. The rape, which she had never mentioned to Odette, came back to her. She felt harried.

She reassured Odette that she could have Paul over by herself. Odette calmed down, her bitterness reduced to an impertinent pout. The elder swallowed her sadness without forgetting the scene. Still smarting, she rearranged the room to facilitate a possible courtship. The tense atmosphere didn't leave her much choice. The best way to deal with a problem was to change your approach, even just a little.

During the week, Laurence got a change of shift in obstetrics, so that she now worked Friday and Saturday evenings. The problem took care of itself.

Paul was as happy with Odette as he had been with both sisters. He had planned nothing in advance, quite simply enjoyed the nice feeling that comes from being desired, content with the idea of a warm evening. He tried to have a discussion with her about the sale of the vast terrain belonging to his grandfather, and she listened with good will, but without much interest. Surreptitiously he moved closer, charmed by the pretty girl. He hadn't appeared hasty, due largely to a lack of self-confidence, which he overcame by chattiness. Odette wanted them to be closer but felt strongly a young girl did not take the initiative. She was no longer a hot-headed adolescent who accepted kisses from men her sister brought home.

Paul was now her boyfriend. Afraid he wasn't being doting enough, he kept his eyes glued on her constantly. It was a bit much for Odette, who got the impression they were acting out the roles of lover and beloved. What she did want finally happened— he took her and held her, unresisting, against him. The warmth of their bodies made him so happy, he couldn't speak. She felt sexy with Paul. He awakened her to the pleasures of the senses, a mutual physical attraction, such as she had never known. Odette was happy, love was on its way.

Odette, who did piece-work, improved her rhythm of production, and with it the pay. Sitting at her sewing machine, she no longer wondered if she was doing the right thing. The job suited her. As she got better, the hard work started paying more than a school teacher would earn. She and Laurence got into the habit of going to a neighbourhood restaurant that served gigantic proportions. They ordered one dish and an extra plate and shared the same cheap meal. Her happiness was a relief to Laurence. Odette was more conversational and volunteered the information that she trusted Laurence's opinion. They learned that Cécile was entering the convent, the same community where Amanda and Aline had taken their vows. The father's letter was full of pride.

Paul brought candy and chocolates that he ate alone. He had grown up at his grandparents, he said, moving between Montréal and the property on the shore of lac des Deux-Montagnes. He said reticently that his parents lived in the city, and he spent time with them when he could.

Odette understood that he had grown up as an only child, a ward of his paternal grandparents. The mother had abandoned her eldest son after three pregnancies, one right after the other. The young child was to stay with his grandmother during the mother's confinement, but he stayed longer than anticipated. They got attached to him so that, although the matter of his returning was raised several times, nobody did anything about it. They just looked after him, brought him up, without any legal adoption, and Paul still lived with them. He held neither his mother nor father responsible for the abandonment. His father, in his opinion, owed him no explanation. Men were useless with children, he said. Paul had had the advantage of a very comfortable life and a lenient upbringing, had not experienced the constraints usually imposed on the eldest. They all knew stories of abandoned children, involving the sad death of a mother, successive adoptions, and most often, poverty. His mother was living and he lacked nothing. He did not hold anything against her, felt affectionate towards her, and wished, without saying so, that their mutual guilt feelings would subside.

There was nothing dramatic about Paul's situation, which, on the contrary, was enviably free, with money to spend and no obligation to earn it. He was part of a privileged group that didn't have to worry about material things.

In a hundred different ways he lavished tenderness on her. The outbursts of emotion were half-hidden in a contagious easy-going manner. He sat close to her. He loved the odour, the colour, the texture of her skin, kissed her. Good-looking sensitive Paul wished to make himself attractive, and he did. Odette looked after her appearance, dressed in simple city clothes. Their caresses and kisses fulfilled their greatest expectations. Their love play made her euphoric. She slept like a baby and, on waking, hummed a little tune, happy after the sensual hours spent with him.

When Paul petted Odette, he was at a loss for words. He didn't know how to speak his pleasure, except by long sighs, little cries, low laughs, gurgles of satisfaction. A false modesty made him avoid tender words. His vocabulary did not comprise sweet nothings, nor even the appreciative compliments a man normally pays to a woman. He had, on occasion, the impression there was a taboo keeping down a vague impulse to say something about her shimmering curls, about how he was attracted to her from the first minute. Love rendered him speechless. Loquacious in any other context, he lost his tongue when it was a question of tenderness, and courted her in silence.

He made no effort to express the many terms of endearment that trotted through his mind. A misguided sense of propriety numbed him into thinking that love needed no words, that words would spoil it. Kisses, a concrete proof of affection, sufficed. Odette appreciated Paul, who was never abrupt with her, for his gentleness. He visited her in the rented room where the two sisters had fixed up what they called their boudoir, hiding the bed with a Chinese screen.

Laurence said how much she liked the gentle young man, who looked after his appearance and spoke well. He seemed to her like a man with whom a woman could get along— if she shared his opinions. They agreed he was a good catch and they were delighted.

The evening he proposed marriage, Odette would have understood better what was going on if she had been more attentive. He wanted to know if she were over past loves, if her heart had been previously broken, if there were still someone.

Odette was laconic, given that her relationship with Lucien was rapidly fading from memory. To save appearances, to show she was in demand, she let on she had already been courted.

Then he admitted that he had a past attachment he wanted to forget. He had met her during a village party which had degenerated into a brawl. Two men who had been mixing their beer with spirits ended up trying to settle their differences with their fists. Other men took sides, stepped into the fray with one or the other of the protagonists. Seven or eight of them were punching each other in the middle of the room, hitting each other with their fists. People shouted from the sidelines. The hullabaloo increased. Paul looked from left to right, undecided about whether to get involved in the fight, which had started with a game of mutual provocation.

In a flash, a smart-ass picked up a chair, knocking over one fellow after another until there were four wrestling it out on the ground. Someone whistled, other men jumped in, the fight intensifying until several women wanted to call the cops. People put off calling them out of fear of reprisal. The strongest guy laid into the smallest, threw a chair at his face, the blood spurting forth as the chair bounced off the wall in a corner where a young blonde girl was standing.

At the sight of the blood, the rampage stopped and Paul, who was leaning against the wall, went over to Simone, who was shaking. Most people were still hanging around out of a morbid desire to see what would happen.

He accompanied her home, himself worked up by the event. Paul told her family about the brawl. Simone's father gave the young man a vote of confidence for his gallantry. His family's good name was already known to him and the circumstances of this first meeting proved he was a gentleman. He was made entirely welcome. For a long time Paul had had his eye on Simone, going to the village on the chance he would run into her. That night Simone consented to the much desired rendezvous, and he was so happy he couldn't get to sleep before dawn.

He visited her, brought chocolates and flowers to her mother, was invited to the midday meal one Sunday. He strolled about the village with the young girl in the afternoon, and people noticed. He introduced her to his grandparents. His grandmother said that thanks to Simone, Paul was behaving like an adult. It was commonly said that going out with someone was a sign of growing up. A month later, Paul was spending Thursday and Saturday evenings at Simone's. The young girl agreed with everything he said, which made Paul inordinately happy. Despite being one of the most beautiful girls in the village, Simone, like her family, was of the opinion that to be happy you had to follow tradition. Her desire to do as others expected expressed a taste for easy village life, free of anxiety. In conforming, she was doing as she wished.

Paul took her for his betrothed. He was so happy that springtime turned into a celebration. He talked endlessly with people, always on the lookout for new companions to sport with, to challenge, to make bets with, sometimes even playing cards all night long. Once, twice, three times, he showed up late or didn't come to see her at all because he was having a run of luck. He was impassioned, enthralled by risk, even by the risk of losing Simone. He would triumph on every front.

Simone broke down and cried. He promised to take her to the beach, to dinner, kept his word, introduced her to his friends and amused her with his quick wit and sense of repartee. He backslid with the onset of summer, neglected to show up for a date, took pleasure in consoling her, in making her relent. The parents were not so ready to forgive his flightiness and their daughter's tears were the omen of a painful future. One evening when he went over, the father opened the door to him. Paul tried to mollify them by being funny, but after three sentences the father's irritation put an end to his naïve attempts. In the future, the door would be closed to him. It was unbearable to see his daughter crying all the time.

Paul didn't sleep that night. He felt in love, desperate, acknowledged he had done wrong. All Simone wanted was for him to be reliable, nothing more. In fact, on the contrary, she showered him with almost motherly attentions. He was looking forward to a happy life with a woman who did not contradict him and who took life as it was. He wanted to improve, thought about how he could change his life, and decided to take a course in radio technology. If he had a job like other people, he wouldn't need to be entertained, to make a career of having a good time. He dreamed of doing things differently, and felt that idleness and love were incompatible. He informed his grandparents of his plans, enrolled in Montréal, and brought back proof he had been admitted to the course.

Document in hand, he showed up at Simone's, and excused himself on the grounds he had had nothing to do, referring in the third person to the young man he no longer was. Now he was a new man, he said. They were impressed by his good will. After all, his only fault was a lack of seriousness. Paul turned over a new page. The ball was in Simone's court. The distance between Montréal and Saint-Eustache meant they would see each other less regularly, and time would take care of things. The lovers made a commitment.

In the morning, when he had to drag himself out of bed, or during the day, when the radio-technology course bored him, Paul dreamed of Simone, of her agreeable curves, of her thick curly hair. His grandmother fell ill. At the age of seventy-five, she said goodbye to the world in the same sweet way that she had worked to her very last days without anyone's noticing she was growing weak. Paul was greatly aggrieved. He loved her, thought her eternal, accustomed for so long to her being old. He felt like an orphan, unable to comfort his grandfather, who took refuge in silence. The emotions and grieving also left Paul at a loss for words. The wake lasted four days, during which time more than two hundred persons paid their respects. Simone stayed by his side, and her face wore a motherly expression. He was so well looked after that he began to think of the possibilities of having children with her. The young girl and her family showered kindnesses on Paul, and he lapped up the pathos, the sentimentalism.

When his radio-technology course ended, he left the apartment in Montréal and moved back to the large house by the lake. Mornings, between wake and sleep, he still heard the footsteps of his grandmother. His grandfather agreed that he needed a break after such a trying year.

Paul took refuge as much as possible at Simone's place, idealized family life, the sense of continuity and security it offered. One June evening, he spoke of marriage to the young girl's parents. It was a spontaneous gesture, stopping short of asking for Simone's hand, and without having asked her opinion. He believed he was being respectful of traditions and customs, yet his way of proceeding trivialized them. Paul went out with the young girl, and neither of the two raised the subject just discussed in the kitchen. He had dared to propose, and she would act according to her father's wishes. Simone comforted herself with the idea that there wasn't the least obstacle, and the good life would come. She would receive her share of blessings, would need for nothing, and what more could she want?

Paul was not expected to help out at home, and didn't want to either. The place was not as comfortable as before, and he had to get used to a certain disorder. But as far his person was concerned, he was better groomed than ever, over-meticulous in his desire to look good. In the village, that summer, he gained the reputation of an affluent city boy. He was flattered by the glances of young girls. His gambling companions thought he had inherited money and he did nothing to disabuse them. He was seen on the main street, the best-dressed of the group, the centre of attention, which pleased him. He hung out with a crowd seeking new thrills. They came up with the idea of playing cards all night long, doubling the bet for each new game.

Paul was one of the group who met Thursday in an empty cottage. Luck was on his side. At dawn, a clever loser came up with a new rule: the winner had to come to the next party, and had to keep betting until he'd lost everything he'd won. That way the money would keep circulating, with no big personal losses. Some bet more than they had and were getting in debt.

They granted themselves a day of rest and said they would meet again Saturday. Paul, instead of protesting, dreamed up some excuse for Simone, maybe an errand in Montréal, which he filed away in the back of his mind.

On Saturday, by the middle of the night, Paul had doubled his winnings.

The indebted player withdrew. The others said bad luck never lasted and decided to adjourn the game until the following Saturday. They had all lost more than a week's salary.

Paul saw Simone in the middle of the week, lied that he had met someone who, he said, promised him work in his field. His voice rose sharply, over-excited, and the young girl believed him. Paul no longer dared to go out. He hid at home.

He entered the clandestine cottage, dazed from lying to Simone, and the possible consequences thereof. The other players wanted to get their own back, and their nonchalance gave way to vindictiveness. Paul, already distracted, found it hard to concentrate when confronted with the others' bitterness, and made mistakes. By morning he'd lost more than half of what he'd won earlier, still not enough for the others.

They were eager for another game the following Saturday, but Paul had the presence of mind to demand it be on Friday. One of the men said ironically they were competing with a woman. They made fun of the idea of having a woman. The following Friday, Paul had the feeling the other players were in league against him, and the thought of being hated gave him the creeps. He considered giving back the money. The game started. Paul lost more than he had won, and wrote an I.O.U. In the middle of the silent night, the players forgot to be careful. Their gestures became automatic. The loser realized he was being cheated by means of the shuffler keeping an ace in his sleeve and passing it to one of the accomplices. Paul confronted the cheater, who responded mockingly. The atmosphere changed from playful to suspicious. Angrily, Paul, in turn, sought revenge. They proposed a game the following evening. It was agreed that he would be able to check the cards before each game. The young man was hurt by the plot hatched by his friends, and no longer thought either of Simone or his debt.

The others lied, played down the number of times they had cheated. They seemed ashamed, each of them, of their brutal behaviour, which none of them found acceptable. Paul counted the number of cards. Luck changed hands and he started to curse, having lost more than he won. They weren't thieves, said one of them in a low voice, returning the lost bills. There remained the sense of disgrace and betrayal of friendship. The others said they were still friends, despite everything. Empty words: his only winnings.

The attractive blonde Simone tearfully reproached him for his inconstancy.

Paul whispered that he wouldn't do it again, told her she was the only person who counted for him, the only one he could trust. Unforeseeable circumstances had kept him at the gambling table the previous evening. He spoke constantly to drown out the sound of Simone's weeping, muffling it by enveloping her in his arms, trying to distance their little scene from the noises he heard in the kitchen, his head turning from lack of sleep.

He took her off to the village. She called him a selfish liar and said she wanted to break up. He begged her not to reject him, feeling embarrassed that the scene was taking place on the main street. He couldn't understand Simone's change of heart, her rational decision to break up, and went home to sleep, dumbfounded.

His masculine pride was wounded. He repeated the scene over and over in his mind and promised to apologize to Simone and her parents. His desire to hang out with the boys won out over his pledges of love when she wasn't around. When he saw her, with her round breasts and tiny waist belted into her dress, he wanted her. He did nothing, unable to muster the guts to ask for forgiveness.

He didn't forget this harmonious family, and idealized them. He watched Simone, calm now between her mother and her father, in step with village life, at peace with herself. Despite his money and freedom, which he enjoyed, Paul had a sentimental attachment to the past.

Paul didn't tell all to Odette, and attributed his weakness for gambling to idleness, and to his radio-technology course, for which he had no inclination. He wasn't gifted with his hands and would not work for anyone else.

His sincerity pleased Odette. Each had had a past love. Simone's face, like Lucien's, were faint etchings from the past. She didn't ask him about his love of gambling, and was in favour of the idea of having a business. He would buy a tavern like the one that had made his grandfather a rich man.

The night he asked her to marry him, she listened to her lover's confession, and felt certain she was his chosen one. They were concerned with themselves and their future. Their respective earlier love experiences put them on an equal footing, an advantage, for they would enter their married life as adults. They were ending their youth, would no longer have to do as they were told, would henceforth do as they pleased. Each seemed grown up in the eyes of the other.

Laurence returned around midnight and was told they had decided. She shared their happiness. She told them they were a handsome, well-matched couple. For Laurence, chemistry, the materiality of the body, took precedence over moralism. She believed in the autonomy of the individual, and that liberty exercised by two was double that exercised by one. She said they would succeed in life. Odette and Paul were thrilled with her words.

Odette gave up the idea that Laurence was an obstacle to her loves, buried it in the back of her mind, saw her evolution as a city woman in a new light, a tranquil series of events leading her to Paul. She had avoided the sexual traps in which women, to their great disadvantage, get caught. Like Laurence, she saw the future as leading her out of the condition of poverty, that of her destitute childhood, riddled with frustrations. A page turned and she felt the strength of her gathering energy, and with it her new faith in the future.

Paul walked through the night, high at the thought that Odette belonged to him alone. He loved her and was crazy with the happiness at the thought he would pass his days with her at his side. They would live together, his inner loneliness would soon be a thing of the past. He would adore her, would not allow anyone to come between them. Their business would be a joint enterprise and its success a guarantee of their freedom. Paul dreamed of daring financial speculations, of little daily risks and of a stable love life. They shared the wish for a lifetime commitment.

Laurence breathed easier, a weight off her shoulders. She remembered Odette's arrival at her doorstep, with her prominent teeth, carrying a suitcase of dirty clothes and a broken comb, and compared her with the hard-working young girl she had become under her tutelage, and without the support of their parents. Unlike herself, Odette was a fine housekeeper. Paul was a loving man who would know how to make compromises for the sake of the relationship. Odette couldn't do better than this.

16

Laurence accompanied Odette when she went to meet the grandfather. Paul had praised her so much that the old man was won over in advance. It was a Sunday afternoon, and a table was set in the living room with chocolate, barley-sugar candy, mints and good porto. The well-built old man held himself erect, was taller than Paul. They spoke of the war and of the young men who were enlisting in the army as much as they talked about the economic turnaround. The old man promised them an apartment when it came time for them to make a home. This would make things easier, a fact Laurence stressed later to Odette, who pretended she didn't care one way or the other.

Paul took his fiancée to meet his parents. Odette felt ill at ease with the mother, who had a young face and a body deformed by pregnancies. Her belly, with its sagging muscles, hung down to her thighs. She was a woman who moved slowly, saving her strength. Her husband served soft drinks and sugared cakes. The mother said she loved her son, that he visited her often. She smiled now, relaxed. Her abandonment of Paul, so far in the past, was blamed on her in-laws, on their insistence, their determination to keep him with them. The same thing had happened to a daughter, now an adolescent, who lived with a paternal aunt, a woman who had no children. Both were pampered, which did not diminish their affection for their parents.

The mother watched lovingly over the household, rocking a crying baby. The youngest drew near the big brother, who distributed coins among his siblings. She did not complain of her multiple pregnancies, nor of her husband's minimal salary. Odette noticed how clean the place was, but felt uncomfortable with the way Paul drank in his mother's every word. She felt left out, a stranger, even if the woman appeared to have no authority whatsoever. Odette looked aloof, sceptical, when she said: you get to a man through his stomach, by cooking his favourite dishes. The woman asked her if she knew how to cook.

Odette suspected Paul's mother had power over him, and felt no affection for the fat woman. The parents' weaknesses, their good relationship, the role of the father as provider, his protective attitude towards his wife, limited the number of things to talk about. It was heavy going to talk only about the little details of daily life. One thing you could say for Laurence was that her perpetual hope for a better future kept you going in good times and bad, and life was never boring.

When she got home from her factory job, Odette cleaned, washed, tidied up, cooked, efficient, indefatigable. Laurence took care of her uniforms, and, if not working evenings, took Odette out for dinner. Marthe would marry René the following summer. Odette would get married in the fall. The young girl from Gaspé surprised the little group when, in a sudden outburst of emotion, she made a speech expressing her gratitude to Laurence. She would never forget

Laurence's consoling words, her moral support, the way she took it upon herself to organize outings for the four of them. They had gained, she said, from Laurence's friendship and advice. René was better for her than her first fiancé. Marthe, in comparing the two men, was glad she had waited.

The age gap between Laurence and the young women seemed bigger now. At thirty-five, she expected to remain single, convinced that most bachelors were like monsieur Brodeur, men for whom other things mattered more than women. For the first time, she mentioned his library of occult science books to her friends. She said she thought it was important to understand the mysterious bonds between humans and the cosmos. She told them she knew she had been indoctrinated in these matters by the Catholic Church, with its overriding notion of blind obedience to dogma, but thought that someday it would be considered valid to work out one's own beliefs, provided one had access to the wisdom of the great thinkers.

The possibility of companionship was the best thing marriage had to offer, she told them. Women in their situation did not yet have access to the nice lifestyle of a monsieur Brodeur. This she thought without saying so.

Odette, Marthe and Lili skied less than in previous years. They knew they would soon give it up all together, and they looked forward eagerly to their new lives. They were bidding adieu to girlhood. Laurence bought herself a becoming, well-cut, red wool coat. Paul complimented her, saying now she looked even taller than he. Red, an unusual colour, played up her strong points, her slenderness. She too was preparing for her new life, that of a woman who lived alone, distancing from the group who were now at home in the city, girls who worked, knew how to have fun and spend money, who went to restaurants, movies, who had explored the city and its surroundings. For economic reasons, they lived and amused themselves in the downtown area, a judicious choice, also, as far as avoiding real and imaginary dangers.

The young girls who were getting married would not limit themselves to the dreariness of housework, to beating a path between the stove and the table. The country girls would not do as their mothers had. Optimism was in the air.

Cécile entered the novitiate at Outremont, and Laurence and Odette went to visit her in the convent parlour. The rich wooden wainscotting and varnished furniture contrasted with the plain white walls. A crucifix and a framed portrait of the founder of the community hung opposite one another, supplying a meditative ambience. Cécile was overjoyed to see them, and immediately thanked Laurence for financing her year in the convent, knowing full well that without her support, she would have been assigned to the housekeeping staff. Now she would have the same teaching status as her sisters. The novice also expressed her gratitude to the father, who had made sacrifices for the third time, in order to provide her with a dowry.

Cécile questioned them about their life in Montréal, in her usual curious and eager way, without casting judgement on their choices. She tried to see the city through their eyes. Laurence described several different urban contexts, replete with details. The future nun yearned to know the city beyond the convent walls, and she hung on Laurence's words. She confessed the rigorous silence, which she associated with boredom, was the hardest thing to get used to. Their warm meeting was cut short by the clock striking the end of visiting hour. They had exchanged a great deal of news, and Cécile was her usual lively self.

Amanda, having called herself Sister Léon-des-Anges, had influenced Aline to choose the name Sister Rosalie, and Cécile to become Sister Isidore. Amanda's idea of choosing names in homage to the father, mother, and the son who died tragically, meant the Naud family had a symbolic presence in the community. The daughters thus recreated a similacrum of their original family unit. To complete the picture would have taken a future priest, which was the fondest wish of the impecunious father, a proud man who would not accept charity, yet demanded money from his children. The son, killed in a work accident in the summer of 1936, transcended his brief, humble life by becoming a symbol. His name's being carried on by Cécile was a way of remembering him in mourning. The religious order was represented by the Trinity, a holy version of the human family. It had been decreed that three daughters would become nuns, a perfect number, Amanda declared.

Paul spent the better part of his time amusing himself. His grandfather was still active, managing some fifteen rented flats. He was teaching Paul the business. In principle, never listen to tenant demands, he told Paul, who collected the rents and checked to see if requested repairs were urgent. The sale of the huge property on lac des Deux-Montagnes took place and the old man paid off all his mortgages. He now had savings in the bank and a monthly income from the city holdings. The nearly eighty-year-old man enjoyed economic security, a security that also benefited Paul's parents, who lived on rue Valois.

Paul hung out with the neighbourhood card players, refused to play for big stakes, and never set foot in gambling dens. He gossiped, played cards, avoided shady types, scheming, suspicious propositions, promises of fantastic sums. Like his buddies, he talked big about dirty dealings or, better, tales of escapades associated with the Montréal mafia, making out as if he had underworld connections. He was attracted to gambling because he had time on his hands, but he no longer felt tempted to miss a lover's tryst for the sake of a card game.

During a get-together, the other gamblers jokingly dared him to tell them about his sexual exploits. They resorted to the language of buying and selling to find out if he had fingered the merchandise and called on him to shop around so he wouldn't be disappointed when he got married. You had to take a woman in hand, the sooner the better, they said. It mattered little whether the confidences they dragged out of each other were true. They had a good time together, and the sexual teasing never got boring. Money and sex were the most fun to talk about, plus partisan politics, added during election times.

Paul felt comfortable with Odette, was devoted to her. He took her to the movies, keeping a clamp on his desire until he understood that his sweetheart was waiting for him to make the first move, which filled him with tenderness. He kissed her discreetly, his hand brushing her breast, his heart throbbing, giving in a little to temptation. Holding back would make it all the better later. Odette, who had had her wild side during adolescence, was a willing partner in the exploration of sensual pleasures, devouring every caress.

Without quite saying so, it was understood they would save themselves for marriage. They flirted with the idea of being sexy, held back the flood of passion, of sensuality, of dreaming and daydreaming that all gathered toward the goal of physical fusion. They entrusted themselves to sighs and touching rather than words.

Soon their evening meetings were for the express purpose of the supreme moment when they progressively undressed, feeling each other up, anticipating new sensations, each stronger than the preceding one. They reached a certain point, stopped, and parted, sure that the next time would be even more intoxicating. A prodigal lasciviousness made Paul proceed slowly. Odette let herself go, not knowing whether she would give in on an impulse or hold back, as they had decided.

Undressing underscored their sense of indulging in erotic behaviour, and the pleasure of transgressing their own promise pushed them ever closer to consummating their union. The difficult first time was compensated for by a flood of positive emotions. The wedding date was drawing near, and no one would know their secret. They belonged to each other before receiving formal sanction from Church and state.

They had a simple marriage, dressed in city clothes. Despite the economic recovery, there was uncertainty in the air due to young men going off to join the army. It wouldn't seem right to be extravagant. Odette accepted a contribution from Laurence, who was the only family member present at the marriage ceremony. She stepped forward into her new role— the role, as she saw it, of an emancipated city woman.

The couple visited Broughton so Paul and the in-laws could meet. He felt like he was stepping into a history book, into a world forgotten by the march of progress. He tried to make friends with the parents. He thought that he could win their respect if he could charm them into liking him. Léon Naud, who expected to be listened to in respectful silence, was disconcerted. All this chattering was beyond him, amounted to disrespect. Odette was indifferent to the lack of empathy between the two men, too busy acting out the role of city woman, a status clinched by her marriage, which consummated her rupture with the past.

Léon couldn't be bothered with a man who would let his daughter live in a rooming house and who promised her an easy life and a business. Paul put it behind him, asked no more about Odette's origins. She had done her bit, as was expected of her.

A month later, the ground-floor flat on rue Valois was vacated, and they moved in, with the grandfather's furniture. Their desire to have a child soon became a reality. Odette was pregnant. They had agreed that they would have children. Odette's self-image was that of a wife and mother, devoted to her task, with a household organized as she saw fit, neat and clean. Paul felt uncomfortable, prevaricated about borrowing money from his grandfather to start a business, and put off making a decision when an alternative appeared.

Members of the army reserves were taking up various posts at the Valcartier military base near the city of Québec. There would be a plebiscite on conscription. Men would sign up even if the province voted against it, even if most people were against it. Everyone was talking about the planned plebiscite, just as two years earlier, everyone had talked about granting the right to vote to women, following twenty years of struggle and debate.

Paul sought Odette's consent for his plan. He maintained that the army would not enlist him since he had flat feet, adding that his father, who had worked for the postal service for more than twenty years, would recommend him for a civil-service job at Valcartier. They were upset about being separated. There was no choice. Paul would volunteer for the war effort like Marthe's husband, already in uniform. They accepted the separation out of necessity. Paul was nervous when he showed up at the barracks. The medical report said he was being turned down due to deformed feet, and to being too obese for a foot soldier. Paul showed the medical document to Odette, but to other people he insisted on the problem with his feet. Too fat! He who wore his roundness with pride, was offended to have it sneered at by the army. He applied for a postal job.

Odette imposed restrictions on the coming and going of Paul's younger brothers, and didn't let them visit unannounced. They didn't understand, and the daughter-in-law explained to the mother-in-law that she needed privacy, and to keep the house neat. Odette knew she would have to watch out for the children if they were playing in the street, a responsibility she refused to accept. The young woman made it clear that she would neither babysit nor cater to their little needs. To each her own bustle and bedlam, Odette concluded.

She maintained neighbourly relations with her mother-in-law. Paul visited his parents more often, noticed nothing unusual, unperturbed by his wife's aloofness. The mother appeared indifferent towards her daughter-in-law's attitude. She had not raised Paul, who was so affectionate toward her, and this in itself made her happy. She asked for nothing more.

The grandfather grew morose, complained he felt isolated. He closed himself up for days on end, but it only took a visitor to get him out again. Then he went to the market and came back with baskets or entire crates of fresh produce that he distributed.

The old man proposed an arrangement that pleased Paul but received an ambivalent response from Odette. He would live with them. In exchange, he would pay for the food the clothing, doctor's visits, births, heat, electricity and telephone. As for the number of children, they could have as many as they liked, and he would provide for them. He told them to think about his proposal.

They didn't talk much. Paul was enthusiastic and Odette, reticent. It wasn't the extra work as much as having to share the space, the loss of privacy. She told him so. When Odette spoke of closing her door to intruders, for her the closed door marked the boundary of their private space. The door, for him, was an opening between the inner world and the outer. He was at home in both. Paul was not speaking entirely in good faith when he said a woman reigned over her house, and this wouldn't change. He took the grandfather's words to mean that he would be considerate, wouldn't interfere in their decisions, would do as the majority wished.

Odette feared a lack of security and Paul, if he saved the money he earned at Valcartier, saw his chance to buy a business. He convinced her that if the war lasted, he would accumulate a sufficient nest egg. They would inherit, one day, and add to their business and properties. He interpreted the grandfather's offer to mean that he had chosen them as heirs. Odette hadn't thought about that. That they were already thinking about the inheritance didn't trouble them. Odette perceived having the grandfather live with them as a temporary sacrifice that would pay off in the long run.

Paul painted a winning picture. Odette played down the consequences in terms of housework, which was light, for the moment. He was probably right about inheriting. The dazzling mantra of supposed advantages was aimed at her weak spot: her longing for affluence.

Odette, intimidated, repressed her doubts, unable to articulate them clearly, suspecting a trap, suspecting she was being taken in. Paul had spoken several times of asking for a loan. When the old man was around, instead of discussing their future business, they spoke only of his tavern and his past successes. She doubted that Paul had told him they needed to borrow. The old man opened his purse when he wanted to, and wouldn't be second-guessing an unspoken request. Veiled allusions, vague attempts to broach the subject, were hardly enough to make the old man think his grandson had serious plans.

Good business sense, said the old man, dictated that a loan to a brother, a son, could cause trouble, or even rifts. Loaning money to a family member should be treated in the same manner as if it were being lent by a bank or credit union, including the charging of interest, and a notarized contract. In America, ownership was governed by formal rules and regulations. In this matter, he shared the opinion of most monied individuals. Paul vacillated between being accommodating and deciding to make an outright request, because he wanted his grandfather to notice, without his insisting, that he had ambitions. The old man remained deaf.

Odette idealized the idea of having a business, but it was not her will but Paul's that would make it come about. She began to feel dependent, helpless. She raised her voice, driven to despair by what seemed like his blackmailing her. He put off making a decision, skirted the issue by urging her to look after the old man in the interest of amassing the initial outlay. She didn't believe in the inheritance and said so.

Paul tried to calm her screaming in his usual jovial manner, which only exasperated her. He went over the advantages of the arrangement again and promised her she would have a salary. She calmed down, but had an angry expression on her face. He smoothed over their first quarrel with tenderness, without asking himself why he was dancing around the issue. He would be leaving, and she would be with the child about to be born and the old man. It was an arrangement that would bring them closer to the goals he had been brewing for years. During the night, he remembered a conversation with Laurence in which he praised Odette's even temper, said how much he liked her personality. Laurence disagreed, and said Odette lost her temper when annoyed, as he would see. One day he too would be treated to her angry outbursts. He, who fled difficult situations and avoided responsibility, preferred to believe this tantrum was unusual.

Odette put up no more resistance, agreed to what the two men proposed. Paul was called to Valcartier just as his grandfather was moving into the rue Valois apartment.

Laurence helped Odette through the long and painful labour. There were no complications. A daughter was born. Odette was happy, and Paul announced the birth to everyone. He told his wife he loved her. Laurence made a formal speech, wishing the best for parents and child. Although momentarily closer to them, her way of speaking showed she was distancing. She was impressed and intimidated by the imperious event, by the appearance of a new life, by motherhood. It seemed to her a metamorphosis had taken place. Odette had earned the stripes of an adult woman, and Laurence no longer interfered in any way whatsoever.

17

The apartment became cramped. The little vestibule encroached on a room to which Odette had not yet assigned a function. An oil space heater stood against the wall opposite the entrance, and there she placed the grandfather's rocking chair and his spitoon. To the right of the entrance, in a recess with a window, she kept her sewing machine. To the left, the double room served as parlour and a bedroom. She meant to put up a curtain to separate the sleeping quarters from the parlour, but never got around to it. The corridor led from the room with the heater, past the bathroom, to a kitchen of modest proportions. Sitting at the table pushed up against the left wall, between the bedroom door and the back door, Odette ate while contemplating a store calendar hanging there. The sole closed bedroom was offered to the old man.

A six-foot basement, dug under the back part of the apartment, was lit by a single bare light bulb of low wattage that threw trembling shadows on the walls. Odette lined up jams and pickles for the winter on the rough boards that served as shelves. On the ground stood baskets of apples, sacks of potatoes, carrots, turnips, yellow onions. She went down there as little as possible— the spiders could have it. She who washed and scrubbed was repulsed by the idea of going down into the basement, down the stairs that led from the den where the grandfather sat, just behind the narrow bathroom.

There was plenty of food, but little variety. The old man, nostalgic for the past, bought produce in huge quantities. He went to the market and had things delivered. His trips there had the air of expeditions that lasted entire mornings.

Paul came home in a khaki uniform and complained he felt lonely, was envious of his wife who had the company of child and grandfather. He gave her his pay, keeping a small amount for his modest expenses. His leave expired quickly. Their exuberant lovemaking kept them long hours in bed, retiring early and getting up as late as possible. Paul was sorry to leave. It seemed unnatural to him to live among men. He was promised regular leaves, and this, coupled with the welcome he got from his loving Odette, who knew how to make him feel longed for, helped him adapt to his new situation.

She knew she was pregnant and the news caused a vague sense of distress. Too soon, murmured a doubtful inner voice. She wanted a second child, but not right away. The young woman kept as busy as possible, forgot about her pregnancy, took the baby out, got to know the second-floor woman, un unusual woman of forty with no children. Madame Chagnon, who was neither a fool nor a chatterbox, made caustic observations about the way people were, and liked her young neighbour for her youth and spirit. They spent time together, taking advantage of the fine weather. You only needed two chairs on a balcony to have a good talk. Madame Chagnon guessed Odette's concerns, and lectured her on the egotism of husbands who didn't get involved with their children, didn't look after them in any way, leaving everything up to the women. With a man like that, better not to have more than two. Odette felt better when madame Chagnon put her inner fears into words.

One afternoon, Odette shared a beer with madame Chagnon, leaving the glasses and bottle near the kitchen sink. Paul noticed them and demanded an explanation. He was jealous that she was having fun in his absence, but accused her instead, rather hypocritically, of squandering their money, of throwing it out the window. He went on and on, saying it was their money, they shouldn't be letting a tenant take advantage of them. A beer shared with a woman she hardly knew was a frivolous expense.

Paul bore a grudge, couldn't stand the idea of his wife sharing something nice with someone else in his absence. Legitimate extras were shared with her exclusively. He said nothing about the group of card players that had started at the military base. He took up gambling again as a hobby, a means of dealing with boredom. His resentment grew, and he gave his wife less money than the previous time. Odette was humiliated. She had kept to her budget since the day they were married, never allowing herself the least indulgence. Paul's obsessive, aggressive behaviour hurt her, embittered her, his accusations, repeated ad nauseum.

She was, since the first day of their life together, in the curious habit of noting every purchase, no matter how insignificant. Odette tabulated and Paul added up the monthly expenses, arriving at an annual amount at the end of the year. With this meticulous approach, they knew what it cost them to live, as they put it, and it gave them a sense of satisfaction. The budgetary restrictions they experienced before the grandfather came to live with them were no longer relevant. They continued keeping accounts as a matter of form, out of a fear of spending more than necessary.

The old man said he was delighted and he promised Odette to look after the first-born when the second came. It was a commitment that she would have liked to hear from her husband. Odette was somewhat reassured by the promise of help. Laurence lavished affection on her and said she should be serene, for there were few women in as comfortable a situation as she. Paul had a secure income and she wasn't obliged to work at the factory. As long as there was war, there would be loss of life. There were young women already widowed, in mourning for the death of their companions. Laurence, by comparing her lot with others', got Odette to admit that so far she couldn't complain. She started to agree, then hedged and stopped short of saying so. Her sister was bugging her. She wasn't going to try and justify herself with a single woman who understood nothing about what it was like to be married and a mother. Sometimes she found Laurence's words inspiring, other times, off-putting.

As long as summer lasted, she went out with her baby, walking it proudly. Odette flourished and had never been so beautiful. Strangers in streetcars and in stores came up to her and complimented her on her child, but the compliment was, in fact, for her. She blossomed, ever more energetic, dynamic. By September, the little home was ready for the new baby. In October, a moment of malaise conjured up the image of her own mother, a woman resigned and self-effacing. She was surprised to find herself calling to her, saying Maman out loud. November rolled around and she went back to the hardest tasks, bringing on the birth early. Her mother-in-law arrived while she was washing the kitchen floor, feeling the first pangs of labour, but she finished the job.

Paul managed to get leave after the birth of his second daughter. His grandfather celebrated the birth, serving porto. He did as he had promised. The child's playpen was stationed at the foot of his rocker and he watched over and petted the little girl, who was now walking. Odette and Paul wanted to prevent a third birth. She confessed to a parish priest, who refused her absolution.

One cold spring evening, the baby asleep, the little girl whined, pouted, because it was bedtime. She fussed and whimpered, clinging to the braces of the old man, who had her on his lap, stubbornly refusing to go to bed. Odette lost her temper, grabbed her as if she were an inanimate object and threw her into the crib, screaming about his habit of rocking her. The child let out a deathly cry, one only, excessive, out of proportion to the circumstances. The mother kept on screaming until her anger subsided, and by the next morning had forgotten her rage. The old man drank his coffee and Odette changed the baby. Towards nine o'clock, the grandfather, trembling with fear, said go and see if she is dead. The mother found her daughter subdued, tamed, quiet beyond belief.

Odette remembered the training she had received at the orphanage, imposed her own régime, no longer giving in to whims. Whether the husband was absent or present, she had free rein in the education of the children. On rue Valois she saw children, half-clothed, sometimes without booties, playing pots and pans in front of an open door. These children became for her the personification of what she didn't want for her own. She detested what she called disgusting urban negligence, hateful child-rearing habits that people in rural areas wouldn't even imagine. Her notion of acceptable norms corresponded to life in a better neighbourhood, and she didn't mind going on about it with Laurence and madame Chagnon. Laurence, more relaxed, confessed that if she had children, they would be more like those playing with pots in the street, and added that it was a good thing she didn't have any. She said nothing about the momentary pleasure she felt when unknown children ran up to her, spontaneous, cocksure. She thought to herself, then, that she would never have children.

Rosalie came to visit Odette during the summer. The woman with her knot of white hair seemed more than ever detached from this world. Odette would have liked to throw herself into her mother's arms. Reunited, face to face, four hands grasped, bodies separate, they looked at each other directly in the eyes. Odette was sorry her brother was there at the moment they saw each other again. Without him, she'd have dared to kiss her mother.

Rosalie wore a plain black dress that fell to her ankles, black lace shoes, and, apart from the bare head, there was nothing to distinguish her from a nun. The woman with her hair in a knot made herself unobtrusive. She was indifferent to the urban surroundings, made no comment on the houses in rows and the paved streets, looked around her with the air of an outsider. She found the different smells, unknown noises, the view limited by the flats opposite, a little suffocating. Whatever the city really was was drowned in an overload of impressions and sensations. Odette tried to convince her about the advantages of progress. Rosalie would not see electricity in her house in her lifetime. But she did not object to an urban way of life.

The farmer's wife only asked for one thing: to visit Cécile. Sitting with her mother in the parlour of the religious community, Odette was moved by the facial resemblance between the two women in long black robes. She listened distractedly to news of people back in Broughton who seemed to spring from another era, another country, and contributed nothing to the conversation.

Rosalie was invited to the third floor of the triplex by Paul's mother, noticed how cramped the kitchen was, and concluded that people must live in very crowded situations. She consoled herself with the thought that Odette, who was so far away from her own family, was surrounded by Paul's.

The old woman was letting go of her maternal role, and absorbing the environment in small doses, without any attempt to love or hate what she saw. After the children went to bed, the two women talked little. Odette would have liked to ask her mother if she wanted so many children. Now that she was a mother herself, a little inner voice told her to learn what she could from her mother, making her want the evening to go on longer. At the same time she was apprehensive about what her mother might say. Odette hesitated to ask, didn't really listen.

Rosalie proffered good wishes for Odette's family. The old lady knew she would not see her again. She made allusions to death that her daughter didn't here. Her departure opened no old wounds, nor any sense of guilt. Odette's youth protected her from the shadow of death. Rosalie died the next summer.

The landing in Normandy took place. People remembered the raid on Dieppe, the crazy military strategy. This time, the confirmation that the Allies were advancing and routing the German troops was welcomed with relief. You had to read the papers to understand how the war was proceeding. Paul read the paper every day, followed the news of the allies, commented on what he read, discussed it with others. Odette turned on the radio, listened distractedly, found it too depressing, and turned it off again. She borrowed phrases from Paul and Laurence to talk about the war. She also suffered from the grim situation, given her absent husband and necessity of putting off their plans until God only knew when.

Odette found herself pregnant at the end of the winter. She wanted a son, so was happy about it. They had spaced the pregnancy, expressed their wish for a son, looked forward to his arrival. Laurence said often, and with conviction, that the couple had beautiful children. She talked of plans for their education, which, in the final analysis, amounted to the single project of music lessons, and promised them a piano when the elder reached the age of six. Laurence felt that good food, sound sleep, adequate cleanliness were all that was needed for mental well-being and good health. Odette was growing more receptive to her notions of what a good education meant, and liked the idea of a piano. The nurse saw, in the children's beauty, the possibility of reclaiming something lost; each child represented a new ray of hope for a more perfect future.

One Friday afternoon in the middle of April, Laurence arrived without forewarning. Odette looked feverish to her, her dark eyes sunken, and followed her into the kitchen. An unimaginable disorder reigned in the place. The dishes from the last meal were still on the table. In a huge pot, a beef and vegetable stew was simmering. Greasy paper and vegetable and fruit peelings overflowed in the garbage can. A large sack of flour was spilling over onto the floor. Utensils for preparing pastry and meat filled the sink, and the counter, where she was making apple pies, was overflowing with peels and cores, half of which had fallen on the floor. Odette talked a blue streak, saying she was using up the food bought that morning. She opened the icebox, pointed to a second piece of beef weighing ten pounds, and, near the back door, a large basket of apples. The old man had again bought enough to feed an army, a habit she hated, a country-dweller's habit. Even in Broughton, they didn't cook in such quantities.

Laurence thought of the scarcity of food that preceded summers on the farm. Her sister had no memory of that. She refrained from bringing it up, nor did she mention all the people living on meagre rations because of the war. She tried to get her to see there must be more to the way she was feeling than an over-abundance of food. Odette's hands fluttered wildly, stirring up a cloud of flour, her face rigid with some unnameable dissatisfaction. She was emerging from a nightmare.

In the middle of the den the two little girls, cuddled against the legs of the old man, were playing with his shoelaces. Laurence was thinking about Odette's volcanic character. In her memory suddenly appeared the image of the first horse shot in front of pregnant Rosalie. Odette was born with a strawberry spot on the back of her neck, just as the horse who suffered from a mortal wound under its mane. She bore the mother's trauma.

The next day, Odette did not understand her panic, and became anxious, missing her husband. In the empty evenings, having no one to talk to drained the enterprising Odette of her energy. Rather than pursue a hobby, she sank into boredom.

Paul appeared, pleased with himself, around nine in the evening. Duty had obliged him to come to Montréal for the night. They drank some beer and moved close to one another. Odette closed the door of the double room and they made love in the corridor. Paul got up early. The postal truck awaited him. The lucky event would have been insignificant had it not been for her father-in-law, who, climbing up to his third-floor apartment, saw them in the throes of making love through the den window. He accused her of having another man at her place, his expression impassive, his tone brusque, to imply his indignation. Odette said it was Paul, was hurt, turned her back on him, angry that he would accuse her of something so serious, that he would suspect her of such a thing.

The war ended. People were celebrating, strangers, neighbours, friends, everybody gave their opinion on the liberation. Odette joined in. Everywhere across the city crowds gathered, cries of joy filled the air, celebrations went on for days and nights. Odette was looking forward to Paul's return. The long separation was nearly over. The first day of liberation broke down her usual reserve and she felt madly gregarious.

Paul's return was duly celebrated. They went out together to cabarets, drank spirits and smoked. In the air of general euphoria, they talked enthusiastically about starting their business. The army was keeping some of its personnel and services for an as-yet unspecified period, and Paul was transferred to nearby rue Hochelaga.

Odette consulted the savings account bank book: there was enough for a down payment. She had deposited the baby bonuses along with her husband's salary. Paul was pleased he had let his wife look after their money, and asked her to turn the bank book over to him.

It was summer. The mother kept her little girls on the balcony. Weeds grew in the fenced-in yard, and she did not pick up the rubbish or rake up the broken glass and cigarette butts. The useless little yard made the front of the house look ugly. The courtyard behind was of packed earth, perpetually in the shade of the sheds, and smelled humid. The children didn't go down there. Odette talked about the beach, about green grass, felt closed in in their apartment.

Working for the postal service was now less demanding. Coming back to Montréal reminded Paul of his youthful idle summers. He got his work done in the morning and took it easy in the afternoon. He was able to slip off, leaving work to stroll around, to hang out in snack bars, chatting with the owners if they were so inclined. Most often, he kept company with the neighbourhood card players.

While Odette served him supper, he recounted the neighbourhood gossip. She knew he was playing cards, and did nothing to retain him after supper. Evenings that he stayed home, he lay around, went upstairs to visit his parents, was bored. There was no point in going to bed at ten o'clock, he wasn't tired. He read right through the newspaper to the very last page.

One Saturday afternoon, Odette washed and dressed the girls in new clothing, put bows in their hair. They were splendidly clean and shining in their new dresses. She said how nice they looked, made a fuss over them. She wanted Paul to get closer to the children.

The mother led the girls towards him, told him to pick them up, sat them on his knee. His arms remained inert and he let them slide off his short thighs, indifferent to the children and heedless of his wife's entreaty. She asked nothing from him save that he be involved with his children, get to know them, that he be an affectionate father, that he take the same pride in his family that she did. Odette was hurt more than she could say. She intuited that if Paul was not interested in his children, their family life would suffer.

Paul's affection was for his wife and she knew it, hoped he would also come to share his tenderness with the children. The scene was short-lived but pregnant with meaning. The children seemed like intruders in their relationship, which she found unacceptable.

18

Laurence had no regrets: for better or for worse, she had given without expecting anything in return. Now it was time to look after herself. Her list of possessions was short— not a single item of furniture in the rented room on rue Saint-Denis belonged to her. Her worldly goods filled two suitcases. A persistent voice in her head said: think of your future, because nobody else will. She was brewing a bold move that finally took her to the shore of lac des Deux-Montagnes. A salary was well and good, but provided no security for the future. She kept reminding herself that she was a woman in her prime, moving toward old age, when one became dependent, an object of derision. She was obsessed by old age, by the recurring image of being bossed around by someone who complained about feeding her and looking after her, a cruel but probable end. Experience had taught her that people can behave unkindly. She dreaded not having control over her life, being told what to do and how to do it. People who had been pushed around couldn't help treating others as they had been treated themselves. Her optimism fed uniquely on her faith in the present. The idea of spending her last years under someone else's tutelage was a dark spot on the horizon. Her exemplary energy spurred her towards a dream that would, had she been born male, have already been a reality. Institutions directed by women had taught her nothing on this score. Nuns excelled in gross ignorance when it came to economic realities, wanting only to have a safe, simple, peaceful life. A recluse was over-protected, was rarely required to take initiative. She never thought of herself as a man, but she desired a comfortable, honest lifestyle, the kind you win through your own efforts, through property speculation, for example. These thoughts had been on her mind for a decade, though law and social conventions were against her.

The salary and working conditions of nurses were improving, including the introduction of the eight-hour shift at Sainte-Justine, where she applied for a job in obstetrics. After her shift, dressed in street clothes, she headed towards a textile factory and did piece-work, sewing frenetically. She worked five nights at the hospital and six days a week downtown. Overcome with fatigue those first months, racing against time, winter seemed endless.

Her daring was accompanied by fear. At the hospital, nobody could know about her day job. At the factory, it couldn't be known she was a nurse. She turned over in her mind the possible consequences if it got out at the hospital that she was hobnobbing with workers, wives and young girls from working-class neighbourhoods, mostly French Canadian. Laurence noticed the strange absence of English Canadians in the factory, and the influx of immigrant women. To her, the word "nurse" implied a certain social status, a world with standards, with specific ways of being, and speaking. It was a milieu not without jealousies, suspicions, denunciations. On duty, she was twice as careful.

She got to know these workers, mothers and young girls, who began in the factories as young as sixteen. The older women were of two minds in their attitudes towards the youngest ones, some maintaining, out of pity, that the work was too hard for them, while others said it was a good job for girls with no education. They earned more than teachers or office workers. Laurence was indifferent to the social stigma of factory work. She was tired, like the other women her age, and no one guessed her double life.

She reluctantly became head nurse, despite her attempts to avoid it. The head nurse had to fill in the register at the end of the shift. Laurence never got over her embarrassment regarding her poor mastery of language, especially when it came to writing down medical instructions. Writing was a trial, it could give her away. She applied herself like a fastidious schoolgirl, but at staff meetings she was full of her usual vim and vigour.

Despite herself, Laurence did not go unnoticed at the factory. She made an educated guess as to the boss's margin of profit. When the boss complained in French that he was the only one without a salary, she ironically blurted out the amount she thought he was earning, according to her calculations. He replied in English: *a smart girl*. He offered to promote her to forewoman, because a woman who knew how to count would see the workload was properly distributed, thereby maintaining the rhythm of production and increasing his profit. She accepted, negotiated the piece rates firmly with the boss. When the parity committee was introduced, with a worker-representative to evaluate the fair value of an item, Laurence made sure she was not viewed as being on the boss's side. She saw her role as intermediary.

Her visceral fear that her double life would be found out obliged her to keep her wits about her. The rented room became a refuge from fatigue, a place she visited in passing to maintain her uniforms, make lunch for the next day and sleep in the evening with the alarm clock set on the edge of the nightstand. In spring she put out new pots of African violets, begonias, impatiens and geraniums. That summer she bought a large piece of land near lac des Deux-Montagnes, unoccupied land where she would build cottages, designed by herself. She spent the money she had saved and looked forward to the possibility of beginning construction the following summer.

She confided the details to Odette and Paul. Together they talked about their future business. Laurence's initiative strengthened their desire to push forward with their own plans.

Coming back from Pointe-Calumet, she felt like drinking a pastis and entered the bar near the station. They were playing Gershwin, which reminded her of monsieur Brodeur, and after a second pastis, Gaston's face floated before her. She checked out the men and found none who measured up to Gaston. The idea of having a little flirt perked her up, but no one approached her. She left, floating, her eyes black and lively.

One night she was eating in the hospital canteen, when she overheard two women sitting beside her discuss an acquaintance on the verge of losing his job due to alcoholism. The man was a conductor on a train running between Québec and Gaspé. They mentioned the name Gaston Ramsay. Laurence was troubled: there couldn't be many Gaston Ramsay's. She piped up and asked where he was from. They identified his home town, described him. He was a single man who drank a lot and became disoriented. In three sentences they described the sad life of a man in his prime. The loneliness of the heart, of hers and Gaston's, deep within them, incredibly painful, seemed insurmountable. She rationalized it away with a generalization: the Depression had ruined many lives.

A young well-dressed man sat down on a streetcar bench, his eyes taking in her every movement. The incident happened again, several times, always discreetly. One October morning Laurence looked straight at him. He was getting out on Phillips Square at the same time as she, and he approached her courteously. He worked for his father on Sainte-Catherine three days a week. He had first noticed her one day shivering in the rain without a coat or umbrella. The following week, on a cold rainy day, they ran into each other again. Laurence thought he seemed well-educated. Adrien Lessard spoke well, was reserved, distinguished. When he invited her out for dinner, she accepted.

He was four years her junior, married, from Sillery. The marriage, organized by the families, hadn't worked. He fled the site of the scandal, settling in Montréal, where he worked for his father's import-export business. Laurence didn't rush into anything. She conducted— as she liked to put it— a character study, intrigued that a rich kid would go for her. With his black eyes, his strong broad shoulders, Adrien Lessard was attractive and his manners showed he came from a good family.

In the stairway of the rooming house, Laurence encountered a very young woman who said hello. A trivial incident, that of the young girl forgetting her keys, brought them together. Pauline was frank, straightforward, and she liked Laurence very much. Her youthful enthusiasm made Laurence talk more than usual. Pauline was surprised, in an admiring away, at Laurence's prodigious level of activity and breadth of interests. Laurence was a phenomenon in her eyes. Pauline Saint-Amant talked enthusiastically to her father about mademoiselle Naud, who built cottages. There were several chance encounters with Pauline's father, and they chatted amicably.

Laurence drew up her plans for two cottages, bearing in mind her financial limitations, but not skimping on the large screened verandah. She sketched in bedrooms and a vast kitchen that would also serve as a sitting room. Léon, in his first letter since Rosalie had died, talked more about Vincent's fruitless job hunts than of his own sorrow.

Suddenly she got the idea of asking her brother to build the cottages the following spring, conditional on Uncle Edmond's also being available. The fifty-year-old uncle had a solid reputation as a builder. Vincent could learn the trade under his direction. Laurence sealed and stamped the letter without rereading it. She felt content, relieved. She was optimistic that this arrangement would work out fine. She would pay the usual carpenter's wages, and benefit her family, instead of people she didn't know. In exchange, Uncle Edmond's presence was a guarantee the work would be done properly. The situation couldn't be better.

Her solitude weighed less heavily, on account of a certain tenderness for Adrien that she started feeling the Sunday she dared tell him everything about her project and the commitment it required. He listened politely, impressed with her spunk. He teased her and asked her why she was doing such a thing. She replied simply: she could count on no one but herself. He was as amazed as he was impressed, and took her in his arms, saying he would look after her.

Feeling close, each admitted to the other they lacked sex in their lives. They became lovers, not too awkwardly, and drank a glass of whisky to drown any sentient guilt after their somewhat predictable brashness.

A banal incident sparked a wry comment. That day, Adrien was unwrapping a package sent by his mother, his fur coat. He searched the outer pockets and the inner pockets of the garment, shook it, and found nothing. His mother hadn't stuffed them with dollars before sending it, he complained, sulking a little. Laurence burst out laughing, and said, sardonically, that he was behaving like a spoiled child whose mother hadn't done as he wished. He stopped sulking.

The letter from Broughton confirmed that the brother and uncle could come, accompanied by a warning that a woman embarking on chancy projects could lose her respectability. The father reminded the daughter that a single woman did not go about with men without hurting her reputation. He took the credit for convincing Vincent and Edmond to come. Laurence, thrilled they had accepted, was disappointed by Léon's spite and his moralizing irritated her. She continued with her damned liaison, an unspoken challenge to his words.

Nothing works like disapproval to bring two people closer. Adrien, who no longer felt lonely, agreed. He seemed to have an open mind, was interested in all sorts of new ideas, and she was sure his bourgeois education had not instilled prejudices regarding the sorts of things people had to do to get along in the world. It was a case of opposites attracting. Adrien was dealing with the failure of his marriage, was in a state of waiting for the long separation process to end. Laurence's energy perked him up.

He accompanied her to Pointe-Calumet. The mud underfoot, the last snow on the ground, the grey of the lake, the black of the trees, the closed cottages, threatened by the rising water, announced the coming of spring. Laurence checked the boundary stakes and the pickets delineating a lot at the edge of her property. By the road, under the one-hundred-year-old maple, she talked of building her cottage one day, with a fireplace and a roof terrace.

Uncle Edmond and Vincent arrived at the end of April with their improvised camping gear. When it came to the purchase and delivery of the construction materials, she had to put up with the misogyny of the merchants. The lumber dealers looked to Edmond for the final decision. She had to write his name on the order sheets. They immediately called them Edmund's cottages.

Under pretext of the standard length of the lumber, the verandah was reduced, but not without an acrimonious discussion between Laurence and her builders. They argued that the verandah should be the same as on the other cottages. Otherwise it would cost too much. She understood they had changed the plans of their own will. She dragged herself back to the city. Everything cost more than anticipated and her bank account was diminishing. It was already the beginning of June, time to rent the cottages.

When she cooled down and could think clearly, she felt like discussing the matter with someone. The only unusual thing about her plans was the large verandah that summer visitors could use in a number of ways. Was she a capricious woman as Edmond thought? Keeping her voice calm, she told Pauline and William Saint-Amant all about her ordeal, looking directly at them. They talked about it at length and she finally concluded that Edmond and Vincent were using the price of wood as a pretext for not doing the cottages her way.

Sundays, in the living room overlooking Park Lafontaine, Laurence and Adrian made love in new ways, surrendering lasciviously. Adrien, in an exuberant frame of mind, spoke of love, affection, praised the things they had in common, hinted at their future relationship. He wanted a modern marriage, a life without children, focused on work and travel. She heard him out with irony, given her humble country background. It was not in the interest of the son of a good family, even if not a very rich one, to make a mismatch. He was insistent, hoping that his arranged marriage would soon be annulled by the Church. Now he felt free from his parents. Adrien, still in a post-coital mood, was dreaming out loud.

At the restaurant, she told him of how the workers were boycotting her plans. He listened distractedly when she enumerated the things that had to be done by the end of the month. He asked, sarcastically, unimpressed by her race with time: why are you bothering? Laurence saw the adult man looking in the pockets of the fur coat for the dollars his mother hadn't sent.

She rented the cottages. The money she got would serve to complete the work. Laurence took an afternoon off to see how the final stages were proceeding. The transparent blue of the sky lit up the trees and brightened the tender green of the countryside. The grass had grown and the odour of chlorophyll made her breath headily. She walked towards the lake, watching the inclining sun spread over the refreshing wavelets of the lake. The sand was hot on the surface and cooler as soon as your foot sank down. She heard a harmonica playing, following the rhythm of the waves that were becoming mere ripples. A boat was drifting along, a man sitting on its bow, dragging his feet in the water, and playing a wild jig. A woman sat in the middle, rowing, while another sprawled on the back bench. The image was over-exposed against the tranquil backdrop. The boat rocked, the player stopped, and the women clapped. She who was rowing turned towards the shore, the man singing a couplet followed by a harmonica riff. Laurence hummed the tune, her gaze widening as she recognized her brother Vincent. Her brother was carrying on with young girls during hours he claimed he worked. She couldn't believe her eyes.

Edmond's pick-up arrived at the cottage lots one hour later. The two men displayed no embarrassment. She accused them of taking advantage of her good will, of making her pay good money for hanging about. Instead of excusing themselves, they glared at her defiantly. They were in it together. She added up their hours and gave them the money from the rent. They knew her bank account was empty. She had told them several times that she was pleased with how the work was progressing. Out of a desire to be flexible, she had accepted various modifications to her plans, not even holding the smaller verandah against them. They couldn't accept that a woman might have power and money.

Two days before the arrival of the tenant, there was no news from Uncle Edmond and Vincent, and she was worried about the state of the cottage. There was no trace of their camp. She entered the chalet and saw that they had abandoned the job without finishing. She was on the verge of despair when she saw the obscene graffiti on the walls, complete with drawings and insulting words. That men in her own family would do such a thing! In a state of shock, she put on an old pair of trousers and started painting the three rooms, putting down linoleum, cutting screens and nailing them to wooden frames. Laurence worked forty-eight hours without stopping, without eating or drinking. She hadn't thought to bring food and there was no water. The hours of the day and night passed by one by one as she accomplished one task after another, without thinking of herself, doing one thing at a time, not noticing how tired she was. The night before the tenants arrived, it suddenly occurred to her they would have no water before the following evening. She was afraid they would ask for their money back. But it was spent. The obsessive worry helped keep her awake, and the unrelenting effort was less conscious because of her anguished fretting. She was putting the last screen on its frame when the family appeared.

They didn't notice how frenzied she felt. She welcomed them, explained that the plumbing was installed, but that it had to be connected to the artesian well. The father said he knew how to do that and would take care of it that very day. She relaxed. The children were running about, she could see them through the mist. In the train, her skin dry, her joints cracked, she dozed, and the streetcars, too slow, jogged her about. She was dying to sleep. By chance, she ran into Pauline in the apartment hall. The young girl had a fright, thought Laurence had been beaten, for she was so bent over. Laurence went to bed in her clothes and drank a mouthful of water. It burned her throat. When the telephone rang, her voice was growing weaker by the minute. Adrien wanted to know how things were and she summed up her forty-eight hours of persistence, without mentioning the obscene graffiti. He said, lightly: why are you bothering? His tone was critical: you really needn't. She broke off with him without further explanation, and felt relieved. A man who got annoyed when his mother failed to anticipate his wishes lacked backbone. It was impossible to get her exhausted body, her trembling knees, her legs, to relax.

Pauline ran to get her father at the garage on rue Iberville. Mademoiselle Naud was sick. They jumped in the little van. William Saint-Amant knocked on her door and saw her state of exhaustion. She poured out her heart in a faint voice. He realized she hadn't eaten and sent out for a roast chicken. A single bite burned her tongue. She cried out in pain, drank a little water, ate nothing. William Saint-Amant was not long-winded. Using a low, even voice, he promised to help her out with the remaining work on the second cottage. The thought of the obscene graffiti made her feel sick. They agreed to meet at eleven o'clock. She would be at her nursing station one half-hour later.

Laurence knew that William Saint-Amant was separated from his wife. Moral considerations didn't interest her. The fact remained that a relationship, even an informal one, between a man and a woman, raised eyebrows. He talked of what people would think, and said he intended to avoid arousing gossip. It would have to be kept quiet, so as not to ruffle the feathers of social convention. She admitted she didn't think like other people.

Odette dreamed of spending time in the country with Paul and the children. Since they had known each other, she had refrained from asking for or doing things that would distract from the achievement of their goals. After the scene that followed her sharing a beer with madame Chagnon, she no longer acted on whim. Her sister's cottages stirred her longing for passing a hot summer with her feet in golden sand, breathing deeply, relaxing. Paul didn't contradict her, but he returned to Montréal for good, and was renewing his acquaintance with the neighbourhood guys.

Sitting around the kitchen table, he trotted out his favourite expression: let's talk it over, and asked what it cost to rent a cottage. Laurence gave a figure. They said nothing. She guessed at the meaning of their silence and said that for the time being, she needed the entire rent. Next year she would lower the price, maybe even let them have it for nothing. Paul did not continue discussing the matter, changed the subject. At the end of the evening he said the rent was too high and no one would pay that much. Odette was of the same opinion, and spoke no more of going swimming.

The fine days exuded boredom, an old feeling that went back to childhood and adolescence. Boredom, coupled with a feeling of not being in control of her life, had driven Odette to the city. When she finished her housework, her intense state of anxiety made it difficult to think. She felt defeated by the sameness of her days, cornered by her everyday life, by doing over and over what was expected of her.

Since Paul had come back, she stayed in the apartment, no longer took her girls for walks in the afternoon, avoided going downtown. From the window she watched the women out with their children, making comments to herself about lack of cleanliness and discipline. She was put off by her neighbourhood. She shut herself up at home. The city became synonymous with all sorts of dangers. Paul read her the local news: a child hit by a car, a child bitten by a rabid dog, a child kidnapped by a stranger in a public park. The less she went out, the more it seemed that to venture forth into the street constituted a risk for her and her children. If out alone, she was not filled with irrational worries, but she was less and less often alone in public places. She started many sentences with: when the children are grown.

Paul did not try to justify taking off at seven. Her conflicted situation weighed her down, affected her mood, stirred a growing rage within her against an enemy she couldn't name, which only increased her disgust. Her confused feelings surfaced as sensations of helplessness. She, who came from a family that encouraged daughters to be nuns, had so much wanted to be a wife and a mother. She had received no guidance or counsel on these matters from other women. She had the impression Laurence didn't listen to her. There had been the warning of madame Chagnon: don't have more than two children if your husband is away a lot. The phrase became prophetic, predicting unhappiness. In the kitchen, she fulminated against madame Chagnon, who had planted the spectre of a disastrous future in her mind.

For the first time, she felt like running away, no matter where, abandoning husband and children. Odette did not see a connection between her youthful fugue and her present state. But having managed to run away once made doing it again seem plausible, a solution to her impasse. She grabbed her handbag, went out the door, walked towards Sainte-Catherine, couldn't decide whether to turn left or right, continued to Notre-Dame, was unable to figure out what to do next. She returned home. Behind the closed doors, the little girls slept.

It was impossible to compare Léon Naud and Paul Vidal. Odette got lost in conjecture when she tried to give the word "masculine" a face. Léon, pious, obeying religious law to the letter, tried to force his children into the mould decreed by his beliefs. He pricked and prodded, refused to accept them as they were. Léon bore the yoke of their poverty as if it were the price of transcendence, and saw himself as a good man being tried by God. A clean, honest reputation was proof of his upright character. The wages of profit are death, he was fond of saying.

Paul was a passionate man, unable to resist a good time, easy to get along with unless crossed, who accepted Odette as she was, better still, who possessed her. For him, the world of women was synonymous with the maternal, especially when he needed approval, or was suffering from wounded pride. When Odette talked about their future business, he glowed. Being in business would be great fun, for he knew how to make a buck, as he put it. His notion of finances started and stopped with a steady income. He would spend little and earn a lot. To date, it was Odette who saw to the economic stability of the family by taking care of the old man. She had despised her father's harshness as much as she deplored her husband's laissez-faire attitude. Neither added up to her idea of what a man should be. Out of a need for models that corresponded to her notion of reality, she focused on the meaning of the word "feminine," and judged women more harshly than men. She pardoned the men for their shortcomings.

Bored to death, she lost the sense of balance discipline provides. The ordered life she strove for fell apart. After her work day, she might have found peace, the simple contentment of an untroubled existence. The absence of inner calm made her desolate.

It cheered her to think she might have a son. The family would be perfect. Her sister's enthusiasm for her children made her feel tense and useless. She would stave off Laurence's raptures by making her explain exactly how to avoid getting pregnant again. The nurse's knowledge of science would be useful to her. Words pertaining to sex, so difficult to discuss, would come up in conversation. Anecdotes about clandestine abortions, discussed covertly, left her cold. She wasn't a medical specimen, but a fertile woman determined not to end up like her mother or grandmother.

Madame Chagnon's sober warning strengthened her determination. She would make it clear to Paul and Laurence. Children were not an end in themselves. They needed to be educated. The word "need" became part of her vocabulary on behalf of the children. One day, they would need to move to another neighbourhood so the children could be surrounded by families who cared about properly educating their children. Paul rejected this value judgement, refused to hear her out, saying there were good people everywhere. You had to think of their education from the time they were very young, she insisted. He disagreed, claiming young children noticed nothing. They grew farther apart. She had notions about manners. Every day she saw people with bad manners, and criticized them, condemned them. Paul made her angry by replying: you don't know how to have fun. She looked down on her neighbours, the other mothers, judged them incompetent, and she refused to keep company with them. She shut herself off.

Odette was not a self-questioning person. She bristled with frustration, now confusing the father's attitude with the sister's, claiming the father's moralizing had deprived her of a sense of self, while her sister had tyrannized her with kindness. Her desire to accomplish something was blocked, nothing was working for her. To think was to beat a direct path to anxiety, or else she ended up expressing needs or desires on behalf of the family.

One day she would have a house for her family, a single-family dwelling, in a neighbourhood of people like themselves. Hers was the dream of the petty bourgeoisie, a dream of living among people who shared their opinions on the rearing of children. A reasonable, well-considered dream. She wanted peace and comfort, a life under control, untroubled by unreliable passions or the threat of change.

When they made a budget, balanced with the help of the old man, when they studied their bank book, Odette saw in the figures the near realization of her dream, drawing closer with each deposit.

During Paul's absence, at least she'd had a reason to feel anxious. Since his return it had gotten much worse, transmuted into dejection. She had handed Paul's responsibilities back to him, but in fact things went on as before. He shouldered none of the concerns nor effort. She knew he would be the one to decide what to do with their assets, and her confidence in him was not overwhelming. When it came time to buy the business, he would play his role of family head. She only hoped he would consult her.

The more fun he had, the more it was up to her to preserve family unity. She did not envy his lightheartedness, save on those rare occasions when she went to the extreme of acting out a kind of gay abandon. Her desire for flight was a figment of her imagination. The need to lighten her burden became drastic. She said: life is not a game. People amount to nothing if they spend their time having fun. To reach her goal implied achieving economic security, middle-class comfort in a context where that was what everybody wanted. The more he went out, the more discipline she applied to her everyday life. She was trying to do it for both of them, thereby concealing the gambler's frivolity.

Life is not a game, she said, convinced that thrift in every detail of daily life was the way to a better future. Sometimes she felt they were lucky that the old man supported them. Sometimes she saw in their good fortune the reason for Paul's slacking off. The former facilitated the latter. Her ambition was to preserve equilibrium.

Odette's way of trying to get Paul to act reasonably was to exaggerate her fears for the future, despite the economic revival. She hated his constant going out, knew he would not change, and despaired.

She thought of her tasks in terms of both old-fashioned and current values. Work had the reassuring rigour of Biblical atonement and structured family life. Odette existed for her family, through hard work, and refused to think of herself as a social being. The same logic led her to reject her street and neighbourhood in favour of a middle-class environment.

When she found herself contemplating her boredom, the same question always came up: who am I? A worrisome, dicey question that undid her completely. Mired in discontent, she repressed her lust for life, held tight to her impasse. She was not reassured by tender gestures. There had never been sweet talk between she and Paul. Paul's sentimentalism, reeking of cupidity, became a kind of blackmail that offered no real access to his person.

Odette's existence was best represented by those hours when she was confronted by emptiness and lack of self-knowledge. She had behaved honourably, given herself respectable goals. Sometimes she admitted that there had been good times with Laurence, and sometimes she accused the old maid of having prevented her from getting enough experience, of having led her, without her knowing, down the garden path. She was not able to determine which version was right, for now Laurence kept her distance. No use thinking about it. Laurence was a good talker, well able to defend her opinions, to argue, and loved discussions. Odette perceived her inferiority with bitterness, a married woman, inadequate, with no proof of social standing.

Evenings, she suffocated as the empty hours ticked by. She had never felt so alone as she did now, wondering who she was, a stupid question, unworthy of someone her age. Her dissatisfaction was the only thing as horrible as the humiliating question. She suffered from a sense of emptiness, and wanted the days to go by as quickly as possible so that she might be free of these perpetual apprehensions, of this painful maelstrom, this immense confusion.

She needed to be able to recognize that she was suffering from mental strain. She buried her troubled moments under ever greater discipline, under a rigidity she had formerly held in contempt. The children's spontaneity horrified her and she drew up lists of rules.

Her desire for a single-family dwelling was like everyone's, which made her feel cornered. She seemed a woman who wanted nothing special, which made her hate the neighbourhood even more. She cloistered herself in the apartment, avoiding madame Chagnon.

19

Laurence recounted her misfortunes with the cottages. Odette thought she was making it up, putting on airs, and her voice joined Paul's in saying cottages weren't as profitable as urban dwellings. Laurence thought a minute, and said she could get a bank loan, using the cottages as collateral. She denounced the stupidity of Uncle Edmond and Vincent, especially the dirty words and drawings, which hurt her as much as did their dishonesty. This way of talking disconcerted them. Paul resorted to generalizations, alluded to how men got their back up when women took charge. Laurence held her ground. She was taking her economic security into her own hands to provide for a comfortable future. She took them to task on the grounds that Paul's grandfather supported them. They were privileged, therefore blind to the realities of existence. Odette watched her sister coolly refute Paul, noticed he was smirking and doing nothing to placate the intense discussion. She refrained from taking sides. She wouldn't disagree with him. Odette was taking another step towards solitude.

It occurred to her that Paul might be wrong. She repressed it. Her desire for peace and order mattered more.

The youngest of Paul's three sisters did not live with the family, but from time to time Odette saw the other two— as different as can be— on the stairway leading to the ground floor. She couldn't understand how one family could create such different beings. The young nineteen-year-old had the body of a movie star. Her pretty face was spoiled by a speech impediment. She spoke little, was reserved and had the kind of manners that Odette, forever worried about doing the right thing, approved of. She dressed conservatively compared to the younger sister, who liked loud colours, nylon blouses with puffy sleeves and flounced skirts. Carelessly made-up with cheap cosmetics, her face looked painted on and her lipstick stained her teeth. With her round face and her plump body, she was a typical neighbourhood girl. She laughed loudly, was full of fun, and people found her easy-going and attractive. Climbing the outside stairs, she teased Odette's little girls on the balcony, whereas her inhibited sister went right on by.

Odette thought derisively it was too bad the former did not possess the easy-going ways and gift of the gab of the latter. She viewed the younger outrageously dressed sister with disdain. Odette swore her daughters would be alike, and dressed them identically, to even out differences. If one was the mirror image of the other, they were off to a good start, suitably protected against neighbourhood vulgarity.

Paul felt it was his right to have fun. Feeling in love and sexually satisfied made him more self-confident. He hadn't lost his freedom, he had gained new privileges. Odette's bustling about washing the children and putting them to bed made it easy to slip off. He felt useless amid the going and coming between the den, the kitchen and the bedroom they all shared. He pretended he was getting in the way. He stepped out now after reading the newspaper, his youthful optimism and carefree spirit returning as he disappeared through the door of the flat.

Depending on how he felt, the man headed for one of his haunts, the snack bar or the pool hall, where he ran into acquaintances with whom he would talk the evening away. He decided on the spur of the moment, didn't commit himself to anything, and cut a wide berth around the serious gamblers, the hardened guys, the true devotees. There were spontaneous card games with amateurs, a few onlookers gathering round. They played for token amounts, while on rue Ontario the habitual gamblers lost their shirts. To play for the sake of playing wasn't really satisfying, and he invented multiple tactics to resist getting sucked in by the sharks who had opened a gaming house.

There was a fierce spirit of competition among he and his buddies. Each guy bragged about his winnings, paraded his ambitions, blew things out of proportion, tried to make the others feel jealous. There was always a pretext to talk about money. Each one was going to make his money by going into business, by dealing in illicit goods, by racketeering. They didn't say so outright, used veiled allusions such as marketing found goods or taking advantage of the largesse of certain individuals. Illegal trade took place in the downtown gaming houses. They all knew of con men and bookies on Sainte-Catherine, and some boasted openly that they had ins with them. When they weren't betting on the horses they were playing blackjack or the slot machines.

They were streetcar conductors, delivery-truck drivers, workers. They didn't talk about their wives, which was considered wimpy. They got together, men with men, to hang out and feel young again. Ambition was fired by the hope of quick and easy gain. They talked about ways and means of making a buck, making little distinction between legal and illegal options. They both envied and despised politicians and their tricks. Paul threw himself passionately into political discussions, referring to newspaper articles, where he read of financial double dealings between the lines. They teased him and told him he should get involved in municipal politics. He was flattered that they noticed he was better educated than most.

Many had not had easy lives. They had started to work at the age of fourteen or fifteen, for rock-bottom wages, during the Depression. Old by the age of thirty, disillusioned, determined to have a good time, they bluffed, substituting showing off for broken dreams, yet still lusting after wealth. They detested the bad hand fate had dealt them, pushed it to the back of their minds, and strutted around like guys who had made it. Paul provided a flattering mirror image with his chubby, unwrinkled face. He was an impressive presence with his good clothing and firm step. He had plenty of time to himself, compared to several of the hustlers and bustlers. It felt good to be envied. Their covetous gazes fed his egotism.

Paul needed flattery as much as he did a good time. His vanity and susceptibility made him an easy target for nasty barbs. His manner provoked jealousy among his companions who tried to take him down a notch or two. The best times were when the braggarts competed on a level playing field. There were enough of those to forget the less successful evenings. He took different routes in his comings and goings always skirting the gaming house on rue Ontario, preferring to make allusions to it at a safe distance. A man could lose his shirt in less than an hour playing barbote.*

As he walked down the middle of the sidewalk, the city was for him the epitome of action. He would be thirty next year and told himself that he was taking a break after the three years in Valcartier, that he was in no rush. The projected business would have him stuck behind a counter soon enough. His habits had been honed in his easygoing youth. A weight was off his shoulders, and he felt like he was recovering an earlier state of mind, made even better by his adult experience. The summer of 1945 had the charm of nostalgia. Time was marked by a sense of floating.

Paul thought of himself as a neighbourhood man. He never mentioned that he had completed grade twelve in the classiest college in the city, that the other students of his year had gone on to university, that they were having brilliant and profitable careers. He played down the value of a formal education in favour of street smarts and clever moves that only the tricky ones, the pros were capable of pulling off when they got a lucky break. For success, there was nothing like a hot tip or a good game plan. You couldn't fall back on education. He was persuaded that the streetwise were the winners, and was fascinated by penniless guys who made fortunes though they hadn't finished elementary

---

★ Barbote is an illegal dice game, requiring a special table quickly hidden away or moved into neighbouring houses through hidden connecting doors during police raids.

school. Paul was sure that it was the neediest guy who turned out to be the smartest, provided he acquired some purchasing power. He saw the illiterate guys he hung out with as self-made men, borrowed from the American dream. The guys who made a lot of money on the black market got the highest points. It was a tricky business that required a good head and know-how that could only be learned in the school of life, for him, the only true school. The advantage of going into business was that it was legal; the disadvantage, that it was less profitable. From the point of view of income, it was as good to be in business as to be a professional.

For Paul, a man was smart in direct proportion to his capacity to earn a buck. Consequently, a good gambler had a fine mind. He had disapproved of Laurence's unrelenting determination, of her forty-eight hours of frenzied labour and the resulting physical exhaustion. Her story about the construction of the cottages was proof of what he despised: excessive physical labour made morons of people. He could not accept that a person be obliged to work like that. Laurence had paid doubly for a disappointing return, and this could not be termed a success. She represented, for him, what not to do. She earned too little, too late, too painfully.

A break with his sister-in-law would have been undesirable. When Laurence listened to his plans, he was absolutely certain she took him more seriously than anyone else did. He knew she adopted an ironic attitude towards his escapism, his bragging, for he had occasionally been the object of sardonic comments. With her he didn't make half the claims he made elsewhere.

To date, he had been spared the hard life, held down a so-so job. His stash was safe in the bank, a goodly sum that he would soon use for a starter business. With a snack bar he would make returns on his investment, because it was a milieu he knew well. He could have fun and make money, too. Paul really dreamed of owning a tavern, but if he were unable to pay off the vendor, he could end up bankrupt.

On the way home from his stroll through the neighbourhood, he weighed the respective merits of snack bar and tavern. The first would be a safe bet, the second would make him rich and grant him immediate social status. The tavern-keeper, given his relationship with the police and the priests, enjoyed a certain prestige. He represented the line of demarcation between order and disorder. Clients spent a lot, and some were good talkers.

Women were not allowed in taverns, which was too bad. He liked to look at a pretty girl. He measured, with his hand, the weight of her breasts, the curves of her hips, entertained rude comments, rolling his eyes like the other guys. If he found the presence of women amusing, it was not the be-all and end-all. His choice was limited by his bankroll: he would buy a snack bar with the intention of re-selling as soon as there was a possibility of buying a tavern at an acceptable price.

Without consulting Odette, he mentally processed the alternatives, considering the pros and cons of each, opening the bank book and noting figures in pencil. He obsessed about the decision at hand. Odette ventured an opinion in passing, introduced by "it seems to me," which he interpreted as an expression of doubt. He needed her presence of mind, her support: total acquiescence. He hated hesitation; her wriggling out of the discussion with a "do what you want" caught his attention, and made him listen.

If he found her anxious, silent, after an evening of inner torment, he turned his back on her and, feeling tired, quickly fell asleep. His day hadn't been bad.

Paul altered his behaviour, sought her participation in the decision-making process. He visited more businesses and would decide by autumn. This gave him an alibi— he was going to check the places out. It was a good pretext for taking off after supper. He needed advice from his father, and climbed up to the third-floor apartment.

The mother and son alone together smiled at each other. With her, he could stand silence, words spoken in half-tones, sighs. There was no guilt involved in their tranquil encounters. Time flew by with her, and he stayed on, his heart beating. She absorbed the proffered love, caught up in the trance created by his presence. He lapped up the charged emotions, whispered so many little compliments and words of adoration, that she was loathe to break the spell.

The father, a postal employee, again told his son he knew nothing about business, and made him promise to be careful and on his guard against fast talkers. All that glitters is not gold. The security of a steady job was worth more than a mediocre business. Paul, who liked the thought of deals and easy profits, was disappointed. The son dug in, debated the validity of his project with his father, who sought to discourage him. Paul lacked convincing arguments, grew impatient, and the discussion did not turn in his favour.

His grandfather supported him as he had promised, paid the bills and asked only to be looked after in return. He did not interfere in his decisions, kept to the only private space offered him, the closed bedroom. The old man, now over eighty and withdrawing from the world, had given his approval; the rest was a question of practical detail and didn't concern him. He had succeeded in business through quiet perseverance, had imposed a discipline on himself that required giving up certain things. Paul, protected by his grandmother, who treated him as an exceptional child, had not learned this lesson. He had been raised alone by an old lady attentive to his needs, reluctant to punish him, a young man with money in his pocket during hard times, a young man people admired, sought out, solicited. He had married a pretty woman who didn't contradict him, whom he loved without telling her so, which was the best way to stay in control.

He never let his daughters sit on his lap, though Odette tried to bring them closer, for children must be reared by both parents. She refrained from expressing her sadness at his indifference towards the girls. He didn't talk to them, didn't say good morning or good night, didn't acknowledge them. They were there beside him, but they asked their mother when they wanted something. He was unmoved by them. Some adults are bored by children, even their own.

The child due in autumn, possibly a boy, would make things crowded in the double room. The apartment was already cramped with children born in their father's absence, who took up their mother's attention. Paul felt suffocated, needed air.

Madame Chagnon, on the second floor, treated him with ironic consideration. She, who had taken Odette's side against him, was an old gossip he avoided. On the third floor was his large birth family, that he was getting close to again after a long absence. Fate had put an economic gap between himself and his working-class sisters and brothers, in front of whom he paraded his privileges. He wondered if they didn't have the best of the deal, compared himself to them, felt increasingly envious.

Too many families lived in the brick triplex. Paul choked on the ever-tightening family bonds. So numerous, so invasive, they stole his privacy, dampened his spontaneity. They each wanted something from him, making it difficult to live an autonomous life, spiriting away his independence. His casual air was sapped by their presence. A sugary sentimentalism softened his attitude as soon as he took a little distance, stepped over the threshold, and he loved them all. Away from them, they constituted in his mind a warm place to go, and he gathered them into his heart, his love for each— which he totted up in feelings as evanescent as air— increasing

One August evening, feeling light and excessively sentimental, he strolled in and out of pool halls and snack bars, looking for a good discussion. Nobody was up to his mettle. He knew in advance what they would say. He walked a long time, away from his usual haunts, and entered the gaming house on rue Ontario, saw some men he knew, and sat down. Someone expressed pleasure at his presence and he felt appreciated. The cigarette smoke veiled gamblers at neighbouring tables, softened the clamour, punctuated with silences. He had his cards in his hand, and the group spirit was so intense that he threw himself into the game heart and soul. Cards were shuffled, a voluptuous sound. He dreamed as he handled the cards that he was handling money, lots of money to buy the business, to buy houses, numerous properties. He had one, two, three and wanted more, a whole street, both sides, east and west.

Laurence had once told him that Odette had fits, that she had a bad temper, that she got carried away with rage. They met at dawn. He had a little smirk, and she was screaming, completely out of control.